Love
by the
Morning
Star

Love
by the
Morning
Star

Laura L. Sullivan

HOUGHTON MIFFLIN HARCOURT
Boston   New York

www.hmhco.com

The text of this book is set in Dante MT Std.

The Library of Congress has cataloged the hardcover edition as follows:
Sullivan, Laura L.
Love by the morning star / Laura L. Sullivan.
p. cm.
Summary: Mistaken for one another when they are sent to the grand English
country estate of Starkers on the brink of World War II, Hannah,
a distant relative hoping to be welcomed by the family, and Anna,
sent to spy for the Nazis, both unexpectedly fall in love.
[1. Mistaken identity—Fiction. 2. Social classes—Fiction.
3. Family life—England—History—George VI, 1936–1952—Fiction.] I. Title.
PZ7.S9527Lov 2014   [Fic]—dc23   2013037690

ISBN: 978-0-547-68951-7 hardcover
ISBN: 978-0-544-54259-4 paperback

Manufactured in the United States of America
DOC 10 9 8 7 6 5 4 3 2 1
4500564301

For Buster

November 1938

Anna, Who Is Not the Heroine

IT TAKES SO MUCH WORK *being better than everyone else*, Anna Morgan mused. *Of course, on one level, superiority is a matter of one's birth. No,* she hastily amended, recalling her father's origins as a grocer: *not birth, but blood. Rank and money don't matter.* What did it say above the National Fascist Front (NAFF) headquarters? "Rank is but the guinea-stamp; the man's the gold for all that." She didn't mind — almost didn't mind — that she wasn't of noble birth, because she had enough pride simply in being British. There was nothing better than that.

But to appear instantly and unequivocally superior to the untrained eye, that took some work.

She had natural advantages, of course, being statuesque and fair, with high-piled blond curls arranged in careful bedroom disarray. Her hourglass lines were achieved through exercise and will; her elegant, floor-length attire suggested leisure and lofty social status. Her features were large, her jaw strongly defined, with those Pre-Raphaelite bones that can make a girl either a stunner or a bumpkin, depending on what she does with them. Anna had been learning what to do with them for seventeen years, and had it down to a science. She knew she was beautiful — if a little frightening, but that was a part of her beauty — and if she ever forgot it she had only to stroll down the street and learn it again from all the admiring stares she received.

From earliest childhood, she'd always had ideas about what she could be, but her seed would have been scattered on barren soil if her grocer father had not discovered his gift for oratory and hate. Several years ago, a Russian Jew had opened a small grocery store around the corner, and through diligence, friendliness, the ability to get oranges year round, and a most un-English lack of rats and black-beetles in his storeroom, managed to lure away a good-size chunk of Mr. Morgan's clientele. From that moment Mr. Morgan conceived a violent hatred of all things foreign and all things Jewish. He threw in Communism for good measure, liberated a soapbox from the storeroom, and began to spout off to anyone who would listen to him.

His eloquent vitriol caught the attention of Reginald Darling, who thought Oswald Mosley's British Union of Fascists too soft and coddling, and he was recruited into the newly formed National Fascist Front. Mr. Morgan marched, he shouted, he smashed windows and broke heads, gradually rising to become

Lord Darling's right-hand man. When laws were passed and public opinion overwhelmingly turned against them, they took the organization underground (which was a relief to Anna, because it meant her father would never again have to wear the blood-red plus-fours that were part of the NAFF's official uniform) and plotted to rid Britain of the parasitic foreigners who were sucking its lifeblood.

Which was all very well with Anna, particularly because it meant a move to London, where she could expand her horizons and learn to emulate the aristocracy. She was one of nature's aristocrats, of that she was certain, so it was only right she should act like them. Her voice became cultivated, she always remembered to scoop her soup with the far side of her spoon, and she learned to apply her makeup in such a way that it seemed she had none on at all. All the while her father worked for the preservation of the true British way of life, and the well-being of the true British worker, and her mother hosted parties in their stylish new flat where people of like mind could plot the overthrow of the government for its own good. Anna kept her eyes open, looking for a "Lord," or a "Sir," or at worst an "Honorable" who might whisk her away to the life she knew she deserved.

Did she too hate foreigners, Jews, Communists? Where there is such self-love there is very little room for anything else, even hate. She did not argue with her father, and she had a general and vague opinion that foreigners were dirty.

Germans, however, did not seem to count as foreigners in the eyes of the NAFF, so when her father received an invitation to be a secret envoy in Berlin, she was forced to revise her opinion slightly. It was not difficult to do. Queen Victoria had married a German.

Now Anna sat before a third-floor window in the Hotel Adlon, letting the streetlights cast her in a silvery outline that she knew was quite becoming. The man her parents were talking with had a Von in his name, which she thought meant he was something aristocratic. Not that she had any plans of settling for a German, but it was good to stay in practice. Though she had no official role in the NAFF, just a decorative one, she could tell that Herr Von Whoever-he-might-be was paying her particular attention. She let a small smile play on her lips, and began to listen to the conversation.

"Thanks to Mosley and his ham-handed tactics, the British have a bad opinion of fascism," the Von said.

"He meant well," Mr. Morgan replied, stung by a barb against his countryman.

"You and I, Germany and England, must be united in common cause. Lord Darling has told you, I've no doubt, of certain operations to place those sympathetic to our cause in positions of power. Unofficial, highly clandestine operations. The Nazi Party itself is unaware of them. The more forward-thinking of us will coordinate directly with Lord Darling. The English people do not wish to be at war with Germany — the Munich Agreement has made that clear—yet led as you are, I think war between our peoples is inevitable."

Anna saw her father's mouth twitch—he was itching to launch into his standard rhetoric, but Lord Darling had been teaching him patience.

The Von glanced at Anna, and she preened her curls. "We are all Aryans, the British, the Germans," he said. "Yet those who are not friends of Germany must perforce be our enemies. We are noble people, soldiers, warriors; we do not recognize neutrality. It is another word for cowardice. If England does not join us, she will fall as the slave races fall . . . which will be a shame. Brandy?" He held out a glass.

"Thank you," Mr. Morgan said, draining it in a gulp, without warming it or smelling it first. Anna saw a fleeting look of distaste cross the Von's face. Unlike Anna, her father had not taken pains to improve himself. But then, Lord Darling liked his working-class charm, offsetting, as it did, Lord Darling's own aristocracy, helping the NAFF appeal to the masses.

"We have the germ of a plan, a master stroke that will ensure that England and Germany are forever allies, and we need your help."

"Of course. Anything," her father replied.

But the Von wasn't looking at Mr. Morgan. He was looking at Anna.

"You have an intelligent daughter," he said, "and a beautiful one." He looked her up and down, lingering too long in the middle, until she felt something squirming inside her, something cold and unpleasant. "She is loyal to the cause?" He turned back to Mr. Morgan.

"Unswervingly."

"We've talked about you at great length, my dear," the Von said to Anna. "And I think you will do. If you succeed, you will be a heroine to two nations. You will have done your part to keep our races pure. Very likely you will have prevented a war. Are you willing?"

The chill worm still wiggled inside her, but something else warmed her now. Was it patriotism or pride? No, it was ambition. The only thing she really heard from him was the word "heroine." Heroines always marry well, don't they?

"I am willing!" she said, low and thrilling. "What must I do?"

"I can't tell you everything yet. Now it is only necessary that you be put in the proper place and await instructions. There is a castle not far from London, a mile or two from Windsor Castle. Starkers is the name. You will be sent there."

For an instant the world around her disappeared. To think, a minute ago she'd been contemplating an alliance with a mere German Von, and now she was being sent to one of the grandest establishments in England, barely a step below the royal residences. Why, everyone knew that Their Majesties went fox hunting at Starkers every winter, that Their Highnesses spent long weekends dancing at Starkers balls and fishing for Starkers trout and strolling through Starkers shrubberies. And now by some miracle she would be a part of it! The cream had finally risen to the top.

"There is a cook at Starkers, sympathetic but not aligned with any organization, who has been at the castle for many years, so she is above suspicion. Through her, we have secured you a job as a kitchen maid. Once inside Starkers, you'll be in a position to—"

"Kitchen maid!" The world crashed back in all its ugliness. "Absolutely not! Do you know how many hours I've soaked these hands in paraffin?" She held up fingers encased in the softest kid gloves, which she never took off in public, and rarely even in private. "My hands are extraordinarily sensitive."

It was the excuse she always gave for her perpetually gloved state. Although she did indeed bathe them in paraffin and lanolin daily, and though they were preternaturally soft, no amount of cream treatment could reduce their size or squareness. They were broad peasant hands, and she hated them. She could exercise her waist into tininess, but her hands, she thought, betrayed her low origins, and she swore she would not remove her gloves in front of a man until her wedding night.

She refused to wither under the Von's scathing look. How dare he belittle the effort she'd put into making her outside as worthy as her pure British inside? Kitchen maid, indeed!

The Von kept his composure as he worked on her; her father did not. She knew she'd comply in the end. That word "heroine" still rang in her ears, and she knew if she succeeded in whatever they had planned, the world would open to her as she had always dreamed. What could her task be, anyway? Passing a message on the sly? Stealing incriminating letters from a guest's bedroom? And then . . . it would be worth the temporary humiliation if she was elevated to the position she deserved.

But she'd make them work for it.

"I suppose I might," she said, cocking her head to catch her reflection in the silvered window. "Perhaps I could wear surgical gloves."

"You'll be posing as the lowest domestic. Chapped hands are a small price to pay for the glory of your country."

"I don't know . . ." She pretended to stare out the window, considering, but she was looking at the full curve of her own cheek, thinking, *No amount of drudgery will mar that. Poor food might only improve my figure.* She'd noticed a disturbing thickening of her waist since her father had gone on the NAFF payroll.

"Honestly, do you think I can pass as a kitchen skivvy?" she asked in her most cultivated voice.

"Perhaps we can get you in a slightly better post — a house-maid, maybe — but the important thing is that you are there at Starkers."

"Why me?" she fished. *Because you're so clever,* she willed him to say. *Because we trust you.*

"Because a servant, particularly a female servant, is anonymous and inconsequential. Especially in an upper-crust British estate, servants are so taken for granted that for all practical purposes they don't exist. They are conveniently invisible. You come from the lower class — no, don't scowl — but you know how to emulate the upper class. You can pass for one of the maids, but understand the masters. That may be necessary. Now, will you do it?"

Below her, through the naked boughs of the few remaining linden trees lining the boulevard, she could see a vague commotion. The window was propped open a crack, and through the gap came a cry, a wail that rose in frantic desperation until it was cut off abruptly to strangled silence. Then the sound of shattering glass, so loud that she was certain her own window had been smashed, and she flinched back. But no, it was in the street. The sound seemed to echo . . . or was it more glass breaking, farther away?

"What's that?" she gasped.

The Von snaked an arm behind her and snapped the heavy curtains closed.

"Nothing that need concern you. Internal affairs."

When he had gone, Anna said petulantly to her father, "I'm happy to help in any way, of course, but really, a kitchen maid!"

Her father slapped her, hard, and that was that.

Hannah, Who Is the Heroine

HANNAH MORGENSTERN WAS SINGING ABOUT SHEEP. Why her audience loved songs about sheep, she was not sure. They were soldiers, businessmen, wealthy gentlemen about town, who had probably never known a sheep intimately. (What a joke her father would make out of that!) Still, when Hannah sang sheep songs they bought champagne and oysters like they were going out of style, and left tips so large that goodhearted Benno the busboy often ran after them, asking if they'd made a mistake.

This was a song about black sheep on the grassy banks of the Danube looking like the freckles on her true love's nose. Since the Anschluss, the annexation of Austria, she was a bit leery of singing songs about that country, but her repertoire of sheep songs was limited. It was either that, a tune about a British shepherdess, which was too politically risky, or one about frolicking Sudeten lambs, which was too fresh, though no doubt popular with her customers. *What the show needs,* Hannah decided as she crooned the final bars to wild applause and tossed flowers, *is a song about a nationless, nondenominational sheep.* A sheep that cannot stir up resentment from any side.

Of course, by now there was only one side, really, and everyone else kept silent if they knew what was good for them.

The next number was the Double Transvestite Tango, so Hannah made her bows, scooped up as many flowers as she could carry (Benno's grandmother would sell the sturdiest of them the next morning, and one might end up the boutonniere of the very man who'd tossed it the night before), and made her way to the wings. Already a couple of admirers were homing in on her. She was used to becoming another person onstage, someone who attracted and compelled. It was good for business but annoying when business was done, when all she wanted was a breath of fresh air and a glimpse of the stars over Berlin.

Her father, Aaron Morgenstern, was the master of ceremonies and the comedian, dressed, as always, in some variation of a devilish costume. Her mother sang torch songs, sad and sultry. Rounding out the troupe were assorted dancers, actors, and singers, lewd or clownish or satiric as the situation demanded. But there was a market for innocence, too, for eyelet lace and braids and shepherdesses in dirndl skirts, for gentler tastes than most of the clientele possessed. Hannah filled that niche. Old men and young soldiers adored her.

Two of the latter, young lieutenants in the Heer, the German army, tried to catch her eye, so she ducked into her mother's dressing room and peeled off her false eyelashes. She slipped out of her dirndl and into a dark wool dress, then pulled off her wig of coiled blond braids to reveal a slicked-back chocolate-colored bob. When she walked by the two eager officers they didn't recognize her.

"Have you seen that luscious bonbon with the golden braids?" one asked her as she passed.

She grinned up at them with such impish mischief that they almost forgot their quest for the singer. "She is with her lover," Hannah said. "But she can always handle one or two more." She winked at them. "Go there, through that door."

She made her escape while the uniformed hobbledehoys gawked and gaped and finally burst into the dressing room where Franz, the three-hundred-pound juggling strongman, was adjusting his loincloth.

"I ought not to do it," Hannah said aloud to herself as chaos erupted behind her. "I just can't seem to help myself. It is a shame, really."

But she did not look at all sorry.

Outside, Hannah leaned against the cabaret's stone wall and tilted her head, taking in the hazy night sky, the lounging neon devil winking insouciantly out at Berlin from the garish sign for Die Höhle des Teufels. She was so lost in thought, she didn't see the middle-aged man approaching, and started at his voice.

"Staring at things that used to be, my pet?" he said. "Where is your imagination tonight? Nineteen twenty-eight? 'Twenty-nine? Come now, you're too young for nostalgia."

Hannah, like a good many other Germans, was trapped in the past. No matter that the twenties had been times of desperation and poverty and rampant inflation, when a loaf of bread might cost ten marks one day and a million marks the next. It had also been an era of wild creativity and beauty, when no one cared about the price of bread because there was art to create, jazz to dance to, satires to perform, debaucheries such as the world has never known to invent. Hannah was a child of that world, born, literally, in her parents' cabaret, learning to walk by hanging on to its gold velvet stage curtains. Her first solid food had been a banana from Josephine Baker's famous skirt, and a visiting Ziegfeld had dandled her on his knee.

Now, in November 1938, that free, inventive, tolerant spirit was gone, surviving in a few relics such as Der Teufel, or more likely, had fled, to Paris, to Russia, to the United States. Bread was cheap, but the golden age was over. Hitler was in charge, and there were plenty of people who liked it that way.

"Good evening, Herr Alder," Hannah said, her small, sweet face scrunching in irrepressible mirth. "Even babies feel nostalgic for the womb, I think. How nice to be toted around and never have to worry about a thing! Now there are battles and revolutions and invasions and horrible discrimination—and that's just among the kitchen staff. Do you know, Chef actually dumped a flambé on top of the waiter Dieter's head because he told a customer the cream therein would make her fat and so she sent it back? Luckily his hair pomade prevented him from catching alight, but still."

Alder took a hopeful breath, but he stood no chance against Hannah's torrent of words. Unless she got the hiccups, she could go on for hours. "Perhaps in other places the wait staff does not make so free, but I like the way we do things, don't you? One happy, outspoken family. Ah, but you asked where I was, you sly man. I was in 1929 for a moment. Do you remember that spring when all the ladies wore violets on their bosoms? They wilted so fast, and Benno and I made all our candy money scouring the parks for new blooms." She sighed. For just a second, the strain of her life showed through the merriment of her face.

"It was a good year, 1929," Herr Alder slurred. "Much like the bottle of cognac I just consumed."

"You're tipsy," Hannah said with mock disapproval. Caspar Alder was almost an uncle to her, a friend of the family who had patronized Der Teufel since it opened. He did something in the government, she knew, though he talked with increasing sincerity of retiring soon.

"I am *not* tipsy," Herr Alder said, pounding the wall with his fist. His vague avuncular air slipped, revealing something hard beneath. "I am drunk. It is necessary to be drunk when you are about to burn the business of your dear friend, and then perhaps beat him in the streets."

"What do you mean?" Hannah asked, her eyes wide and luminous in the devilish neon gleam.

His voice dropped. "It has started already, across town. There's not much time. They were only waiting for an excuse." He growled the words like a caged dog, and Hannah cringed, catching fear as if it were a fever, though she had no idea what he was talking about.

"They *planned* it," he went on. "They want it to look like a spontaneous uprising, but they planned it, weeks, months ago. I should have warned you sooner, but I lived in hope that mankind isn't quite so foul as it seems to be." He took a long swig from a pocket flask. "Get your parents, my little kitten. Go to a friend's house — don't tell me where — and hide until it passes. If it ever passes. Damn it, I should have made you leave! Damn your stubborn father and his art, his calling . . ."

He dragged her, almost violently, back inside, and, bewildered, she followed him through the backstage corridors. He knew them well. He'd paid court to many nubile performers over the last seventeen years.

Onstage, Waltraud dipped Otto . . . or was it the other way around? She was so nobly built, he so sveltely beautiful, that in the sensuous, sinuous stalking of the tango it was hard to tell who was who. Each was dressed in bifurcated drag, male on one side, female on the other, and as they danced their hips pressed close, their legs intertwined in a glorious pansexual blur. The

Nazi Party inspectors had come to observe the pair but declined to censor them. A man who dressed as a woman because he enjoyed it was decadent and obscene. A man dressed as half a woman, they decided, was worth watching.

Waltraud and Otto bowed and curtsied, then curtsied and bowed, and Benno, who doubled on the fog machine, made a great sulfurous swirl rise through the suddenly dimmed red lights. A violin off scene played a diabolical air, and Aaron Morgenstern appeared as if from the abyss.

He was always the Devil, sometimes a caricature in crimson, though more often Lucifer in his less obvious guises as a sophisticated roué, handsome and irresistible, which closely resembled Aaron's real self, or a jaded old man with a patriarchal beard, bent and weary with the sins of the world. He was the ancient tonight.

"I've seen it all before," he sang, waggling his eyebrows like a dirty old man at the park when young girls in pinafores arrive. *"If there is nothing new under the sun, do you think you will find a novel sin in this, the Devil's cave?"* He stroked his beard and leered at the audience. Then he seemed to fix them with eyes as deep and black as chasms. *"When you come into the Devil's hole and enjoy yourself, aren't you doing to him what he would like to do to you?"* He broke character and laughed, a young rich baritone. *"Bend over, Devil! We will give you a surprise, in the end!"* he sang, and made a rude gesture that set everyone laughing—the closet Communist and the Jew on forged papers, the local head of the SS, who had sent someone to his death that morning (though his hands were

so clean now) and his subordinate, who would soon commit suicide when he finally realized what he'd signed up for.

All political reference had been banned from the German stage a year before, which had killed most cabaret. Aaron Morgenstern survived, in part because he cultivated many influential friends, but mostly because he could couch his bitter opinions in comedy so perfectly balanced that every side thought he was praising them and condemning their opponents. The SS man nodded and thought, *Here is one Jew who knows his place,* seeing in this Devil every enemy of the German state. The man with the forged Aryan papers knew the Devil was the Nazi Party, and delighted in seeing him bend over. Coming into Der Teufel, catching the coded secrets of Aaron's diatribes, was the only way that he could fight. It helped him keep a seed of rebellion in his heart, one that might never sprout so long as he and his were safe, however tenuously, but all his life he could say that seed was there—that inside himself he fought, by listening to the Morgenstern Devil.

"Get your father," Herr Alder whispered as Aaron hobbled offstage in his old-man disguise. He was replaced by a plump Bavarian who played a molting bird, her strategically placed feathers falling off here and there, to the delight of the men in the audience.

In the dressing room, Hannah saw her glorious mother in triptych in the hinged dressing mirror. "Am I late for my cue?" she asked her daughter in English as she smoothed the edge of her dark peekaboo waves. Born Caroline Curzon, she had come from

England after the Great War and married Aaron when she was barely out of her teens, then adopted the stage name Cora Pearl Morgenstern.

When Herr Alder came in she made a little moue, thinking only that her performance preparations were being disrupted, not her entire life. Hannah took her mother's hand and they listened while Herr Alder drunkenly, incoherently explained.

A Jewish boy in Paris had shot a German diplomat. Why, no one was sure. Was it a lovers' quarrel? Was he angry that his family — Polish Jews living in Germany — had been deported? No one knew, but it was called a Jewish conspiracy and there had been orders . . . no, not orders, but official collusion, Nazi Party encouragement, to seek retaliation on all the Jews in Germany.

"They are coming now," Herr Alder said. "The SS and their minions, in plainclothes, and I have been ordered to . . . to not interfere. To not interfere in such a way that I might render all assistance necessary. Every Jewish business is to be vandalized, burned. The synagogues destroyed. Men arrested for the labor camps." He went to take another gulp but, finding the flask empty, flung it across the room, where it crashed into Cora's dressing table, smashing a crystal vial of scent. Though harsher smells would permeate the coming tragedy, Hannah would always recall that whiff of Sous Le Vent's tarragon and iris, disturbingly tropical on that chill, cut-glass night.

Hannah saw the tremor of terror cross her father's face, but it passed almost at once. "You should take your turn onstage, old friend. You're overreacting. You've been predicting doom since 1932."

"And it has been coming. Now it is here. They say they'll destroy every Jewish business, imprison you, send you to Poland . . ."

"We've lived with that threat for years," Aaron Morgenstern said lightly. "They won't touch me."

But Cora's pale brow furrowed. "Maybe now it is time, love."

"It was time long ago!" Alder said. "When they cast your people out of the civil service, you said only, 'Good thing I'm not a civil servant,' and the Devil laughed. When they forbade your people to teach in the universities, you said, 'Well, I'm no intellectual, what does it matter?' Do you think because you can make a Gestapo brute chortle he won't send you to Buchenwald? You'll laugh your way to the grave, and take your family with you."

Aaron looked at his wife, her powdered porcelain face a deliberate mask of calm, and at his daughter, whose slight frame seemed to him now so terrifyingly fragile. But Der Teufel! Its bricks could endure anything, filled as they were with the goodwill of all the powerful men who had eaten and chuckled and grown tipsy within its walls in the two decades since its founding. He was host, he was jester, to the most powerful men of Berlin. He'd been safe so far. Surely his luck would last. About one thing he was adamant—he would not leave his cabaret. He had built it—not its walls, perhaps, but its reputation, its glamour—and it was his lifeblood.

Still in costume, he stroked his beard, pulling the tip into a sharp point. "I won't leave," he said. "I'm a German. They'll come to their senses eventually. But, Cora, I think you and Hannah should go back to England for a while."

"Hannah, yes," Cora said, giving herself a little shake and turning away from them all to apply her lipstick with a slim golden brush. Anyone watching her would have thought her cold, indifferent, but this was the only way she knew to tackle her deepest troubles, to shoo them aside as if they were a cloud of summer gnats, and deal with the task at hand brusquely and efficiently. Hannah always thought of it as her mother's Englishness, that ability to balance problems so that a scuffed shoe and an impending disaster were almost equally distasteful, but both were borne with aplomb.

"But I have too much to do," Cora went on. "Who will keep the Edelweiss Twins in line if I'm in England, eh? Who will remember that oysters must be ordered on Thursday, and langoustines on Friday?" She shrugged her bare shoulders, then dusted them with shimmering gold flakes. "No, it is ridiculous to think I'd leave. Our business would crumble without me here."

Hannah could see the pulse racing in the hollow of her mother's throat, and knew she loved her husband too much ever to leave him voluntarily. The couple joined forces and turned on Hannah.

"You, however, will go to my brother-in-law's house. He will be perfectly happy to take you in," Cora said, with far more confidence than she felt. "That should be easily arranged, no? Documents and such?"

"I will see that it is done," Alder said. "But, Cora, you must go too. You are an English citizen still, so you will have no trouble. Our government is most adamant that foreigners not be inconvenienced. You, Aaron, will be harder to place, but perhaps if you go first to France—"

"I told you, I'm not going. This is my business and—"

"Fool, what have I been telling you? The tide has turned, the deluge has come. There will be no more Jewish businesses. They are being confiscated, now, tonight, next week. It is the end for you. I'll help you with money, but—"

"They can't do it!" Aaron shouted. "I own it free and clear. I don't owe a cent to any man. They can't steal the property of a German citizen!"

Alder took his old friend by the shoulder. "The Jewish people are no longer citizens of Germany," he said gently. "You are an undesirable."

Aaron could hear the muted cheers from the audience, officers positively glittering with medals and insignia, industrial giants in bespoke suits being insincerely adored by women their wives did not know about. All the power of Berlin trickled in through his door. They had toasted him. They had shaken his hand.

"I am an undesirable," he repeated, trying to make sense of it.

"Der Teufel will be gone. Be smart and go first."

The greatest men, Hannah remembered reading somewhere,

make the greatest decisions lightly. She saw something come over her father then, a strange mix of resignation and triumph. "As it happens," the Devil said, "Der Teufel is no longer a Jewish business." He brushed past his family and out of the dressing room, taking the stage just as the buxom Bavarian shed her final feather. "My friends," he cried, "as the good lord gave plagues and pox to his most faithful Job, I, the Devil, must be a contrarian, and to my friends give gifts. Benno, come onstage, if you please."

Whoever is in charge of such things had been sparing with his blessings at the moment Benno was born. He had neither looks nor wit nor skill. He was not large or strong, he could not sing; in fact, he had a stammer, which on most occasions left him self-consciously mute. One gift only had he been given, a gift as simple as it is rare: the gift of pure goodness. He knew, unerringly, what was right, what was kind, what would make people happy, and he did it without fail. His goodness took no effort; there was no internal scale to be balanced. He hoped for no reward and feared no hell. He was not clever — in his final year of school before the teachers despaired of him, he was asked how he would equitably divide a half-pound loaf of bread among himself and two friends. He said he would go without and his two friends would each have a quarter pound, and neither threats of failure nor the switch could persuade him to change his answer. He had done odd jobs at Der Teufel ever since, supporting the grandmother who had raised him after his parents' death.

"Dear souls who are mine for this night, is there a lawyer in the house?" Aaron asked. There were several, and one, chivvied by his friends, gamely hopped up onto the low stage, thinking he'd be part of a burlesque. There was a quick, whispered consultation, and then Aaron called for paper and pen. "Riches are a curse in disguise, the camel through the needle's eye and all that, so the crafty Devil gives away his wealth. Perhaps if I am a pauper, I can sneak into heaven behind the camel's hump, eh?"

Aaron bent over and invited the lawyer to use his back as a desk, while the audience, perplexed, waited for the punch line and poor Benno lingered in the shadowed wings, hoping he wasn't really expected to do anything.

"There!" Aaron shouted. "All perfectly legal now, save for the signatures. Come here, Benno, and make your *X*."

Benno pushed his wheat-colored hair away from his face and sheepishly came center stage. "Der Teufel is yours, my boy," Aaron said, too softly for even the lawyer to hear. "I hope you'll let me stay on." He smiled beneath his gray beard.

Benno's face fell. "N-no!" he gasped, but couldn't get any more out. He didn't know what it meant, but he didn't want it. Then he looked into Aaron's eyes, glistening bright, and though he didn't understand what was happening in the least, suddenly he knew on which path goodness lay. He signed his name.

"Witnesses!" Aaron called, shooing Benno out of the spotlight. "Champagne for everyone who puts his name as a witness on this deed of sale!"

In the end there were thirty signatures crammed at the bottom of that document: the SS officer, a member of the Luftwaffe High Command, the richest hotelier in Berlin, the city's most notorious madam. They did not know if it was avant-garde art or absurdist comedy, but the transfer was real, and Der Teufel belonged to simple Benno, who, after all, had one more gift, one of particular value in the years to come — he was Aryan.

THEY CAME LATER THAT NIGHT when Hannah was onstage again, singing one of her sweetest love songs. As the young couple's fingertips touched for the first time with poignant minor notes that boded ill for their future, the door was shoved open and a group of armed men stormed in. They weren't in uniform, but most were party men or SA or SS members, and after their first bullhorn announcement that this Jewish-owned establishment was hereby shut down, were rather chagrined to be told by patrons who happened to be their superiors, *Shut up, we're enjoying our champagne.* They smashed a window but were disheartened to learn that despite what they had been told, Der Teufel was no longer a Jewish cabaret. They checked a few papers, referred to their list, then summoned Aaron Morgenstern to join them for a conversation outside. Hannah tried to cling to him but he brushed past her without appearing to recognize her. None of the mob paid her the slightest attention. She was dressed once more in her blond wig and dirndl.

They kicked her father to the gutter as she watched, while

her mother dug her nails into her daughter's arm, pulses of pain sending the silent coded message: *Do nothing. By law you are Jewish too.* Down the street, all through Berlin, worse was happening. Storefronts were smashed, inventory burned. A synagogue two blocks away was in flames, its relics plundered or destroyed. Dimly, Hannah saw someone surrounded, heard laughter, saw a ghoulish figure raise a sledgehammer. Old women were thrown out of their homes in their nightclothes, their teeth still in jars at their bedsides. Young men were rounded up for Dachau. A shot rang out. Another. And through it all, like the crackling of a wildfire, breaking glass.

Aaron was lucky. Seeing an old man in this Devil's disguise, they decided he was unfit for labor and set him loose with no more than a split lip and a cracked rib. Der Teufel's juggler and two of the waiters were taken to labor camps, and only the juggler ever returned, years later, gaunt and lash scarred.

Near morning, when all was still at last, Hannah crept out to the street. The infernal gasses of the neon devil still glowed above her, pulsing red, leering at the river of glass shards and knocked-out teeth and once-prized possessions littering the boulevard.

This was mine, she thought, looking out at Berlin. *This was my city. I loved it. It loved me.*

Numbly, she found a broom behind the door and tried to clear away some of the rubble, murmuring all the while, "My city . . . my city . . ." Before long, a middle-aged man came by, a man with kind, tired eyes, a baker or grocer up early to open his store.

"Don't bother with that, *Fräulein*," he said pleasantly. "A nice girl like you needs her beauty sleep. They'll drag out some Jew dogs to clean up the mess soon enough." He tipped his cap to her. "Good morning!"

She watched him pick his way carefully through the glittering glass fangs, a typical Berliner, who smiled at pretty young girls and worried about his neighbor. A good man, except for one thing.

When he was gone, she ripped the forgotten blond wig off her head and flung it after him.

December 1938

Hannah, the Unfortunate Fruit

HANNAH STOOD AT THE GATE of Starkers and watched her cab
motor away. The driver had been paid by the Jewish Aid Com-
mittee to deliver her from the refugee agency, and he was not at
all pleased to have to go so far out of his London route with no
possibility of a tip from what was so obviously a penniless waif. It
was only when he was gone that Hannah realized the castle was
half a mile away from the gate.

"Oh, well," she said aloud. "Makes me rather glad I don't have
any luggage after all." She straightened her travel-shabby hat and
contemplated the dusty trek to her new home.

She'd been forced to stay at the refugee agency for several days
after all of her baggage and money were stolen. She tried to pay
them for their help. Cora, though scrupulously loyal to Aaron,
was after all beautiful and popular, and it was beyond her power
to refuse the strands of pearls that many admirers, inspired by

her name, forced on her. She had perfected the art of saying *no* in a tone that implied *if only*, and even as she aged, the pearls continued to come. Most had been sold through the years to pay for the cabaret, but she'd sewn the remainder into Hannah's skirt seams.

The refugee agency refused to accept them, saying she should save them for her parents when they finally followed her to England.

"His Lordship will pay you back, I'm sure," she told them.

Now she pushed open the heavy iron gate and stepped onto the grounds. In the distance she could see the crenelated heights of Starkers Castle.

For a second, she forgot shattered glass, distant family, the terror of the last weeks and the loneliness of the past days, and surrendered to the magnificent absurdity of it all. To think that because her mother's older sister had been married to a little man called Peregrine for a few months before she and her baby died in childbirth (*A few months only?* Hannah suddenly wondered, counting to nine and discovering possible scandal), she should have an earl's estate as a sanctuary.

"You must accept any treatment, be prepared for any harsh words they might throw at you," her mother had warned. "My sister was not considered a suitable match, and then, when she was dead, they didn't approve of me moving to Germany. I had become family through marriage, you see, and they thought they should control me, for the sake of the family's reputation. They've acknowledged your connection and have agreed to take you in, but don't expect them to be kind. It will only be for a while. Whatever happens, however they treat you, you must promise to stay at Starkers until we come. I need to know you're safe with family. Even an unloving family."

Hannah didn't believe her mother's gloomy prognostication. She stood still on the frost-browned grass at the winding roadside and knew exactly what Starkers would be like.

"It's straight out of P. G. Wodehouse," she said aloud, too loud, grinning for the first time in weeks.

"I live in hope," said a voice behind her. She hadn't even heard the car, it was so quiet, a sleek black Bugatti coupe looking like a panther stretched full-spring. Inside the rolled-down window, a rakish face looked up at her. "We have the aunts, we have the valet, we even have a silver cow creamer." He pushed his floppy, too-long chestnut hair out of his eyes. "But no matter what pains I take to set up a clever screwball comedy, my family remains steadfastly pedestrian."

"Except for you," Hannah said, eyeing the Bugatti.

He laughed, the freest laugh she had ever heard. It would knock down prison walls. "No, I'm rarely a pedestrian. I imagine myself taking long woodland strolls, but like the Wodehouse, staging it never quite happens. I'm always behind a wheel or atop a horse. You must be a new one."

"Rather new," she said, blushing.

"From Germany?"

She nodded, reminding herself to sound English. She could,

of course, but since even her mother spoke German most the time, her English tended to be accented unless she thought about it.

"We just got another one last week. Hop in—I'll take you to the door."

Hannah ran around to the other side.

"You read Wodehouse, eh? I hope this doesn't sound too bigoted, but I never thought of a refugee maid reading . . . oh, hullo!"

Hannah was so entranced by his poetic way of calling her a maid—for *maiden,* she assumed, another example of ever-changing English slang—that she found herself holding the car door open for the large blond woman who had just pulled up outside the gate in a second cab. Her hair was twisted into fantastic serpentines, and her very long dress was a shade away from white, just enough so that her attire suggested virginal glamour, not nursing. Her gloves, however, were pure white and immaculate. She slid into the two-seater.

"Thanks," the woman said, to the driver, not to Hannah. "Oh, you're not a chauffeur."

"Lord Winkfield, at your humble service, madam."

"Winkfield?"

"I know, embarrassing to no end, but what can one do? Still, ever so slightly better than Lord Liripip, what? May it be many years before I accede to my father's title, for more reasons than one. My mother is expecting you, I believe."

He seemed to suddenly remember Hannah, standing at the car-side, a shadowed little obscurity. "I'll be back for you directly," he said, with a smile that had the decency to be contrite.

"But I —" Hannah began, only to be cut off as the blond woman slammed the door. The Bugatti sent up refined puffs of dust, which settled on Hannah's travel-stained suit.

She waited . . . and waited . . . and waited, staring hungrily at the castle, thinking, in an abstract sort of way, about the young man she'd just almost met. As glib, but not, she thought, as foolish as a Wodehouse hero. He was Lord Liripip's only son and heir.

Her mother had given her a rundown on all of the family, from pottering old Liripip, who had married and buried two wives in quick succession before finally producing an heir, to Lady Liripip, who, unlike the more congenial wives before her, steadfastly refused to expire. There were two married daughters by the first late wife who, with their broods, often occupied Starkers. There was the obligatory eccentric uncle best known for riding to the hounds à la Godiva, minus the hair. All this Hannah's mother had gleaned from the society pages of English-language papers that trickled into Berlin a few days out of date. Of personalities, though, she could offer little, except to say that Lord Liripip almost always meant well, and Lady Liripip didn't.

The line of kicked-up road dust between Hannah and the castle had time to rise and settle again, and still no one came for her. She could have walked — she was bone weary from her journey, and from a fright she hardly let herself acknowledge, but she could have walked. However, he had said he would come back, so out of courtesy she waited. There was a square hunk of rock outside a faux guardhouse. She sat upon it and, to pass the time, took out an oft-folded copy of the letter Lady Liripip had sent.

> *You should know, Caroline, that my husband has never*
> *forgiven you for leaving England when he was in mourning*
> *for your late sister. It showed a most irresponsible and, may*
> *I say, unkind spirit. And to marry a foreigner, a stage jester*
> *no less, when Lord Liripip would have been so pleased to ar-*
> *range a union more suited to your fine family connections!*
> *And now you say the unfortunate fruit of that mésalliance*
> *must come to England? You never lacked nerve, Caroline.*
> *Very well, she may certainly come, but mark my words, we*
> *will teach her better than anyone ever taught you about*
> *what it means to be an Englishwoman of good blood and*
> *family. Here at Starkers, she will learn her proper place.*

It was a hard letter, from a hard woman, Hannah could see that, and rested on her mother's assurance that Lord Liripip was a gentle, easygoing man. No one had ever been unkind to Hannah, and she imagined Lady Liripip as a character, a stereotype, whose company one endured stoically, but whom one laughed at behind her back.

Hannah and her mother had had a good laugh together over

that term, *the unfortunate fruit,* and Cora had taken to calling her daughter by that name, with wry affection. She'd been wary of putting Hannah's full name in any of the letters, never being quite sure what the government might read. A neighbor had been taken in for questioning after writing to a Russian acquaintance about beet-seed, though her only Communist leanings were toward the neighborhood's communal vegetable garden. If anyone knew Cora was desperate to get her daughter out of Germany, it might attract attention. If she wanted to get out so badly, could it be because she was hiding something, selling secrets, dangerous in some way? The world was changing, Cora knew, and one couldn't be too careful. So she used her maiden name, Caroline Curzon, and Hannah's first name alone, giving a hotel as her return address.

Hannah had a particular aptitude for being sanguine in the face of trouble. Looking at the castle, at the grounds, she couldn't help but believe that Lady Liripip would be far less formidable than she appeared in her letter. Her parents would leave Germany in a few weeks without a hitch, and they would be together again, free of all danger. Why, in a few months Germany would probably come to its senses and a change of government would leave them free to go home again. Meanwhile, she was on holiday.

So she told herself, and tried to believe it. Then the sun shifted, casting clear slanting light on the dewy grass, and each silver drop shone like shattered glass. She shivered, feeling a gimlet of panic prod through the assurance she'd wrapped around herself. Was it here too, in this idyllic spot? The hate and the pain and the fear?

It couldn't be, because here, suddenly, was music, lilting over the grounds, and where there was music those bad things could not exist. The past days of travel were the first she'd spent in her entire life without being constantly enveloped in song. There was always someone practicing at Der Teufel — comic songs, ballads of tragic love, wry and subtle political songs that hid their jabs in syncopation. Scales rose and fell in the background of her life as birdsong does for a country dweller. And Hannah herself was rarely without a tune, murmuring songs as she bustled through her work in that low contralto so startlingly at odds with her slight form. Among the things she had given up — family and home — was music. In addition to her cabaret performances, she'd been taking private lessons most of her life, and her teacher thought it might be time to collect on the favor the director of the Vienna Opera owed him and send his young protégée.

She'd resigned herself to the loss of her career, because she told herself it was only a temporary loss. Even if she couldn't go back to Germany, even if Austria never welcomed her, there was opera in England, wasn't there? At worst she could take supporting roles in Gilbert and Sullivan operettas — they, along with Wodehouse, were her standard for interpreting the English. But it was only now that she realized how acutely she missed music in her everyday life. There had been no singing on the train, where she'd trembled at every stop and checkpoint. There had been no singing on the Channel crossing, during which she had been most humiliatingly ill. The refugee office had been all bustle and efficiency, everyone far too busy to pause for a song.

Now, as the uplifted voice reached her ears, she felt she was breathing for the first time in days, and gasped it in eagerly. She saw him then, a strapping fellow a little older than she, with that typical floppy English hair, a shade or two darker than Lord Winkfield's. He was pushing a wheelbarrow, belting out a song she'd never heard before but that she instantly wanted to steal and translate for Der Teufel.

She was still puzzling out how she could change it to German, the impossibility of it making her mouth curl most becomingly, when the man parked his barrow at her feet.

"You're the new maid?" he asked.

It occurred to Hannah that either she'd missed some colloquialism in her mother's English or expressions had changed since her mother had left the country. She knew women were called bird, chick, hen. It sounded so medieval to be called a maid, but if that was the slang of the day . . .

"I am. I've just arrived."

He grinned at her. "I know. If you'd been here already you'd already be my girl." He winked at her, and it was so like the backstage flirtation, which never meant a thing, that she felt instantly at home. "Just remember, I've called dibs. Why have a footman when you can have a gardener? Well, under-gardener."

"Does that mean you just do the potatoes and bulbs and such?"

"Under-gardener for underground things! Oh, you're a doozy, you are. And not quite as scary as the other new refugee maid. Whoo-ee, but she could eat a man alive! You're a much handier morsel. Now, where are your things?"

"I don't have any. They were . . . lost." She was ashamed to admit she was foolish enough to have let them be stolen. No, the truth must be faced squarely. "When I was getting off the boat someone in an official-looking cap took my bags and said to follow him to the cab. He wove through the crowd and I never saw him or my bags again."

"Cheeky. But not so cheeky as me. I would have asked for a tip. I'm Hardy, by the way. That's your cue to play Nelson and say *Kiss me, Hardy.* I tell you in case you don't know, being a foreigner. Though you hardly speak like one. I will, you know."

"Will what?"

"Kiss you, of course."

"No, thank you," she said amiably.

"Suit yourself. Hop in." He tipped the barrow.

She glanced up at distant Starkers. What would they think? Suddenly, she didn't care. She was herself, Hannah Morgenstern. Let others take her as they may.

She slid her tush into the wheelbarrow, crossed her ankles neatly, and began to sing, catching the words easily.

A few minutes later, Lord Liripip, nursing his gout and scribbling away at his memoirs in an upstairs library, heard the melodious uproar and heaved himself to the window, ready to yell or chuck a volume of Trollope at the offender. He froze as soon as he drew a preparatory breath, for below him was nothing less than a memory made flesh, a delicious and painful spirit coursing down his throat, warming and intoxicating and befuddling him. There, cavorting on the green, was his youth. There, raising her voice in unselfconscious song, was the love of his life, many years gone, made fresh and new again. The resemblance was only superficial, he realized a moment later—a small, lissome, vibrant form, dark hair parted virginally dead center over quizzical black brows. What really caught him was her animalistic joy. Like another girl, many years before, she seemed to have a sense that no one else's opinion mattered in the slightest, yet combined with that, a total lack of selfishness. *I will make myself happy,* her free voice and body seemed to say, *and through that, may you be made happy too. If not* . . . a shrug, a gay laugh, and on with the Maenad frenzy of sheer living.

It hurled Lord Liripip into his past, to a time when he still had hope of happiness. Now, all he had were the things that made other people assume he was happy: vast amounts of money, a secure estate, and a son to carry it all on after he was gone.

Leaning out the window to see her better, he twisted his big toe at a painful angle and staggered back, crystalline needles stabbing his swollen joint. "Damned hooligans," he swore. But he did not hurl the Trollope.

Hannah and Hardy reached the front steps. "Is that an actual portcullis?" she asked in awe.

"That gate thing? No, this castle isn't real, you know."

Hannah cocked her head up at the massive edifice. It looked real enough.

"It's neo-romantic," Hardy said, pronouncing the term carefully, as if it might get stuck on his tongue if he wasn't careful. "Built not more than a hundred years ago, after they knocked down something *really* old, and made to look like five hundred. 'Cept the heating's better, a bit. That's what Umbel, the head gardener, says, anyway, when the ladies from the gardening clubs come on tour days. That's only once or twice a year, though. Lord Liripip hates outsiders."

"What will he think of me, then?"

"Fancy him thinking of you at all!" Hardy said, laughing. "Hey, where do you think you're going?" For she'd mounted the smooth-edged marble stairs and grabbed the velvet bell-pull. "Stop!"

She turned back to him, wondering why he looked so aghast. Was she supposed to wait for him to ring the bell for her? She had no patience for inaction, or the indolence of propriety. Hannah acutely remembered going to her mother in tears of laughter one time when she'd read some English melodrama in which the heroine had never once in her eighteen years of existence put on her own stockings. *It is true,* Cora had said with a rueful smile. *English ladies—real English ladies—are notorious for doing as little as possible, except ride to the hounds. There are servants for everything else.* Young Hannah had scrunched up her face into unaccustomed earnestness and said, *Then, Mama, I am glad you moved to Germany. I should not like to do nothing all day. And shouldn't the servants get awfully tired?*

There were workers in Der Teufel, of course, and she supposed technically they were servants, but they were employees who became friends and happened to sweep and wash dishes, not some lesser form of life evolved to do all of the unpleasant chores. She had no class divide in her life. Certainly, her father had owned the cabaret, and if a city official was sick behind the potted palm Mr. Morgenstern wasn't the one to clean it up, but when they celebrated some new act, everyone from the busboys to the stars drank champagne and kissed one another.

"Thank you so much, Hardy," she said. "Perhaps when I have the leisure you can show me around the garden. I am so fond of flowers, though I know nothing about how to grow them, only how to catch them." She closed her eyes a moment, recalling a massive bouquet of golden roses an old man had shakily thrown to her after (what else?) a sheep song. She'd buried her face in the blooms, dizzy with sweetness, the petals like a lover's fingertips . . .

Dreaming, remembering, she pulled the bell.

She raised her beatific face to the answering butler, Coombe, who thought he had seen something similar reproduced in one of the improving circulars to which he subscribed, a portrait of Saint Someone in Ecstasy, perhaps Theresa, or Cecelia, or even Francis. He was so taken by her shining, transported countenance that it was a full three seconds before he noticed her shabby clothes, the dark circles under her eyes, her gloveless little paws, and mustered a severe frown that still contained, visible only in a twitch in its sinister corner, a hint of avuncular benevolence.

"We do not use the front door," he said, the *we* sounding more royal than inclusive.

"What door do we use, then?" Hannah asked, sounding once again quite German in her perplexity.

"Back entrance only, strictly observed," he said, then, allowing himself a little joke, "except, of course, on stair-scrubbing days." He shut the door in her face.

"But . . ." Hannah attempted.

He opened it enough to point to her right, and shut it with stern finality. Then he went to inform the housekeeper that the new kitchen maid had arrived, and was going to need a good deal of watching.

Mrs. Wilcox, the housekeeper, sighed deeply, a luxury she only allowed herself in the company of her old friend Coombe. "It's Himself's digestion will suffer for it. Cook's in such a state, I don't know how she'll ever cope with an untrained creature."

Cook was on the verge of a nervous breakdown, or quitting,

or perhaps jumping for joy, or all three, because only a week before, she'd been humble under-cook Sally Mayweather, a step above kitchen maid, a vast canyon below the lofty Cook. But the old cook, Trapp, had fallen ill and been sent to a sister in Lyme Regis to recover, which, the doctors owned, she might never do, and now her underling had taken her position. It was an honor, a significant increase in salary—and a job of terrifying responsibility requiring the strategy of a general combined with the steady hand of a surgeon, the aesthetics of an artist, and the human understanding of a Viennese psychiatrist. She had two other kitchen maids to help her, but neither was competent enough to fill her old position of under-cook, and they had to be chivvied through even the most mundane tasks. Now she moaned to whoever would listen that she could not possibly prepare daily feasts for the Liripips, never mind the absolute banquets when there were guests, with an incompetent staff.

But she had, for the past few weeks. The kitchen maids had gone to sleep after midnight on tear-stained pillows, but every bite, from delicate crustless cress tea sandwiches to haunches of venison to a splendid charlotte russe, had been perfection.

Coombe, remembering that ecstatic Cherubino face, said, without much hope, "Perhaps she'll do."

She would no doubt do for something, but probably not for kitchen maid.

Anna Is a Kissing Cousin

LADY LIRIPIP LOOKED THE NEWCOMER up and down, as if she were a Chippendale cabinet of dubious authenticity. "You look English enough. I remember your mother as a brown girl. I suppose your father is blond. How fortunate for you—his sort are so often swarthy, I gather." She sniffed, and that sniff conveyed volumes.

Only Anna's strict self-training kept her from responding. Knowing her inadequacies, her gaps in learning and culture, she tended to remain silent whenever she was not absolutely certain what to say. Her mother did have light brown hair, though she could not imagine how Lady Liripip could have encountered her, and her father was indeed blond. And why should she not look English?

"I have decided that if you are to be here it is absolutely necessary that we do not speak of your family. I will not do you the discourtesy of speaking ill of your father, and the easiest way to do that is to not refer to him at all. You are not responsible for the sins of your parents—*sin* is a hard word, I own, but there it is." She sniffed again, and Anna wondered if she'd trodden on something when she'd exited the car.

"You are family, of sorts, and I embrace you, and forgive you for what you could not help. But while you are here you will be strictly English. I do not want to hear you converse in a foreign language. That is not done in this house. Even when we entertain ambassadors they are requested to speak our mother tongue. You will kindly not speak of Germany, or the stage. Follow those rules, comport yourself like a proper Englishwoman, and you will fit in quite nicely. I will guide you, my dear." Lady Liripip smiled, and the effect was ghastly, like a mummy Anna had seen in the British Museum, its lips in a permanent rictus over too-long teeth. "Now come and kiss me, Hannah dear."

"It's Anna, my lady," she said before she could help herself. "Anna Morgan."

Slowly, she was beginning to think that Lord Darling and the German Von had exerted rather more influence on her behalf than she'd dared hope. Where she was expecting to be incognito in the kitchen, here she was being welcomed by the lady of the house, into the very bosom of the family! Had Lord Darling revealed his plan to them? No, he wouldn't have. Even if he had, it would be imprudent to speak of it. Had he given them a code name for her? Was that where Lady Liripip had gotten Hannah?

Though if that had been part of Darling's scheme, he surely would have prepared Anna to answer to a different name.

This, at least, did not appear to be a blunder. Lady Liripip's smile — which now looked almost predatory, so long and so numerous were her gleaming teeth — grew even bigger, and she said, "How sensible of you. Anyone would mark you as a Jewess with the name Hannah. I'm sure you had no say in the matter when your mother named you." Anna had bossed her tractable mother from a very early age, but not so early as that. "But it is right and just of you to adopt a more English-sounding name now that you are free. We shall get along very well, Anna, I am sure of it. Only you must take pains to learn how a respectable Englishwoman behaves. Gloves, for example, should not be worn indoors."

Anna clasped her hands. "I'm very sorry, but I have . . ." She somehow thought the excuse she usually used — sensitive hands — wouldn't fly with Lady Liripip. "I have an . . . unsightly condition on my hands. I keep them covered to . . . preserve your sensibilities."

Lady Liripip looked slightly alarmed, as if she might be thinking of leprosy. Then she calmed. After all, Germany was not quite Molokai. Almost, but not quite.

"You are a considerate child. Come, we will have tea. Do you have a lady's maid? No, of course not; what am I thinking? You are penniless." If it smarted, she did not care, and Anna did not show it. "We will have to see about finding you a husband. I did so well for my stepdaughters. The children of Lord Liripip's first marriage, you know. Your mother's sister, his second wife, had no living children, and I have only my darling boy. You shall meet him soon."

"I believe I have met him," Anna said, with a look Lady Liripip did not at all like. Then she gave a dry little laugh, dismissing her fears. This continental Anna was pretty enough, in a blousy, overblown way, she supposed, but not the sort to interest her son. Lady Liripip had been gathering titled young heiresses of impeccable lineage ever since Theodore, Lord Winkfield, known to everyone except his mother as Teddy, had been delivered far enough for his gender to be determined. Her life was devoted to the intellectual pursuit of arranging for him a wife who would be perfectly suitable in every way, not the least important trait being that she would make no effort to supplant her mother-in-law. Lady Liripip was twenty years younger than her husband, and assumed she would end her days as a dowager, a most uncomfortable position if one has not cultivated one's daughter-in-law with great care.

No, Lady Liripip thought she knew her son well enough to believe she had nothing to fear from Anna. She took her arm and led her to tea, where she was pleased to find the young lady knew how to handle the Limoges. Anna ate one apricot biscuit with delicate exactitude, nary a crumb to be seen. She made pleasant conversation about flowers in a general way, was vaguely disparaging about modern art, and praised her hostess's dress, cameo brooch, furniture, and coiffure in the sycophantic manner that was exactly to Lady Liripip's taste. She was not one for subtlety.

Lady Liripip found she was pleased with the arrangement. Every woman in her position wants a companion, one she can bully but who will never turn on her. Poor relations are easy to find, if one scours the family tree carefully, but dependent companions are usually old, or frail, or uneducated, or in some way unfit for society. Anna was pretty enough to be an ornament, and her mother was of good stock, but she was poor and solitary and, apparently, desperate, though Lady Liripip only dimly understood what was happening in Germany. (In that she was certainly not alone, in England or the world, or even in many parts of Germany.) Lady Liripip, for reasons she could not begin to fathom, did not seem to attract any female friends. They came to her house with their husbands for her lavish events, paid the requisite social calls, but they did not gossip or scheme. Their flattery was perfunctory, and came mostly from those who had eligible daughters. Anna, gracious and free with her compliments, with a knack for sounding sincere, would be a pleasant diversion for a while. Then, when Lady Liripip was tired of her, she could be married off to a country attorney or a parson.

The ghastly smile twitched again. Lady Liripip had hated Caroline Curzon and her modern, wild sister, Lord Liripip's unfortunate second wife. It pleased her to have her dead rival's relative under her thumb, even if she chose to stroke her with that thumb.

The door, its hinges weekly greased and then cleaned again to render the grease invisible, opened with respectful silence, admitting a not so silent or respectful Teddy. "Hullo, Mum. What ho, long-lost cousin. Didn't greet you properly before." He took Anna's unprotesting hands, hauled her to her feet, and gave her a kiss on the cheek, releasing her so abruptly afterward that, whether through astonishment or mere lack of support, she toppled back onto the springing cushion, where parts of her continued to bounce in a way that did not please Lady Liripip at all.

"Anna is not your cousin, dear," Lady Liripip corrected.

"Of course not. Still, some sort of relation. I can never fathom second cousins and thingumies once removed. Can I puzzle it out?" He cocked his head and regarded Anna, making her suddenly too warm, stirring feelings that had nothing—or at any rate very little—to do with Teddy's wealth and title. "I've got it! You're my step-aunt!"

"I am?" Anna asked.

"Your mother's sister was married to my father, so . . . no, your *mother* would be my step-aunt. You must be my step-cousin. Or my kissing cousin, to use that American slang Mum detests."

"What is a kissing cousin?" Anna asked, to cover her confusion about something much bigger than mere slang. Her head was swimming, she was foundering—or floundering, she could never remember which word it was—and she needed Teddy to keep babbling to give her time to catch up.

Teddy blushed, glanced at his mother, then remembered he

was at Oxford and a man, and soldiered on. "First cousins can't marry, so a cousin you can kiss is anyone more distantly related. Ahem. I'll dress for dinner, if you don't mind. Are we *en famille* tonight, Mum? Make sure I'm sitting next to Anna. I have so much to ask her about Germany. Toodle-oo!"

When he was gone, Anna breathed, "Oh my!"

Lady Liripip examined the girl's face carefully, determining whether the hot flush of her ears was instant infatuation, ambition, or shame. She saw Anna's lip tremble, and decided on the latter.

"I do apologize for Theodore. He has cultivated a most free and cavalier manner. They let practically anyone into Oxford these days, and I fear he might be associating with a literary crowd." She gave a delicate shudder, like the withers of a thoroughbred when a fly alights. Then she fixed Anna with a penetrating look. "He is so friendly, so chivalrous, so polite, that he is always giving ladies the wrong idea, the poor misguided creatures. I hope you never delude yourself into mistaking his kindness for anything else."

"Oh, no, Lady Liripip, I would never presume!" Anna said with such vigor that the older woman's fears were entirely quelled. Anna lowered her long golden-brown eyelashes for good measure, and tried to look every inch the unassuming relative.

"You are a good girl," Lady Liripip said, rising and then patting her on the head as she passed, as if the young woman were a spaniel who could reasonably be expected not to mess on the

Persian carpet. She looked at the soft, fair, upturned face, comparing its roses and cream, its large eyes and full lips, with the narrow, horsy, aristocratic faces of the assorted girls she'd selected as proper mates, girls with faces and breeding much like her own. No, she told herself again, Theodore would no more yearn after this girl than he would the kitchen maid.

Anna, trying and failing to discreetly fix her disarrayed high-piled curls, followed Lady Liripip to the bedroom she'd selected for her guest. She'd actually ordered two made up — one quite grand, quite near to her own, with a view of the terraced gardens, another cramped and insignificant, overlooking some gloomy yews. The girl was well spoken, showed none of the bohemianism or defiance she expected in the offspring of Caroline Curzon, and seemed to have no designs on her beloved boy. She put her in the larger room.

"Dinner is at eight," she said, and swept out, thinking she had done an act of almost saintly charity and goodness, yet still relishing the sense of triumph over the girl's mother and late aunt, her erstwhile nemeses. *How bitter it will be for Caroline,* she thought, *to know that her daughter is safe only because of me, that she owes the clothes on her back, the very food in her stomach, to my generosity.*

And so, doing good but meaning ill, she sat to her toilette in perfect spiritual contentment.

As soon as she was alone, Anna collapsed into the deep eiderdown of her bed, breathless, giddy with elation. The bright golden arrow of her life had been aiming for this ever since she could put her desires into coherent thoughts. Her father, rising higher than his birth and education ever led him to expect, had pulled her up on his coattails to what she had once thought were lofty heights. But this! A castle, an estate — a titled heir! All placed in the palm of her gloved hand. She had dreamed it might be possible, had schemed to make it so, but here she was, almost without her volition, placed squarely in luxury and position.

Anna squeezed the downy voluptuousness of the thick bedspread and laughed, softly at first, then like a maniac. She sprang up and ran to the gilt-edged mirror hovering over a most elegant vanity table and looked at her beauty, regarding it as a beloved old friend, a loyal companion, a partner with whom she would make her fortune.

He adores me already, she told herself, mistaking his humor and native friendliness for passion (just as Lady Liripip said she would, though one would hate to admit she might be right about anything). *Kissing cousins!*

Then, before she even realized she was afraid, she saw the roses flee her cheeks, replaced by ivory pallor. Her body knew before her mind that she was sailing in dangerous waters, under false colors. How on earth had she been mistaken for a — what had Teddy decided on? — step-cousin! Was it all part of the machinations of the Von and Lord Darling, in which Lady Liripip and family were complicit? It seemed a rather complicated cover story. Perhaps they had decided that for whatever service to cause and country she needed to perform, she must be sitting on the parlor couch, not plumping its cushions; that she must be eating succulent mock turtle soup, not preparing it. She would just have to play her part, and all would no doubt become clear in time. Meanwhile, there was Teddy, Lord Winkfield, to ensnare.

That, however, was looking on the bright side. There was another possibility. What if there were indeed, somewhere in the world, a step-cousin? Lady Liripip had said she was not to speak of Germany, or the stage, that her name was meant to be Hannah, a Jewish name. Lady Liripip did not appear to be acting a role. She seemed to really expect a Jewish girl to appear on her doorstep, to be taken under her wing.

Father wouldn't like that, Anna thought. One of her father's favorite rants of late was about Jewish intellectuals (how he spat those words, one more abhorrent to him than the other) sneaking into the country and stealing the honest livings from good English girls. Let a Jew into your scullery and you might as well invite the rats and beetles, he would shout (forgetting that his own English grocery had been the one with the vermin). Let a Jew cook your supper and you'll be poisoned. How he would roar at the notion of Jewish girls being taken into aristocratic families.

Anna, to the best of her knowledge, had never met a Jew. She looked at herself in the mirror and thought, with about as much generosity and milk of human kindness as she possessed, *If I can be mistaken for one, they can't be* that *bad, can they?*

And so, in loving herself, she almost loved her fellow man.

Uncertain, she drifted away from the mirror and looked out

the window. There, below, she saw a manly form. Teddy, she was certain, and rapped on the window to try to catch his attention. But when he turned and looked up, she saw it wasn't he. This man was of a height with Teddy, had his same broad shoulders and floppy hair, but his locks were browner, his brows heavy and dark, his appearance more intense, compelling. She felt a familiar weakening somewhere within her. It was a failing that had plagued her for years, absurd longings for the wrong man. But lord, he was handsome, even at this distance! Alas, he carried a pot of chrysanthemums under each arm. He was only a gardener, and thus beneath her notice. She turned away abruptly and tried, and failed, to picture Teddy's face.

I'll play my part as long as I can, she decided. *And if I get unmasked before I can do what Lord Darling demands, perhaps I can still be a step-cousin long enough to snag Teddy.*

All things considered, she'd much rather be the wife of a lord, eventually wife of an earl, than a heroine. Heroines, she seemed to remember, sometimes wind up dead.

She shivered, and pinched her cheeks until the color came back.

Hannah Meets the Heir of Trapp

ECCENTRIC, HANNAH DECIDED. That was the only explanation: the family was eccentric. The trait ran in aristocratic blood, apparently—she'd learned that from Wodehouse. And there was the uncle who rode to the hounds in the nude (or occasionally, on a good day, in one of those pink coats that was really scarlet, and nothing else). So it stood to reason that the family should have some peculiar traditions. She unfolded that little inward crumpling that had begun when she was turned away from the front door and marched gamely to the rear.

Behind her, Hardy tut-tutted. "Just my luck—the prettiest ones always get axed," he muttered as he pushed his barrow.

"This house is as big as a city block!" Hannah said as she dragged each weary leg a step further around Starkers's walls.

"It almost *is* a city," Hardy said, wondering if he could steal a kiss before Cook heard about this girl's effrontery and sent her off without a reference. "Well more than fifty on the staff, if you include the foresters and gamekeepers. We have our own laundry, our own plumber, an electrician, and a few carpenters. And of course if you include the village of Winkfield, you have everything else you might need. Lord Liripip owns Winkfield too, you know."

"And I'm to be a part of it all," she said wonderingly, craning her neck to look up at the crenellations chiseled against an iris-hued sky.

"For a minute or two, anyway." Just long enough to get chewed out. Hardy tipped his hat regretfully. "I'll be back and forth from the hothouse. They want chrysanthemums in the drawing room. Come and see me right before you leave." He pointed to a crystal-line wonder gleaming like a huge cut diamond in the late-afternoon sun.

Hannah looked perplexed. "But that might not be for a very long time." Perhaps the family wasn't supposed to mingle with the servants, but she liked Hardy's easy, friendly ways and hoped to see him much sooner.

"Not nearly as long as you might think," he said.

She closed her eyes again, briefly, ecstatically, to see that world in her mind where her homeland was restored to its senses, where people were not imprisoned for their last names, where her family would be together again. She'd braced herself to wait, to endure as long as it took for her world to set itself aright, but could

Hardy be correct? Maybe it wouldn't be so long after all. "How *kind* of you to say so!" she said, and ran up to give him a feathery kiss on the cheek.

Hardy walked off in a daze, and Hannah rapped her knuckles on the white-painted wooden door. A chip flaked off and fell to her feet.

"Yes?" came a harried voice before the door even opened. Hannah saw a girl about her own age, tall and scrawny, with her hair slicked back tightly under a white cap, and a sheen of sweat on her brow. "Oh, you're the one old Trapp said would come. Inside. Where's your things?"

"Lost. Stolen."

"No mind. You're to get two dresses while you're in here, returned upon quitting. You don't need no best as you won't have no time to yourself. Least, not 'cept when you're too dead on your feet to think of fun with a young gentleman." She heaved a mighty sigh, then perked up. "Oh, but with you here to help . . ." Her hips gave a suggestion of a sway. "Maybe I'll have the strength for a turn or two about the village hall after all. This way."

She led Hannah through a spacious, spotless kitchen and pointed to a little antechamber where a pleasant-faced woman was sitting at a table, thumbing through accounts. "Cook," the girl called out, "got a new leveret for you to skin and roast." Distantly, a little bell tinkled. "Damn. I mean jeepers," the girl gasped as she raced toward the dying peal. "This will be your job soon, leveret!" she called over her shoulder. "Hope you're as fast as a hare."

"Less of your cheek!" Sally Mayweather snapped at the girl's backside. Then she looked the newcomer over.

Trapp—the old cook—had been a martinet of the highest degree. She didn't actually carry a little whip on her belt, but the unlucky souls who worked under her might have preferred corporal punishment to the stinging lash of her tongue and the sometimes arbitrary discipline she doled out. By her word her minions might be denied their weekly afternoon off or their alternate whole day Sunday. They would be set to performing the same mind-numbingly dull task—polishing the stove or scrubbing the steps—over and over again until she deemed it perfect. Like nursery ne'er-do-wells, they might even have their pudding withheld.

Sally and the ever-changing bevy of kitchen maids had put up with it all, though, because Trapp was the best in the business. Other grand estates insisted on having a male in the kitchen, an impressive continental chef with airs and an accent. That was only because they couldn't steal Trapp away from Starkers. She might have been a beastly old harridan, as mean as a vexed badger, but she could single-handedly coordinate and cook the most elaborate and delicious meals anyone had ever tasted. When she prepared a banquet she went into a sort of frenzied daze, almost mystical to witness. Surrounded by her ingredients and equipment, she would pinch and slap anyone who didn't do precisely as she was told. Once she even stabbed Sally with a fork—not severely, though that was more through Sally's agility than Trapp's intent. In the end, everyone (except Trapp) was in tears and utterly exhausted, bruised, and swearing to give notice. But the meals were brilliant.

And the thing Sally learned early on about being a cook was that in service, it was absolutely the best job with absolutely the worst training period. A kitchen maid was a slave, pure and simple. In the old days they had scullery maids, at least, stunted and dimwitted drudges who could do the really unpleasant things. Now that they had fallen out of fashion (no doubt being too depressing to the upper classes when they had to read about them in those novels the rich write about the poor), their work fell to the kitchen maids.

But on the glorious day that a kitchen maid transmuted into a cook, ah! Suddenly she had power, money, status. She ruled her realm absolutely, and overruled the housekeeper and even the lady of the house in matters of the kitchen. She had time off whenever she liked, so long as there was no meal to get ready or she could leave an under-cook in charge. She got tips and bribes from every merchant, for she decided which businesses got the biggest accounts. If she was good she was courted by other houses, and could demand raises accordingly to stay in her place.

Other servants would serve all their lives, even the highest. A cook was a queen.

Now Sally was queen, a quivering blancmange of a queen who could cook like a champion but was terrified of the prospect of bossing people around. She was not a natural leader, so with Trapp as her only model, she was doing her best to emulate her.

It was certainly effective — the kitchen maids wept at least as much as they did under Trapp's reign — but keeping up the tough act was driving gentle-natured Sally crazy.

"Well?" she said, cocking her head up at Hannah. "And what are you supposed to be?" It hurt to snap at another human being like that, especially one who looked so small and perplexed and pretty.

Hannah gave a slow, heavy blink. "I'm *supposed* to be a debut coloratura contralto in the Vienna Opera House," she said with deep melancholy worthy of the best tragedy or the worst farce. "But how many people are what they are supposed to be? Good morning. I am Hannah Morgenstern. I've come here to stay."

She held out a delicate, expressive little hand, and waited.

What would Trapp do? Sally wondered. Could she possibly shake the hand of an underling?

The hand hovered in midair, palpably yearning to be clasped, cupped slightly upward, offering a benediction as much as a shake.

Knowing she'd cry about it later, Sally glared at the hand until it fell, as dispirited as a baby bird tumbled from the nest.

"Stay or go depends on me and no other. You're a refugee, aren't you?" Trapp had mentioned hiring a girl before she was carted away to Lyme Regis, but she'd said nothing about her being foreign, as this girl so plainly was. They had been streaming into England for weeks now, and every household that took them in complained about their uppish ways and absolute ignorance of proper service. Just what she needed. "Hannah, you say? The last three maids were Jane. I ought to call you Jane too."

"I'll never answer," Hannah said, summoning a laugh. "Whenever I had to act—I mostly sing, you know, but at the cabaret we all do everything, and I was the understudy for five of the ladies—I would always miss my cue if it meant someone calling me by the character's name. In the end they just named all the girl characters Hannah in case I had to step in and play them. Jane is such a lovely name, though, isn't it? So plain and simple, but noble, you know, like Lady Jane Grey, and Jane Eyre, and Jane—"

"Tongues are for tasting, not wagging," Sally said with as sour a face as she could muster, though she secretly decided Jane would never do for this girl. "No jibber-jabber in my kitchen."

"Oh." Hannah sighed. "I'll just have to stay out of the kitchen, then. I'm afraid there's no chance that I'll ever stop talking, unless I'm singing, and that's just as bad, I'm sure, if you prefer silence. My father used to say I never heard of a full stop. Though I'm much better now. At least I take a breath now and then so other people have a hope of breaking in. What a shame! The kitchen is my favorite room. At home we'd always gather . . . Yes, I see your look and I remember now, no jibber-jabber. Shall I go up to see Lord and Lady Liripip?" She supposed she should call them

Peregrine and . . . what was his wife's name? Enid? Edna? But it was probably better to err on the side of formality, since relations were historically strained. No doubt they'd want her to call them Aunt and Uncle, or something quintessentially English like Gaffer or Guv'nor.

The poor little foreigner, Sally thought. *She has no idea what's in store for her.* Already the girl's cheerful patter was lightening the kitchen, making that day's vast and heavy labors seem slightly more possible than they had lately. But Sally knew from Trapp that where there was spirit it must be crushed, and where there was frivolity it must be bent and twisted into drudgery, else dinner would never be served.

"You will not be seen. You will never be seen by Lord Liripip. As for Herself, on most days she summons me to her morning room to discuss the menus, but occasionally she comes to the kitchen and talks with me here. She will not speak to you. She will not notice you. For her, you do not exist. Just consider yourself fortunate that you have a place at all, and don't trouble your betters."

To think that only a few weeks ago Sally had been talking to Coombe of servants' unions and the equality of all people, servant or served! She did not believe for one moment that Enid Liripip (it was Enid after all) was her better, or this new lass's for that matter. Why, this girl had brought more nice things into the world in the last two minutes than Lady Liripip had in her whole life.

Very politely, very diplomatically, Hannah folded her hands and said, "I understand that she might not want to spend a great deal of time in my company. I do not wish to impose. But it is only civilized that I thank her in person for her kind hospitality in allowing me to live here during my time of trouble." She had rehearsed the speech, and thought she carried it off well. "I . . . we . . . my family and of course I am . . . are . . . Oh my, I have it muddled now. Let me begin again." Her accent was encroaching. "Ahem. I know: hush. I mean you want me to hush, not that you should hush. I'm rarely rude except accidentally, and that doesn't really count, but if I might just get through my speech to you I'll do a much better job when I see Enid."

Enid! Trapp would have boxed her ears for that, though no one had had their ears boxed outside of stories for fifty years. Sally only just managed to suppress a smile and said sternly, "You will never dare to speak to Her Ladyship, or to any of the family. In fact, you will rarely be permitted to leave the kitchen."

It began to dawn on Hannah that something was most emphatically not right.

"You mean . . . they won't see me? Not at all?"

I won't do it, Sally told herself when she saw Hannah's large, luminous eyes begin to well. *I can't* do it. *I'll be a Trapp later, promise, but not right now.* "What did they tell you when they arranged for you to come? Did you think you would be part of the family?" Trapp would have said the same thing, but the sympathy in Sally's voice made one fat tear roll down Hannah's cheek.

"I didn't think they'd love me," she said, her rich, low voice cracking. "But I thought they'd at least see me. How can they be so cruel?"

"They don't view it as cruelty. Come now, buck up. I put just the right amount of salt in all my dishes—I don't need your tears brining everything. You're German, are you, and a Jew?"

Hannah nodded.

"I've read about some of the unpleasantness going on in Germany, and I do think it's a shame. But you're safe here now. All you have to do is work hard, and maybe one day you'll be a cook like me. There's no better place to train than Starkers." She forced herself to become Trappish again. "If you don't obey, you'll be out on the street. If you're here on a work permit, that means deportation back to Germany."

"They would do that to me?" All her mother's warnings came rushing back to her. She hadn't believed it. People might be grumps, ignorant and selfish. They might not *want* to take in stray members of their family. She'd braced herself to be lectured and insulted and given a tiny room and relegated to the worst seat at the table. She was ready for all sorts of criticisms of cabaret life. *Don't expect kindness from them,* her mother had said.

Not kindness, no, but civility. Human decency. Hannah remembered that night of broken glass, and wondered if such a thing as human decency still existed. Had it withered away in the human spirit, victim of some insidious modern disease?

You must accept any treatment. Her mother had said that, too.

Hannah smoothed the single fallen tear into her cheek until it disappeared. "To be sure I understand," she began, her accent thick now as in her mingled fury and disappointment she reverted to her more natural pronunciations, "you mean that I am to work in the kitchen? To be permitted to live here but only to work?"

"To serve, yes."

"Like a penitent," Hannah said, settling her heavy-lashed dark brown eyes on Sally. She composed herself, making her small body somehow even more compact, folding in on herself to become an organism of profound self-sufficiency and inwardness.

Sally felt a sudden, almost overwhelming urge to fall on her knees before the girl and beg her forgiveness. But Trapp whispered in her ear: *So she thought her life would be easy and it is hard. Should you care? You scrubbed your share of grates and slate floors. Your knees still ache with it. So she's some European bluestocking with soft hands and too much to say. Peeling potatoes and plucking pheasants never killed anyone. Better than whatever is happening to her sort in Germany.*

"Shut up," Sally muttered under her breath, too softly for Hannah to hear.

"I beg your pardon?"

"Nothing. One of the housemaids will show you to your room and fetch your uniforms. Two print, one blue, the other pink." Horrid things they were, too. "Plus aprons and caps — cap to be worn at all times — and towels. Return here for lunch and you may begin your duties assisting at dinner. Fortunately it is only the family here tonight, and one houseguest, a distant relative of some sort. Tomorrow you will begin your official daily duties. Here is a list. Wait out there, and close the door behind you."

When she was gone, Sally had a quick therapeutic weep, the second of the day and by no means the last. Then she splashed her face, dusted her nose with powder, and set about making other people cry, as Trapp would have wished.

Hannah May Eat as
Many Bugs as She Likes

HANNAH HAD JUST BEEN DECIDING with what exact degree of stiff, formal politeness she would greet the designated housemaid when she heard more singing—throaty, abysmally untalented singing in ribald German. She took a swift, sharp breath. It could not be . . .

The door swung open, and in came Waltraud, the (mostly) female half of the Double Transvestite Tango.

"Traudl, could it be you? Oh no, it couldn't, really, never in that outfit." Hannah's mobile face incandesced into joy. She took her friend by the arms. "What do they call this?" She rubbed the rough black fabric between her finger and thumb.

"Linsey-woolsey," Waltraud said with an exaggerated English accent, then switched immediately back to German. "Isn't it a scream?"

"I hardly knew you without silk and sequins. How on earth did you get here?"

"Oh, *Liebchen,* it was terrible. I had to sell all my costume jewelry to that horrid Bavarian hen, and my only consolation is that she can't tell glass from diamonds. Still, they were all such pretty baubles, and now they adorn her fat neck. Do you know she took a Nazi lover? Perhaps he will strangle her with my faux sapphires one day. One must always look on the bright side, no? I got just enough for all the bribes and there I was, on a train at the border, absolutely penniless but with one very valuable piece of paper giving me permission to work here in England. Then—oh, Hannah, how it shames me to tell you!"

"As if anything could shame you, Traudl," Hannah said with an impish grin. Waltraud had never shunned a dare, never followed a law if it did not please her, rarely bothered to determine the gender of a pretty lover before turning off the lights.

"Wait until you hear this, though. All my money was gone, and there, at the very border, a guard demanded one more bribe. 'But I'm broke,' I protested. He claimed a woman always has a way to pay. My dear, do you think I clawed his eyes out? Do you think I ripped off his little counterfeit family jewels so those baubles could replace the ones I sold?"

If she had, Hannah knew she would never have made it to England. She'd be in Buchenwald. Still, she could not imagine her friend yielding to coercion what she loved to give so freely.

"I did not. I reminded him that I am Jewish and it would be

a crime for he, an Aryan, to, ahem, collect that particular sort of bribe from me. However—and this is the shameful part, *Liebchen*—there was in my train car a horrid personage of about sixty, an aunt or governess in charge of a gaggle of children, who had spent the entire ride lecturing her brood about the unnatural vileness of the Semitic people. You know her sort. I'm afraid I told the guard that she was of our party, a full-blooded Aryan turncoat smuggling out Jewish children, and she would be more than happy to pay our bribe."

"You never!" Hannah gasped.

Waltraud shrugged her shapely shoulders. "You would not believe a sixty-year-old woman could slap a strapping guard so hard he'd fall on his derrière. In the confusion I found another car with a kinder guard and went on my merry way. And la, here I am, cleaning fireplaces in blue in the morning, changing to black in the evening to fluff pillows and stalk those delicious young footmen in their dandified uniforms. There is a quite pretty chambermaid here too, with lava-colored hair and freckles like little red ants crawling all over her face, but it seems English girls have never heard of Sappho. Pity. But what are you doing here in the kitchen? I'm to find the new kitchen drudge and show her to her room. Have you seen her?"

Hannah gave a hysterical hiccup of a laugh. "It is I!"

"You? But I thought you were the prodigal third cousin once removed, come home for the fatted calf? Was that just a story you cooked up for customs?"

"It's true enough, for all the good it has done me. Perhaps if I'd cooked up a better story, I wouldn't be here in the kitchen. Could you show me to my room, please? I'm very, very tired."

"Tell me *everything*," Waltraud said.

"No, please, just let me endure. I'll be fine if I don't have to talk about it. Talking makes me think, and thinking makes me talk more, and if I'm not careful I'll storm up to Lord Liripip's bedroom and kick him in his gouty leg. And I *promised* Mother and Father that I would come here and be safe, and surely they would send me away if I kicked Lord Liripip, so I must not even let a *thought* of the vast unfairness of it all creep into my mind."

But of course she told Waltraud everything.

"I shall put sticks of strychnine trees in their fireplaces!" Waltraud swore, pounding her thigh with her fist. "I shall put pins in their pillows!"

"No, you mustn't, or we'll both be banished from Starkers."

"Let them banish us! We will form our own act, the angel and the devil, the lamb and the serpent. We would have all the laureled heads of England eating from our hands. Come, doesn't the stage call you?" She grabbed Hannah in her strong arms and dipped her, as she had once dipped Otto.

"England is our sanctuary," Hannah said between giggles as she regained her balance, "and Starkers is where we must stay until it is safe to go home. You know you won't be allowed to stay in the country without a job."

"I don't know why you are putting up with it so calmly, *Lieb-chen*. You have an iron core of pride in you. All of you opera singers do, I think. It helps a little thing like you resonate up onstage." She kissed her friend's cheek. "But don't let pride and stubbornness keep you from happiness. Seek out Lord Liripip. His wife is a fright, but he can't be as bad as all that. Kneel at his feet, put your head in his lap, sigh prettily . . . believe me, it is a strategy women have been using with men for centuries, whatever their relation. Ah, *scheise*! I am to lay the napkins out for lunch. After the masters eat, we underlings get our nibble, so I will see you soon downstairs. Your frocks are over there, you poor thing. They're worse than mine."

She clicked her heels, gave a martial bow, and marched down the narrow staircase.

Alone, Hannah sat down gingerly on the dirt-colored blanket that served as a bedspread, half expecting dust to puff up around her. But no, it was perfectly clean, only so, so ugly. "It was *dyed* this color," she murmured, patting the blanket as she would a pug puppy who couldn't help being born unattractive. "If they were going to go to the trouble of dyeing it, why wouldn't they make it scarlet, or plum, or anything other than dirt-colored?"

Besides the bed there was a three-drawered dresser, a tipsy chair with an enamel coating that had worn off in places to reveal rusting wrought iron, a rag rug, a mirror just big enough to reflect one cheek, and for decoration, a mockery of a painting: a garish pink-cheeked servant in a crisp white apron and cap skipping through a pastoral landscape as if she'd never done a day's work in her life.

Two dresses hung from hooks on the wall.

"They're not hideous at all," she told herself gamely. Perhaps they had even been pretty, once. The blue floral one might have looked like Delft china . . . three or four owners ago. The pink floral gave a vague impression of spattered blood that had been scrubbed and scrubbed but had never quite come out.

She stood and crossed the room—it took only a step—and opened the dresser. The top two drawers were empty. The bottom drawer had mouse droppings in it.

"No underthings," she said to herself.

Then she covered her face in her hands and, just for a moment, blotted out the whole horrid world.

"I don't care!" she insisted, throwing out her arms and baring herself to the truth again. "Let them hate me. Let them punish me. Here I was sent and here I stay until my parents come to England." She looked again at the shoddy ugliness around her. "I wouldn't care if they were poor. If this were all they had and they took me in with love, I swear I would never make a single squeak of complaint. But to live in a castle, and treat me like this . . ."

She swallowed hard and knitted her dark brows. "There. That was my last bit of whining. I won't complain. Not to the Liripips, not to the cook, not even to myself. And I'll die before I ask them for new underthings. Why was I so stupid at the station?

No, never mind, that's only complaining about myself, and I'm not to complain anymore. Or talk to myself."

She made a motion of locking her mouth and throwing away the key. Then, since no one was watching and she could be as silly as she chose, she scrambled on the floor to pick up the imaginary key and slipped it into her pocket, just in case she changed her mind.

Resolutely, she slipped into the blue print dress. It was miles too long, but she managed to hook it up under her apron so it hung higher, though unevenly. The cap was trickier. No matter how she placed it, it either tipped forward over her eyes or tumbled backward off her head entirely. Finally she spied an old hairpin wedged into a corner on the floor, relic of a kitchen maid past. With that she contrived to secure the cap at a rakish angle so it dipped down over one eye. It was the best she could do.

Then she carefully stowed the few mementos of her past life. She hung her light coat neatly on one of the hooks, and folded her jacket, and the matching skirt weighted down with strands of pearls sewn into the seams. Beneath them in the top drawer she tucked her mother's letter from Lady Liripip, and a picture of her parents linked arm in arm on the stage, taking a curtain call. Finally she settled her passport and visa in her lap and looked at the little *J* stamped on them.

She had never been religious, and her parents' only faith was in the stage. Aaron Morgenstern was a member of the local synagogue because his parents had been, because his friends were, because it took his donations and put them toward good deeds. His was a Jewishness of history and culture and sociability, not of faith. Spiritually, he was an atheist. That did not matter to the state.

"From now on, for the sake of my fellow Jews who are suffering, I will be as Jewish as I can." Hannah did not speak Hebrew, knew few of the rites, but what she knew, she would practice. "It will be a lie of a sort," she admitted to herself. "But a good one. A lie of homage. A lie of solidarity."

She shoved her cap more firmly on her head and hiked up her trailing hem, determined to do whatever she had to until she could be with her parents again.

"Though I hope it won't be *too* long," she said as she closed her door behind her. "I don't know how many washings my one pair of underwear can survive."

The family's lunch was over by the time she descended, and the servants were just sitting down to their own repast. Dozens of pairs of eyes whipped around at her entrance.

No need to be afraid of them. It's only a stage, she thought to herself (fortunately remembering not to say it out loud, for once). *I am just acting a part. An Aschenputtel part—no, in English it is Cinderella. Only my father will be my prince when he makes it safely to England, and I have a beloved mother instead of an evil stepmother, and . . .*

"Ahem," she said after a long and uncomfortable silence. "My name is Hannah and I suppose I am . . . no, I *am* the new kitchen maid. I am also Jewish, and I'm sorry, but I won't work on a Saturday because it is a holy day. Also, sausages and other pig things are not to have." In her confusion she was thinking in German and translating to English. Her accent was creeping up on her and she fought it back, her face scrunching with determination. "I am very happy to be here and hope to be your good friend. Oh, and shrimp. I must not eat shrimp. Or camels. Or insects." She was very hazy on dietary laws, having spent her toddler years wandering among the tables at Der Teufel, sneaking diners' shrimp cocktails. But it would have to do. She had made her point.

She bobbed a curtsy because she had seen it in a movie about English servants once. "Thank you."

One of the parlor maids tittered, and this started a chain reaction of giggles and guffaws until Sally barked, "Silence!" and told Hannah to sit at the end of the table.

"You work on Saturday like everyone else. Do your praying Sunday when the rest of us are at church. As for shrimp, *my lady,*" she added with an echo of Trapp's withering scorn, "you shan't be offered them. Eat as many bugs as you like, though. Sup now, and you'll set out the kitchen table in preparation for dinner afterward. Tomorrow your work begins in earnest."

Feeling like a cad, Sally immediately turned to chat with the housekeeper, who usually deigned to eat with them. When one of the kitchen maids served them and Sally saw the chubby, still-sizzling pork sausages she had prepared not ten minutes earlier, she felt a terrible urge to leap up and make Hannah a special omelet all for herself, but she manfully controlled that impulse. *Best the girl get used to it now,* she thought.

Hannah, who had dined lightly the night before and breakfasted not at all, almost drooled at the fragrant, fatty smell of sausages. *No,* she told her salivary glands sternly. *People are being persecuted for having Jewish blood. I have never been particularly Jewish, but I will do my best. It is the least I can do.*

She reached for the potatoes and ate them in silence under heavy stares.

Hannah, Who Tried to Be Helpful

"I INTEND TO MAKE MYSELF as helpful as possible," Hannah said after the servants had dispersed to their varied duties and the lunch table was cleared. "I know very little of cookery but I can make a few things. *Pfannkuchen*, of course. Crepes. No, that is French. I'm sorry, my English sometimes runs away from me here and there. Pancakes!" She laughed. "The word might run but I always catch it. My legs are short, but fast. I do not care for the sweet *pfannkuchen* so much but rather the ones you eat for a meal, with bits of bacon and cheese and scallions. And when they are in season the plump white asparaguses. Asparageese? No, one asparagus, many asparagus. They are like fish and sheep."

Sally could not see at all how asparagus were like fish or sheep, so she only said, "Can you lay out a table for dinner preparation?"

"I have laid out many tables," Hannah said, thinking of the

napkins she'd coaxed into the shape of swans or crabs or Viking longboats every night at Der Teufel.

"I'm going to run to the village to get a few ducks. Herself changed her mind and needs roasted mallard tonight, and if I let one of the girls pick them out they'll take whatever they're given and never ask how long they've hung. Himself won't eat a duck that's hung less than a week." Sally stopped short in her bustling, amazed at her own jibber-jabber. The foreign girl was getting to her. Could it be that Trapp was wrong? Maybe talking didn't get in the way of an efficiently run kitchen. It felt rather nice.

"You have the cook's table set out for me," Sally went on, "and while the girls and I make dinner you can watch and learn. The most important things are to do what you're told and stay out of the way. And see Judy or Glenda about a few more hairpins."

Sally reached for Hannah, and for one tender instant the girl felt loved as the older woman adjusted the unsightly white construct perched on her head. She caught Sally's hand. "They won't say anything, will they? I can bear it. I *have* to bear it. But they won't be so unkind as to tease me about it, will they?"

"What, about where you come from? Who you are? Oh, they'll tease you without mercy. You just give as good as you get." As she looked down at the dark-eyed little morsel of a girl, she felt more of Trapp slip away. *This is my kitchen now,* she thought. *I can be kind if I want.*

But when Sally came home with a basketful of perfectly hung ducks she was not inclined to kindness. Hannah, her cap askew again, was standing beside the vast cook's table with a pleased expression, while Judy and Glenda smirked in the background. "I told you to have my table set up!" Sally thundered. "I have to start dinner now. Not in five minutes, *now,* for if it's not ready the instant Lord Liripip sits down, the entire lot of us will be sacked."

The table looked very pretty, with its single knife and fork, its slotted spoon and its ladle, its large mixing bowl and its tea towel cleverly rolled into the shape of twins sleeping in a hammock. Dead center, in an empty Bovril bottle, was a cluster of late, bedraggled wild asters cheerfully shedding pollen all over her pristine work surface.

She rounded on Hannah. "You *said* you could set a cook's table. Have you never seen a cook's table?"

"I . . . I thought I had. There was a chef, and he . . . well, he drank quite a bit and things were a mess afterward but he did wonders with one knife and a towel." Then she added, quite unhelpfully but very hopefully, "I can make cocktails."

"Get those things out of my kitchen!" Sally shouted, hurling the flowers toward the scullery. The dinner frenzy was upon her, and like a berserker she snatched up a cleaver and jabbed it in Hannah's direction. Trapp had rarely been without a weapon. "You, back against the wall and don't dare make a move unless I tell you to. Glenda, you get my table ready. Judy, get those ducks plucked and scalded. Herself demanded *pommes soufflées* tonight, and you know what that means."

As Hannah was to discover, it meant volcanic eruptions of

blistering oil, copious cursing, and in the end, ballooned golden potato fingerlings that were worth the burn wounds they inflicted. Not, Hannah mused from her corner, that the people who suffered to make them got to so much as taste them. Sally tore one potato in half to make sure its innards were properly puffed, then served them. The ducks likewise were prodded for doneness, but not one morsel of crispy fat-backed skin passed the lips of any of the servants. Sally did taste the mushroom consommé, adding a smidge of salt, and nibbled a bit of the warm pear and onion salad, but for the most part, one half of the house cooked and the other half ate.

Sally had turned into another creature entirely, a focused general doing battle against ingredients and time. Feathers flew, steam made everyone look like damp beets, and no one stopped moving for even an instant. Only Hannah was still, holding up the wall and watching, spellbound, the frenetic activity that, under Sally's supervision, produced perfection from chaos.

They'll chop their fingers off, she thought as she watched the shining blades rise and fall. Judy almost got gutted when Glenda, knife in hand, dashed off for one more pear, and a tall and comely footman in archaic breeches and hose only just managed to avoid being doused with scalding water.

Somehow it all worked. The table, properly laid out now, had a dozen knives, twenty bowls, spoons of every shape and size, but Sally grabbed what she needed almost without looking. At the precisely right moment, after just the right amount of shouting and tears, threats of firing and vows of quitting, each dish was ready and handed to a footman, who carried it off to that rarefied ether in which the aristocracy dwell. The soup, a delicate sole in tarragon butter, the ducks and their supporting cast of vegetable matter, all left their humble origins to nurture the masters.

Finally, a moment of calm. Only dessert remained, a chocolate timbale, and Sally had that well in hand. The spare footmen were chatting up Judy and Glenda; the butler Coombe, who was overseeing the wines, was beginning to think of the pipe and mystery novel waiting for him on his bedside table. Sally took what felt like her first breath in the last two hours. The terrible ghost of Trapp began to retreat. Sally wiped her sweating brow and spared a glance at Hannah, still gazing wide-eyed at everything. "See," she said, diminishing to mere Sally again, "it's not so hard once you learn. Tomorrow you'll—"

Late that night, sitting like a trim little lotus on the floor while Waltraud sprawled on her bed, Hannah recalled how at that moment everything had gone to hell. All at once the battle of dinner, so near to being won, was a rout. The asters, wilted and forgotten in the scullery doorway, started it all.

"It wasn't really my fault. Flowers, in themselves, are innocent, and if their yellow eyes looked particularly baleful that didn't mean they had tripped that gangly footman *deliberately.* Who would be such a goose as to trip on a flower? But oh, Traudl, he simply went flying. I never knew one human being could have so many arms and legs. Dozens, at least, like a squid."

Flailing as he fell, the footman knocked Judy over a stool, where she crashed on top of another footman with black hair and very interesting sideburns.

"I bet she was pleased with that," Waltraud said. "She's been trying to straddle him for ages, I hear, but he says that she is a nothing of a creature who has more bosom than brains, and he will only marry someone with the potential to rise to housekeeper or cook so he can be a butler or valet and make them a package deal."

"You've been here a week and you know about everyone's personal lives?"

She shrugged her shapely shoulders. "Of course. I do not care for novels, so I must have human drama. Go on, ask me what love song Lord Liripip sings in the bath, or what they say about Lord Teddy's dearest friend from Oxford. But no, Judy was straddling Corcoran—I must know what happened next."

"Nothing lewd," Hannah assured her. "I wish it had. Better that than what really happened. Corcoran—and thank you for telling me his name, because I've forgotten everyone's already—pushed her off and grabbed at whatever he could to pull himself up. Unfortunately that was the tea towel, the one I'd folded so cleverly into sleeping twins, and somehow it went flying right onto the range, where those poor sleeping innocents went up in an absolute holocaust. I have heard the phrase 'chickens with their heads cut off,' but I had never seen it until this day. Glenda had the presence of mind to fetch a pail of water from the scullery, but it was a soapy one, and sadly she flung it on yet another footman, the one with eyes like a lizard and no lashes to speak of?"

"Samuels," Waltraud supplied.

"Yes, him, and he was absolutely soaked, and two other footmen went down in the slipperiness, and someone's tails caught on fire too, and poor Sally, who I must remember to call Cook, was moaning that His Lordship was ready for his pudding and someone had to take it out *right this second,* even if all the servants were drowning and burning to death, or the world would come to an end."

"She didn't!"

"Well, that's what it sounded like at the time. Which is how I made my most terrible blunder." Hannah turned down her lips in a pretty little mock frown, but her eyes were merry.

She had promised to watch, to learn, above all things to be useful. While the world dissolved into injury and anarchy around her, one clear mandate rang through: The dessert must go out. While Cook was fuming and the footmen were burning and drowning, Hannah did the only practical, logical thing that could be done. She picked up the chocolate timbale and carried it out to the dining hall.

"No one ever thought to tell me that it is a mortal sin for a woman to serve at the dinner table!"

Anna and Hannah and the
Gross Social Blunder

〜✕〜

LORD LIRIPIP SAT AT THE head of a table as long as a tennis court. His foot, swaddled like a particularly colicky and troublesome infant, was propped up on a velvet tuffet. His wife, his son, Anna, assorted visiting married daughters, and the eccentric uncle (happily clothed) sat far enough away so that there was no danger of them accidentally jarring his gouty extremity, and incidentally out of spitting range—for Lord Liripip was wont to talk with his mouth full when excited or angry, as he almost always was. Beyond the small cluster of humanity stretched dozens of mournful empty chairs that seemed to remember all the titled—and even royal—buttocks that had filled them in happier days.

"Must you go away so soon?" Anna asked, keeping her voice low and dulcet. Her natural voice was somewhat shrill, but if she tried she could keep it in an aristocratic, cultivated register far below her usual squeak.

She was sitting across from Teddy and his mother, in a perfect position to let Teddy's gaze linger. Taking minuscule bites and appearing to chew only with her front teeth, she was doing her best to throw herself at the son without attracting the attention of the mother. Teddy seemed so charmed with her, she almost forgot her true purpose in being at Starkers. Almost, but not quite. Coombe had delivered a letter to her on a silver platter. ("Misdelivered downstairs; apologies, miss," he'd said.) *Good luck in your new position,* it read. *Sincerely, N.* N for NAFF, of course. She had torn it into bits.

"I'm afraid I must," Teddy said. "Oxford waits for no man. But I'll return at Christmas and be here until Hilary term begins in January, I hope." He crammed in a mouthful of duck. "What an absolutely magnificent breast," he said, chewing slowly and twitching his eyebrows at Anna.

Anna flushed and looked down. For five years at least she had attracted every nearby male gaze, and she never let it arouse in her more than a passing curiosity at most; more often, contempt. Those men had been practice. They hadn't mattered. Lord Winkfield — *Teddy,* she corrected, with another blush — did matter.

"We will have quite a large house party arriving the day after Christmas," Lady Liripip said. "Things being what they are, we do not entertain quite so much as we once did." This was as close as she would ever get to talking about money. The global financial crash, the decline in land value, the shift from farming to manufacture, had all taken their toll on Starkers, as they had on every landed family, from the lowliest baronet to the king himself. Not that they were poor, of course. They just couldn't prove quite so frequently or ostentatiously how very rich they were.

"They come for the Servants' Ball," Teddy explained.

"Is it a costume party?" Anna asked. "Do we all dress as servants?" She found the idea distasteful, but then she remembered that Marie-Antoinette had often dressed as a milkmaid or shepherdess. She had a pretty little book at home about great queens of the world, and had been fascinated by a picture of Marie-Antoinette dressed in peasant garb made of silver and blue watered silk. She hadn't actually read that chapter, so she didn't know what sometimes happens when the lower classes resent being aped by their betters.

"No, no. On Boxing Day we have a grand festival to honor the servants for all the work they do through the year. We serve them tea earlier in the day, and then in the evening there is a banquet for them, and a ball. The local tradesmen and some of the villagers are invited too."

"Mingling with the servants," Anna said. "How . . . delightful." She had almost forgotten that until a little while ago, she had been supposed to be a servant. Now she was adapting so well to her new position that she probably would not correct anyone who called her *my lady*.

"Simply everyone will be there," Lady Liripip said. "They clamor for an invitation. Shall I wear my sapphires, do you think? So suitable for winter. But Their Majesties might come, and she will probably wear those tired old sapphires of hers. Why she does not put the state jewels to proper use, I cannot claim to know. No, I shall wear my pearls. Anna, perhaps I will lend you a strand. They are considered quite the best collection in England. And Theodore, some of my dearest friends' daughters will be here."

Lady Liripip gave Teddy a pointed look. He ignored her insinuation—he had a lot of practice in that, having been told since he was fifteen that he must one day marry this girl or that. It had become background noise.

"Splendid girls, every one," Teddy said, thinking of their horsy faces and identical minds and hips designed for the sole purpose of bringing forth an heir. "But my dear step-cousin will be the belle of the ball. And by the way, coz, when I return for the holidays I plan to monopolize all of your free time."

He smiled at her, gazed at her with his earnest hazel eyes in such a steady, intimate way that the dining hall seemed to dissolve all around her. She leaned her chin on her gloved hand, her elbow on the table, and stared dreamily back, thinking in the corner of her mind what a nice ring *Lady Anna* had. Then she remembered how very lower class it was to put her elbow on the table and sat up straight, primly folding her hands in her lap. "You do?" she asked.

"Yes, I plan to be quite a pest and a bore. I've been studying German, you see, and though I speak it excellently—that's not bragging, I'm just repeating what my professor says—it seems I have the most appalling accent. My goal is to sound exactly like a native. I figure if we spend several hours each day chatting, I'll pick up a proper accent in no time. You lived in Berlin, right?"

Oh good lord! No, no! Who on earth do they think I am? Damn that Von! Why didn't he tell me what to expect, and who was in on the secret? She took a sip of wine to steady herself. *I am clever. I am a heroine. I will one day be Lady Liripip. I overcame a Cockney background and I straightened my own teeth with rubber bands. I can carry this off.*

She knew she was masquerading as a real person, though one whom none of the Liripips had ever met. She could tell them almost anything. Then she caught Lady Liripip's stern, puckered frown and saw her salvation.

"I'm so sorry, Teddy." She made her eyes moist and melancholy. "Your dear mother, who has been so kind as to welcome me into your home, has asked me not to speak of Germany during my stay."

"Oh, but surely . . ." Teddy began.

"And I must say I agree with her. My life in Germany has been so unpleasant, every day longing to be an Englishwoman — I have made a vow to put it all behind me and devote myself to the land where I belong. Germany is dead to me, and if you are kind you will not ask me to speak the language." There: that might be poignant enough to put him off.

Lady Liripip nodded. "How terrible it must have been for you to be kept away from England," she said. She turned to Teddy.

"The Germans are practically savages, my dear. Why, I remember reading of the things they did in the Great War. Huns, they called them. I don't know why you study the language of those uncivilized people."

"Goethe," he said, with a smile he seemed to expect Anna to share. She did not recognize the name but gave a little smirk. "Schiller. Hesse. Mann. Rilke. Well, Rilke gets on my nerves a bit, but I read him passionately in order to dislike him passionately." Suddenly his flippant, devil-may-care demeanor dropped. "Besides, everyone at school says we'll have to fight them again someday. My friends and I thought it might be a good idea to know how Germans think."

Remembering what the Von had said, Anna offered, "Perhaps there doesn't have to be a war." Before sending her to Starkers, the Von had promised there wouldn't be, if she could do her job properly — whatever it was.

"Yes!" Teddy cried, pounding the table with his fist so vehemently that the eccentric uncle woke from his doze and mumbled "Tally-ho!" before nodding off again. "You're exactly right, Anna. There doesn't have to be a war at all. Not if right-thinking people in England and Germany take action now and unite to—"

"Pudding!" Lord Liripip shouted.

"Husband, please," Lady Liripip whispered, trying to hush him, but he was having none of it.

"Don't you 'husband' me — it's time for afters. Am I or am I not the earl? Do I or do I not pay the salary and room and board of that pack of wastrels and ne'er-do-wells who call themselves servants? The least I can expect is to get my sweets in a timely fashion."

Anna tried not to stare. For years she had been working on her impeccable manners, yet one of the leading members of the aristocracy was allowed to behave like a spoiled child?

Teddy winked at her and whispered across the table, "We all think he'd be better for a good spanking, but who would dare give it to him?"

Lord Liripip started banging the table with his fork. "I swear I'll sack every last one of them!"

"The royal family likes to come for the show," Teddy hissed confidentially. "It's amusing for outsiders to see his tantrums. Less so for his family, though." He rolled his eyes to the sparkling chandeliers that dangled dangerously above their heads.

"What good is it to be a lord these days?" Lord Liripip roared. "There was a time when being the lord and master meant you didn't have to wait for anything. You got what you wanted, and everyone bent over backwards giving it to you."

He was ranting so loudly that no one heard the door swing open, or noticed the small, dark personage who entered rear first. When they finally heard her voice, it was more shocking than Lord Liripip's tirade. It was as if a hound had spoken, or Liripip's tuffet had interrupted him.

"Having people bend over backwards for you was called *droît du seigneur,* and it was a most terrible thing," Hannah said in her clear, penetrating stage voice. "Some say it wasn't ever so—the right-of-the-first-night part, I mean—and my friend Otto said that with many of the old lords and kings they were just as likely to take their right with the groom as with the bride. But in any event, to think of a lord having rights, those or otherwise, more than any other mortal, just because he is a lord . . ." She made a little *pff* sound. "You would not like to be that sort of a lord. Truly you would not. People would write satires of you and the anarchists would do you in. Timbale? I have not tasted it, because of course I must not, but it smells so heavenly that I'm sure you will like it."

When she noticed that every single mouth was hanging open, she realized something must be dreadfully wrong. *They are embarrassed to see me, of course,* she thought. *Shamed of not embracing me as family, of making me work. Well, I am not ashamed of work. Labor is ennobling.*

She would not say a single thing to the Liripips about her position, would not utter a word of complaint. She would show them by her cheerfulness that she didn't mind at all. She would be just like a waitress in Der Teufel, vivacious and talkative. The family might be unkind, but she was not.

Utterly struck dumb, Lord Liripip accepted his portion of timbale and stared at the girl who reminded him so acutely, so painfully, of another girl from long ago. *She's the little singer, the one from the lawn this morning,* he thought. *Just a servant, beneath my notice. Yet here I am, noticing her again.*

"Who's next?" She spied Anna. "Oh, hello again. What a lovely frock you are wearing, and you wear it so well. I, alas, lack the accoutrements for such a dress." Hannah sighed, raising her meager accoutrements with her breath. "Here you go."

She continued on to the next diner, one of the married daughters. "I'll give you a bit extra," she said confidentially. "I see you hardly touched your duck. Don't you care for duck? I knew the most lovely ducks who lived in a little park but liked to cross traffic to paddle in the fountain. Perhaps you have a friend who is a duck? I can always eat animals even if I am friends with their brothers. It is too terrible if you think about it, so you must *not* think about it. If you did, before you knew it you would make friends with a carrot and never be able to eat again. Here, have some of the raspberry goo from the inside."

Hannah was beginning to believe that the English did not talk very much. Perhaps it was a mass eccentricity of the aristocracy. She tried with the next sister, chatting about the raspberry cane wall one of her neighbors had planted around her small garden to keep marauding children away. "A sort of guard and bribe all at once," Hannah prattled. "The children would be placated by the berries and pierced by the thorns. I have a scar—I bled like a stuck pig. In fact I looked rather like this timbale, leaking red juices."

Nothing—not a single response, only stiff, paralyzed stares, gaping mouths, wide eyes. The odd uncle peered at her, trying to puzzle out whether she was a hallucination. The other sister looked steadfastly at her dish as if none of it were happening. Poor Hannah's voice grew weaker, filled with ellipses as she broke off one unsuccessful topic and launched into another, hoping to get something, anything, out of these hard, cold, unfeeling aristocrats.

They hate me, she thought. *Why did they take me if they were going to treat me so cruelly?* There was not even a faint look of acknowledgment, not one indulgent nod recognizing the unfortunate fruit. No guilty smile. Not even a word of rebuke for inflicting herself on their presence. That would have been better, somehow, than being utterly shunned. Half of them looked at her as if she were some improbable and unattractive creature that had heaved itself up out of the muck, and the others appeared to have entered a fugue state, pretending not to notice her at all.

Her eyes were feeling hot by the time she got to Teddy. *I'm angry,* she insisted to herself. *Not sad. Not at all sad. There are too many horrible things happening in the world for me to be sorrowful over a little coldness.* Anger made it better, though. Let them be disagreeable — she would be happy nonetheless, and entertain herself by thinking of all the nasty things that might happen to them. In the books, bad things always happen to bad people, though it sometimes takes ever so many words before they do.

She was lost for a moment in her reverie, thinking of cruelty near and far, of the helplessness of each person to fight it.

"What, no floor show for me?" came a gently teasing voice at her elbow. "I particularly like stories about aunts, and valets, and cow creamers." Teddy, easy in his lordship, free with his friendship, was the only one of all the family looking at her as if she was an actual human being, a person and not an automaton on the fritz.

There is always a light in the darkness, Hannah thought. *However small, it is always there, and it makes the darkness disappear.* Teddy's bright hazel eyes shone with earnestness, laughter, camaraderie, sympathy.

Then he looked across the table to the stunning blonde who had usurped her seat that morning, and Hannah saw that his countenance was exactly the same for her.

He is the world's friend, not mine, Hannah realized, and though that made him a better human being, she found it pained her somehow, a little hurt as if from a splinter that cannot quite be grasped and pulled.

Suddenly, she found there was one thing she could not manage to forgive. "You never came back for me," she said, knitting her brow so furiously that her cap slipped dangerously askew. "I waited at the gate for you to come back and you never did."

"Damn!" He looked sincerely contrite. "I had this niggling feeling in the back of my head that I was forgetting something." He seemed to examine her more intently, and his expression shifted from that generic geniality to something more intimate. "I can't imagine how I could have forgotten *you.*" He lowered his voice, but Anna, straining, heard him say, "I never will again." More loudly he went on, "Why, with that chocolate lump of whatever it might be on that plate, and your eyes flashing Old Testament vengeance, you look a perfect model for Judith with the head of Holofernes. I have an artistic friend coming for Christmas who will be delighted with you. He has a knack for capturing fierce women. Somehow I don't think I want you, of all people, to be angry with me. If you don't forgive me, I doubt I'll sleep very well tonight."

Hannah felt warm and peculiar. What did he mean by that caressing look, that intimate voice?

"You don't know who I am, do you?" she asked all at once. There was something so honest and upfront about him, she couldn't imagine him not acknowledging who she was. He might flirt with a real servant, be kind to a real refugee—that was his nature, she could see that—but he would not pretend that a relation, however tenuously related, was a servant.

His mother, though, had finally found her tongue. "Don't speak to her, Theodore. Not another word. I've heard about these foreign girls. Communists and anarchists, every one. Did you hear her threaten your father?" She turned her ire on Hannah. "How *dare* you show yourself here among us?"

"The footmen were occupied, and I—"

"Silence, creature! Your place is in the kitchen. Return there at once. I shall speak to Cook about you, and if I ever see so much as a glimpse of you again, you can go back to whatever slum you came from." She sounded exactly like a fishwife. Then she flutteringly fanned herself with her pristine napkin and turned apologetically to Anna. "So difficult to find decent servants, my dear," she said with syrupy sweetness. "And foreigners are the worst of the lot. Excepting you, my dear. How clever of you not to have any accent at all. One would almost think you had spoken nothing but English your entire life. But you must not forget about your elbows, my dear. Only merchants' daughters put their elbows on the table."

Smiling and simpering, she returned her attention to her family, and Hannah ceased to exist.

I'm leaving, Hannah swore to herself. *Even if Waltraud doesn't come with me, even if I have to beg in the streets, I won't stay another minute in the same house as that wretched woman and that childish, petulant man!*

Then Teddy changed her mind. He stood and deftly lifted the platter out of her hands. "Yes, *Fräulein,*" he said to Hannah. "How gauche of you to have been born in another country. It is almost a capital offense. Here in this house we believe that one must be severely punished for the happenstance of one's birth." His face was a jester's mask of mockery, but there was a tightness about his eyes, a tense set to his smile. "What a dilemma for the English, though — we agree with Germany on so many things, including the patent inferiority of anyone who is not *us*. Darling Mum, did it ever occur to you that to the rest of the world, *we* are foreigners?"

"The very idea!" Lady Liripip said with a nervous titter.

"Just a silly philosophical notion. As you say, Oxford has been the ruin of better men than me. Serve from the left, *Fräulein*, and remove from the right." He dumped a ludicrous portion onto his mother's plate, then took Hannah's arm and marched her out of the dining hall, silently seething.

"Are you angry with me?" Hannah asked when they were in the narrow stairwell leading to the servants' chthonic realm.

"With you? No, of course not. With the world, I suppose. Poor Mum is of the world. Still, I am too, and you don't see me being such a towering clod. Maybe if Mum had gone to Oxford — there now, I'm merry again already, just thinking of that — or talked to anyone without a title or a fortune, she might see things a little differently. Don't worry: I'll make sure you don't get fired or sent back to Germany. No one with an ounce of compassion or common sense should be there. Not to mention a drop of Jewish blood. Is it as bad as they say?"

She nodded. "My mother is there, and my father. They're supposed to follow me to England but I haven't heard . . ." She fixed her eyes on Teddy's shirt studs.

He took her chin in his hand. It was rougher than she'd expected. She thought a lord's hand would be soft, but his had calluses on its palm and fingertips. He tilted her face up to his.

"What do you say I look into it for you, eh? I'm sure they have things well in order, but I have a few friends in the government and . . . elsewhere. Maybe they can hurry things along. What are their names?"

"Aaron Morgenstern, and Cora Pearl Morgenstern."

"I'll remember." The names didn't seem to strike a chord with him. *He really doesn't know who I am. Did they never tell him we existed?*

He was still holding her face in his hand, examining her. He leaned closer. "I'll help you, if you'll do something for me." His voice was low and caressing. "Something personal."

She pulled away and slapped him as hard as she could.

"How do you dare! You would be so mean, so base as to bribe me with my dear parents' lives to win my attentions? Do you think that just because I am low and you are high you can gallop over me like I am a little fox? I do not sit at the table with your beast of a mother and your child of a father, but I am no vermin, and neither is a fox. They are beautiful and clever. Not to say that I am, though you'll never find out if you try to threaten me into tumbling into your bed or a closet or the summerhouse or wherever you have in mind." Her eyes flashed darkly.

"I never meant—" he began, his cheek turning scarlet.

"Do not attempt to deny it—I have read all the right novels. You silly lord, do you not know that you can win anyone with kindness, only it takes a little longer? Do you not think I would allow myself to be seduced as well as any other girl if you gave me sweets and told me my hair was pretty and perhaps wrote a bad poem, or stole one out of a book I have not yet read, though I have read a great many, so there you would not succeed. Still, I might be charmed by your buffoonish attempts and yield. But to hurry things along with threats? For that I will slap you again."

She did, on the other cheek.

"Are you quite finished?" he asked stiffly.

Standing out of reach, Hannah crossed her arms over her accoutrements. "I wish to add that I do not *want* to be seduced by you, only that I understand human nature, and mine, enough to say that should you earnestly attempt, you would likely succeed." She frowned. "Would likely *have succeeded*. Now that you have threatened, of course that is no longer possible. Good day." She curtsied. "You see, I am polite, not menial. I do not bend over backwards for you."

With that, she ran down the hall, and did not hear Teddy mutter, "But I only wanted to speak German with you!"

Hannah told Cook about her gross blunder, but not about Teddy's.

Sally mustered as much ire as she could so late in the day, and told Hannah that if she ever again did something so foolish she'd be let go on the spot.

Then, after the servants' dinner, when she was alone in her comfortable little bedroom, she laughed herself into a jelly at the thought of her chatty little kitchen maid discomfiting the Liripips. The girl might not be made for service, or have any kitchen skills whatsoever, but all things considered, Sally was rather glad Hannah had come.

It was only as she was drifting off to sleep that she remembered one little thing Hannah had said, about the pancakes she liked to eat. The ones with cheese and scallions and *bacon* . . .

TEDDY RETURNED TO FIND the dining hall empty, and joined his family in the drawing room for coffee. Anna, licking her lips and watching the door with predatory attention, spotted him instantly, and glided toward him. But she was not more alert than the butler, who intercepted him first and handed him a small envelope on a silver tray. Teddy read it swiftly and crumpled it.

Anna sidled up to him. His face was flushed, she noticed. She had not at all liked the way he'd been looking at that mousy little maid, that dusky foreigner. Still, she kept her voice sweet and said, "How kind of you to help that poor unfortunate girl. Why, she must be a simpleton, though I'm sure she meant well."

There was something in Teddy's eyes, a sort of anger and amusement and determination, that alarmed her. *Surely not . . . not that little nothing of a servant. Oh, but she's German, isn't she, and he wanted help with the language. Help that I refused to give. Can't give.*

Recklessly, before she could change her mind, Anna laid a hand on his arm — what a strong arm, too, she thought, as muscled and sinewy as those of the dockworkers who used to sometimes paw her before she realized she shouldn't be flattered by that sort of attention. "I was selfish," she said to him, taking his elbow and leading him away from the others. "I will help you with your German, if it is important to you."

He seemed to shake something off, and it was a moment before his face lit with its usual open, affable grin. "Bully! We'll start tonight."

Hiding her panic, she said, "No. I've promised your mother I'll help with the . . ." She drew a blank.

"The village fete, I'm sure. She recruits everyone to do the work, and keeps all the credit for herself. When I return for the holidays, then?"

"Of course," Anna said, trying to find a graceful way to slouch. In her heels she was as tall as Teddy, and she had practiced all of her most appealing expressions looking *up.*

"I have to leave tomorrow, early. I just got word." His balled fist uncurled, revealing the crumpled slip of paper. Anna, twisting her neck, read: *Qui tacet consentire.*

"What does that mean?" she asked. It was the sort of ignorance she did not have to hide. Even now, women rarely learned Latin, though it was still mandatory for schoolboys.

"'Silence means consent,'" he said. His grin was still there, but his eyes were focused far away, unsmiling.

She tried it, consenting to everything he might ask of her as silently as she could, but it produced no measurable result.

"We've been silent too long," Teddy said harshly, still looking beyond her as if he were talking to someone else.

"But I don't have to tell *you* that. Your parents are still there, suffering."

They are? Anna almost said. Then she caught herself. Of

course, he believed she'd just escaped from Germany, leaving her parents behind. She tried to look suitably sorrowful without making any wrinkles in her perfect skin.

"Never fear," Teddy said. "I'll search for Mr. and Mrs. Morgan while I'm in Germany. My father mentioned which cabaret they run—they should be easy to find. You must be so desperately worried about them." Then he turned on his heel and left.

I only have a few weeks to learn enough to fool him, she thought. *Once we're spending hours alone together, I know he'll fall in love with me. Why, he's halfway there already. Then when we're married, it won't matter what I really am. I'll be Lady Winkfield, and I'll never look back.*

Tomorrow, Anna told herself, *I make friends with that mouse of a maid.*

Lord Liripip Berates a Star

TEDDY WATCHED HIS FATHER METHODICALLY smooth the wrinkled paper on his library desk. *It is so strange,* he thought, *how a man can be both what he is and what he was at the same time.* Lord Liripip was a ruin of a man now, plagued by gout and a dozen minor ailments that robbed him of his digestion, his sleep, his breath, his comfort.

But he had been a giant once, one of the great liberal lords, an oratorial power in Parliament. He had been the terror of foxes in three counties, and such a ladies' man that he was officially declared *not safe unchaperoned in carriages* by two generations of debutantes.

Teddy had never known that man, but he heard it in the whispers of the oldest servants, and from his father's brother, the loony who rode in the nude. Thumbing through ancient scrapbooks kept as curios in dowagers' parlors, he had run across clippings of society columns depicting quite a different man from the temperamental, decrepit creature who smacked his gums and looked at him with rheumy, anxious eyes. Exactly when his decline had begun Teddy didn't know, but from gossip and guesses he thought it must be either when Lord Liripip fell in love with one woman when he was fifty-five, or when he married quite a different woman when he was fifty-six. Or perhaps even when that woman died in childbirth not long afterward, and he had married the current Lady Liripip.

Difficult as it was—and difficult as Lord Liripip was—Teddy loved the man his father had become. In his alternating gruff and petulant way he was a kind and generous father. And of course, Teddy was his father's future. Through him, Liripips would go on. Sometimes Teddy caught his father examining him incredulously. He used to think his father was marveling that after all those years he'd managed to produce an heir. Then one day, a bit drunk, his father had said, "Damn my eyes, how a miserable prune like your mother ever managed to squirt out a noble specimen like yourself is beyond me."

"I can forbid you, you know," Lord Liripip said now, a trace of his old power and canniness flashing in his pale blue eyes.

"No, sir, you can't. I've reached the age of majority."

"All the same, I think if I forbid you, you won't go."

Prevaricating, Teddy said, "I would not like to disobey you, sir."

Lord Liripip laughed, which he had not done in a long while.

"But you would, wouldn't you, and what am I supposed to do about it, eh? Disown you? Couldn't even if I wanted to, and wouldn't even if I could. What, give Starkers kit and caboodle to that yahoo up in Edinburgh? Har!" If Teddy had not been born — or if he should die — the entire estate and title would pass to a distant relative no one had ever met.

"But think about it, boy. You'll be leaving Oxford . . ."

"Not at all! This is officially part of a study program. I'll be there under school auspices."

"But not doing schoolwork. Teddy, you don't have the makings of a proper spy. You're too friendly by half. I've seen you, making the housemaids smile and chatting with Caroline's girl." He winced. "Don't care for that one, even if she is Caroline's get. Looking about with those big cow eyes of hers as if she'd like to eat the place up. Her father must be a piece of work. Bah!"

He was prone to inarticulate exclamations, and went on in that vein for a while — *pah!* and *humph!* mingled with his hacking cough — before remembering the matter at hand.

"People *like* you, Teddy, which is well enough for skullduggery, but you like them back, which is fatal. You're not hard and calculating and cold."

"The world is hard and cold enough, sir. I think I can change it by being something else."

"And get yourself shot, no doubt."

"Did you get shot in Mafeking, or the Great War?"

"Only shot *at*, but that is neither here nor there." Lord

Liripip slapped the paper on his desk. "Does Burroughs think you'll do for this kind of work just because I did? These are different times."

"Yes, sir — worse times, and that's why all good men have to act. Now, before it escalates. War is coming. Any fool can see that. There's an entire continent at risk right across a ribbon of water."

"That's their business."

"It's our business to keep this world peaceful," Teddy said. "And it's an awfully skinny ribbon."

"I still say Burroughs has some nerve recruiting my son and heir for spy work."

"I'll just be a student, making friends, learning the territory while it's still easy to get into Germany. I won't be doing anything dangerous."

" . . . Yet," Lord Liripip said darkly. "They don't take you into the fold if they don't mean to put you to use."

"Look on the bright side, sir. Maybe we can put things right enough so that Germany gets a new regime and everything gets better. Maybe it won't come to war after all. Then I can go back to reading poetry and rowing crew."

"Wipe that cocksure grin off your face, Teddy. There's a man over there with a puny heart and weak brain and dreams as big as Alexander or Napoleon. You won't get rid of him so easily. Do you know what they do to spies in wartime? You'll be tossed into some black pit of sadists and set to work upon, and when they've milked you of all the things you've sworn you'd never tell, when they've cut off bits of you that you never thought you could live without, they'll shoot you in the head and dump you in an unmarked grave. Then won't that Edinburgh blighter laugh his head off?"

Unflappable Teddy said only, "I'll be back by Christmas. I told you, sir, I'm there as a student."

"Where you'll get lost, or set yourself up with a false identity, or marry a Communist farm girl for cover."

Teddy threw back his head and let loose his free and beautiful laugh. Then he kissed his father on the brow. The old man tried to brush him away . . . but he didn't try very hard.

"Just be sure you come home safely," Lord Liripip said with growling affection. "I don't like to think what your mother would say if I told her we needed to produce another heir. On the other hand, the shock might kill her." He seemed to perk up, then: "No, wouldn't be worth the unpleasantness I'd have to go through doing my marital duty. Har!"

Teddy, who wasn't any fonder of his mother than he absolutely had to be for the sake of propriety, took this in stride.

"It's near dawn," he said, drifting to the window. "I'll have to leave soon."

"Dawn, hell! It's the middle of the night still. Look at you, already skulking like a proper spy." He looked oddly proud, and not for the first time did Teddy wonder exactly what his father might have done in his youth to serve his country. Neither he nor Burroughs, his father's old friend and now Teddy's professor of German literature and secret handler, would say, though they hinted broadly at great deeds and derring-do. For all Teddy knew, it might have been anything from fetching coffee at an embassy to political assassination.

"Throw open the window, would you?" Lord Liripip said, shifting uncomfortably in his chair. It was painful to walk, and nearly as painful to sit all day and half the night. "I want to feel the night air. I've half a mind to make you push me around the grounds in my bath chair."

"Another ploy to keep me home?" Teddy unlatched the window and swung it open, leaning out into the starlit darkness. *Can I be nostalgic for something I haven't lost yet?* he wondered, affected more than he realized by his father's grim warning about the fate of spies. The night was cold, clean, with delicious earth smells rising from the landscaped and wooded grounds. In full light the land had the melancholy grays and browns of the decaying season, but when it was blanketed in night, only the best of the turning year remained. The autumnal world was drowsy and bittersweet, like a child's tucking-in after a long day of play.

Only, Teddy thought, *a child is always sure there'll be a tomorrow just as crisp and bright.*

Behind him, Lord Liripip closed his eyes, lost, as he was so often lately, in a memory. There had been another night such as this, chill, starlit, just before the dew had risen on the crisping leaves. There had been a girl, singing . . .

And then, there she was, or her voice, in any case. It was a different voice, but he was familiar with the ways of those reminiscences that were half dream. Details were different, merged and oddly juxtaposed, but he could always tell when something was meant to be a sign of the woman he had loved and lost. She had been a singer, untrained but with the purest voice, as light and flirting as birdsong. And like a bird she would lead him on a chase through the forest, singing her siren melody, luring him deeper into the trees and, at last, into her arms.

This singer, though — her voice was much lower than the one he remembered. Where hers had been a bell, a flute, this one was an oboe, a bassoon, but somehow still feminine. A voice deep with emotion, with secrets and longing, singing a low, caressing whisper loudly enough for all the world to hear.

She was singing in German.

That makes sense, Lord Liripip thought, believing he must have slipped into a dream after all. *She fled from me, from my proposal and my title, and went to Germany.* Back then the language had been English, her spoken voice showing her aristocratic blood, her singing voice shifting delightfully from sweet pastorals to "Cockles and Mussels" fishwife songs to bawdy ballads that even he had blushed to hear. She had always been so free, so unashamed. *There must have been something of that in me, too, that came out in my son,* he thought. *Why didn't I show it to her? She might have stayed.*

"It's she," Teddy said in wonder, leaning as far out the window as he dared. "Have you ever heard such a voice, sir?"

Lord Liripip's half-mast eyelids sprang open. "You hear it too?

It's not a dream?" He was still drowsy, confused. *It's she, Teddy had said. Can it be* my *she?*

"It's my step-cousin-in-law-thingumie. Anna." Teddy grinned into the silvered darkness, searching for her. Her blond hair must positively gleam in the starlight. But though the voice was quite obviously coming from near the gargantuan Liripip Yew, he couldn't see so much as a golden glint through its thick evergreen needles. "It must be. Mum said she's a singer, though from the way she said it I fancied she stood on tables in her scanties and sang 'A Guy What Takes His Time' in a Mae West impersonation. I never dreamed she sang like this."

"What is she singing?" Lord Liripip demanded, struggling to his feet and crossing to the window in an undignified, agonizing hop. He had learned a bit of German in school, but it, along with his French, had largely deserted him. (The Latin had been beaten into him so severely by various headmasters that it stuck.)

"It's Brahms's Alto Rhapsody," Teddy said. "The lyrics are by Goethe."

"How on earth do you know that?" Lord Liripip snapped, almost resenting his son's erudition. "When I was your age we didn't have to know so much, and someone punched us in the nose if we let on we did. What are the words? Tell me!" Would there be some balm in them to ease his heart? A visitation—not from beyond the grave, because Caroline was alive—but from across the years?

Teddy closed his eyes, listening intently to the low, reverberating words that seemed to echo off every dying leaf. "'Who is that apart?'" he quoted, then paraphrased. "It is about a man, a misanthrope, walking through the wild. The foliage all closes behind him, leaving no sign he's been there."

To his utter astonishment, Lord Liripip felt a tear course down his cheek.

"He was scorned, so now he himself scorns the world," Teddy went on. "Then the singer begs the Father of Love to help him. To open the clouded eyes of the thirsty wanderer, so he might see the thousand springs surrounding him."

His eyes burning and wet as that thrilling voice sang on, Lord Liripip knew his best days were behind him. His love was gone, belonged to another, and his pride, his joy, his son, was embarking on a dangerous new journey that might well end in death. But was there a way to seize both of those things, the lost and the soon-to-be-lost?

Vivified with a sudden inspiration, Lord Liripip felt young again. The perpetual throbbing in his foot receded, his breath came easier. He knew what had to be done.

No one, not even Lady Liripip, would ever work with more determination as matchmaker. He decided then and there that, come hell or war or revolution, Teddy would marry Caroline Curzon's daughter.

Then he would never risk himself in spy work.

Then Lord Liripip would have a piece of his lost love after all, grafted onto the family in perpetuity.

"Go to her, my boy," he said throatily. "No girl sings like that without calling to someone. It's you she hopes hears her. Go!"

"I thought you didn't take to her," Teddy said with a grin.

Lord Liripip didn't, really. He never could quite care for that big, busty blond sort, and there was something in her manner—exactly what, he wasn't certain—that he didn't trust. But he dismissed his concerns. *That was only because I loved and hated her mother,* Lord Liripip thought. *And because she is so different from what I'd imagined. I'll cultivate her, I'll be her friend. Between the two of us, we'll make Teddy marry her.*

But since he knew that children thrive on opposition, he only backpedaled and said with a shrug, "She'll get by with a good shove."

"Goodbye, Father," Teddy said, taking the arthritic fingers tenderly in his own oar-callused hand.

"Don't rouse your mother, boy, but as she's awake, you might as well let your cousin-in-law, or whatever she might be, know that you're leaving."

Teddy left without answering.

"She's not really a relative, you know," Lord Liripip shouted to the closed door. "Not by blood." Then he staggered to the window and watched. The anodyne of hope fled, leaving his gouty foot to throb again, but still he stayed standing until he saw a shadow he thought must be Teddy slip out the door and stroll into the garden.

"There," Lord Liripip said. "Night and solitude and stars.

Drink that potion and anything can happen, even in a few moments." He looked up and saw one star, particularly bright, the diabolical morning star.

Lord Liripip glared up at it with an old man's anger. "I asked you," he told the star. "I begged you for it, and you wouldn't give her to me, damn you. You owe me now, star!" He shook his fist at the luminous dot hanging in the plum-dark sky just over the grand yew. "You owe me one loving wife, one happy marriage."

The little boy in him, the part that made him whining and petulant, also made him steadfastly believe in the power of a wish made on a star. It was the part of him that Caroline Curzon had loved. But she had not loved it enough to marry him.

The morning star winked at him, but it made no promises.

Teddy and Hannah Are Not Formal

THOUGH IT WAS CALLED the Liripip Yew, it was not one yew but two (a tongue twister Hardy the under-gardener had perfected for his occasional tours), growing so close together that they had merged before Caesar's troops set foot in Britain. Now they were barely distinguishable, their lumpen, gnarled trunks fifteen feet wide with a hollow cave big enough for a hermit's comfort in the bole. It was a squat tree, fat at the bottom, dense at the top. It was not nearly as tall as some of the nearby firs, but they were callow youths, a mere two hundred years old. It was smaller even than some of the old oaks, enjoying a spry middle age of five hundred years. But it was dense with years and patience, well rooted.

Teddy ambled with his hands clasped loosely behind his back. Another time he would have whistled, but he was too charmed by a reprise of the Rhapsody, breathy this time, broken at odd intervals, as if she were talking to herself. He could hardly see;

the moon was new, and what had been a gently starlit garden of mixed geometric beds and isolated specimen trees from above was now dim as a cave. He knew the paths intimately and he did not hesitate, but still he walked slowly, and even when he was quite near he couldn't see the singer. Her voice had taken on a strange muffled quality.

"Anna," he called into the darkness as he neared the twin yews.

From very near, the singing stopped.

"Anna?" he called again.

Another moment of silence, then, in German, "Is that you, Lord Winkfield?"

He answered in the same language. "It is, but you must call me Teddy."

"I can hardly hear you, which I think is a good thing after what you have said today."

"Where on earth are you?" Teddy asked, circling the bulbous trunk.

"In my concert hall," she answered. "I am trying very hard to make a joke of it, but I'm afraid I can't quite. The acoustics are lovely, but the audience is so small."

"It has grown," he said. "I was listening upstairs in Starkers. My father, too."

"You could hear me? Ah, I'm not supposed to sing. Or talk, more than necessary. I thought that the garden was big enough, your stone walls thick enough, that I wouldn't bother anyone. If you're not to let me sing you may as well shoot me. It would be kinder." She gave a little laugh to lighten it, but again, it fell flat. "I forgive you, you know," she added.

"You do?" he asked, bemused. For what, exactly, was he forgiven? For his little scene at dinner, he assumed.

"Yes. One must be allowed to say what one thinks and do what one likes. Now more than ever. Others have the right to disagree, but you have the right to say such things, I suppose."

"And do you agree that the lower classes are a different species, and that everyone is foreign except the English?"

"Oh, your poor mother!" Hannah said with a low giggle. "Despite everything, I almost feel sorry for her."

"I am not a good son," Teddy said, mock solemn.

"But I think—also despite everything—you might be a good man. Too flippant and flirtatious, but perhaps good, too."

"I try," he said.

"It is a start. But you must do so much more than try. I wish there were something I could do. I am safe, and I have my troubles still, yes, but there are so many who have not been able to leave, or who, like my father, will wait and wait, never believing the moment for running has come. Your family doesn't care for my father, I know."

"I don't think any of us knows your father," he said to the talking tree, trying to see her in its pit, wondering if he dared join her. There was plenty of room for one, but it would be a tight squeeze for two. Particularly if one of the two was so amply buxom.

"But still you condemn him, because my mother married him. Which is silly, because if she hadn't, she might have married your father, and then none of us would have been born. Do you know, your accent is truly atrocious. Where did you learn German?"

"At school. My first teachers weren't natives, and I'm afraid I've gotten in bad habits. What do I sound like?"

"Like a turnip-headed child. People would hear you speak and think, *The poor thing—when he was a baby his mother picked him up after making sausages and he slipped right out of her greasy hands and landed on his head.* And then you leave off bits of sounds, and add others. Quite as bad as dropping your *H* in English, which I do not like to point out, but you also do on occasion."

"Never!" he said, delighted.

"You do. You just did a moment ago." It had been hard to hear him from her little cavern, but he had definitely mangled her name. Still, it was sweet, somehow, to hear her name on his lips at all.

"Will you correct me?" he asked. "In German, I mean. I need to develop a very good accent, and quickly."

"Perhaps. If I have time. I have a great deal to do." Sally had written out a list of her daily chores, a shocking schedule that had Hannah rising at five and laboring until the family had gone to bed. She was so nervous she'd oversleep that she got up at three, splashed water on her face, and paced her tiny room before finally succumbing to the calls of music and the outdoors and slipping outside.

"My mother can be very demanding, but surely you can find a little time for me." He leaned his head into the hollow but still couldn't see her, though he caught a faint whiff of strong lye soap, a jarring, unexpected note where he had thought to smell violets or lavender.

"I have time now," she said.

"So do I. But only a little. I have to go."

"Back to Oxford?"

"No . . . not exactly. To Germany for a while. I wish I could tell you more. You of all people would appreciate it."

"Ah, is it an assignation? A secret lover?" Hannah giggled.

"What? No, of course not! Only, a friend and I are traveling . . ."

"And this friend, she is beautiful?" Hannah made sure there was not the slightest trace of pique in her voice.

Nonetheless, she was relieved when Teddy said, "This friend smokes a pipe and wears bespoke suits from Savile Row with creases sharp enough to cut a good steak."

"Sounds like a dear friend of mine, and *she* is quite beautiful. Though she cannot afford good clothes these days."

"Well, my friend is named Maurice and he is also quite beautiful, but since the days of Wilde we in England don't admit to such things."

"Oh, are you Wildean?" She felt another little quiver of alarm.

"No."

"Ah, good." She paused. "Not a good in and of itself, because there is neither good nor evil in desire. But good because you seem to have a knack for making women smitten with you on short notice. Even by insulting them you seem to attract them." She sighed.

"Are you smitten?" he asked.

"Would I be such a fool as to admit that? You are charming. I say no more. It would not be appropriate to feel a jot of anything for you. What would your mother say?"

"I figured out long ago that only one of us could ever be happy. When I was a child I tried to make sure it was her. As I grew up, I realized it had to be me. We cannot live our parents' lives." Even as he said this he had a vague romantic notion, the same his father had had not long ago. *My father loved her mother and lost her,* he thought. *What an interesting idea it would be if I loved Anna.*

Gregarious, joyous, vital Teddy liked nearly every congenial person he met and fell half in love with every attractive woman. That first half always came easily, the second half, never. In the last week alone he had been momentarily enchanted by four women. There was a femme fatale in clocked stockings whom Burroughs had brought in to teach them some of the most common slip-ups for an Englishman masquerading as a German— forgetting to slash their sevens, looking the wrong way before crossing a street. There was a piquant redhead in a coffee shop. There was the extraordinarily loquacious servant girl who looked like a small, dark bird. And there was his glorious, golden kissing cousin.

The more they talked, speaking always in German, interspersed by her gently teasing corrections, the more he forgot everyone but Anna. It was better, almost, to hear her without seeing her. Her beauty was so incandescent that if he could have indulged his eyes he might have fallen for her looks alone, and he was idealistic and self-analytical enough to know that this would not do. All the same, as she spun her delightful stories of cabaret life, of the lost bohemian Weimar era, he did enjoy knowing that concealed within the intertwined yews was one of the great beauties of her generation. It was like talking to a dryad, a nymph, a secret voice that transcended flesh . . . though the flesh was there too, waiting to be touched.

To his astonishment they agreed on nearly everything, and where they differed it was only that she pushed him beyond the places where even the most liberal aristocrats dare to go. *Yes, believe that,* she would tell him, *but believe it more intensely! I feel that too, but you must think beyond that, to the next step!* Nothing shocked her, except when they discussed their species' capacity for stupidity and brutality.

"And even that is not so surprising anymore," she said. "That is the worst sign. Those things should always shock, completely and absolutely. If I, a victim, am hardly surprised, only think what most common people in Germany, in England, feel. Oh, another twenty professors fired for being Jewish? Another thousand people rounded up and sent to labor camps? The paper says it every day and it becomes commonplace. Then the paper stops saying anything, and no one cares."

At last, with dawn creeping closer, Teddy said, "These have been among the most delightful moments of my life."

He heard a little catch of breath from inside the tree's hermit hole. Then, softly, shyly: "And mine."

"I have to hurry or I'll miss my train. I'll be back for Christmas, though, and the Servants' Ball afterward. Will you give me the first dance?"

To dance again! She could waltz, of course, and knew some country dances, but what she really loved were the smoky golden nights in jazz clubs. She danced the Lindy, the shag, the Balboa—all kinds of swing—and in the Berlin clubs even the old Charleston and Black Bottom could still be found. It had all come from America, and officials had been looking at it with suspicion for years. *Do they still swing in Berlin?* she wondered.

"I would love to dance with you," she said from her hiding place.

"And may I write to you?"

"Yes, please," she said, feeling happy, giddy. She thrust her hand out of her burrow, reaching for him.

Teddy clasped the hand in his. She had removed her gloves at last!

It was such a little thing, but so firm, so strong. Other hands he'd held lay still and placid in his, but hers was a living creature, scampering over his knuckles, feeling him, learning him. The world was lighter now, the sky grown pearly, sending all the stars scurrying except the bright morning star. He could just see the little paw that played in his, the neat, clipped nails with their large moons, a little scar at the slim waist of her thumb. He ran his hand over that scar, wondering at the story behind it, reveling in the delightful knowledge that this was one of the ten thousand other things he would learn about her when he returned home.

He kissed the scar and released her hand. It hovered midair for a moment, then fled back into the cavern. Almost . . . almost he reached for her, for all of her, to take her in his arms and claim her mouth, her throat. But there was no time for that. He knew, from that brief conversation, that this was a woman he would not grow tired of.

"*Auf Wiedersehen,* my morning star," he whispered.

To which Hannah replied, "No, you ass, a native would say *tschuss* unless he was being formal." Then she added very tenderly, "We are no longer formal."

Hannah Utterly Fails at Domestic Service

PLEASANT AS THAT PREDAWN ENCOUNTER had been—and she called it only *pleasant* in an unsuccessful attempt to take away some of its intimidating gravity and the odd ecstatic joy it had engendered—Hannah regretted it almost immediately.

As soon as Teddy had gone far enough away not to be reasonably recalled, she remembered her parents and had to pinch herself quite hard for forgetting them even for an instant. Being with him had temporarily driven away all of her varied fears, but as soon as he was gone they all rushed back. He'd said he would make inquiries about her parents. She had slapped him afterward, but still, he had said it. She knew now that she had been dreadfully mistaken in his intentions. Even though they'd not talked about that, what they did talk about had been enough to make it patently obvious that he was not the sort of fellow to blackmail a girl for her favors. What he had wanted her to do for him, the personal thing, she didn't know, but it was not *that*.

I should have given him their address, told him the name of the cabaret, she thought. *I should have told him again and again how very important it is that they get out of Germany.* All he had were their names. Would it be enough? Of course, if all went well, they would follow her easily to England very soon, but if all did not go well . . .

She would get a letter from them shortly, she knew. Soon there would be a note from her parents bearing happy news, and one from Teddy, in which she would be very curious to see the word that came before his signature. *Yours* would do, but there were several others that would be better. Then, depending on the contents of her parents' letter, she could write back to Teddy and urge him to help.

They'll be safe, she told herself. Her mother would see to that. Aaron might persist in staying in Berlin out of some perverse stubbornness and hope, but Cora would convince him. As a last resort, she'd make him leave for *her* sake.

But it was not only for neglecting to press her parents' cause that she regretted talking to Teddy for so long. As soon as she crept back into the kitchen, she realized she desperately needed a few more hours' sleep. *Even romance cannot keep me awake today,* she thought, stifling a yawn before tying on her apron. She'd been up late, slept badly, and risen early. Now she faced her list of chores.

"'Number one,'" she read. "'Tend the cooker.'"

Well, that at least was easy. *"Tending* has such a pastoral feel," she said as she looked around the kitchen trying to figure out exactly which piece of equipment was the cooker. "Perhaps I can make believe I am tending sheep. Not," she added rather sadly, "that I know anything about tending real, actual sheep. I probably would not enjoy it. I'm sure they smell, and not like alpine flowers or new hay. Still, I will name the oven and pretend it is a sheep. Thank goodness no one is awake to hear me."

Nothing looked at all like the svelte electric oven and range at Der Teufel, on which their chef had prepared all of his brisk and simple masterpieces. There was a roast warmer and a squat, wood-burning cast-iron dwarf that looked so archaic, she was sure it must be strictly decorative. There was a sort of electric heating cupboard for sauces. Ah, there it was. With its cream-colored enamel front and little square doors, it looked more like an old-fashioned icebox than an oven. It was also already warm. There didn't seem to be much to tend, so she wiped its surface with a cloth and slid her finger down to the next item on the list: *Light the kitchen fire.*

She found a stack of newspaper in the butler's pantry and crumpled it all into a ball, then tossed it into the hearth. She struck a long match, and the flame crept and then caught in a cheerful blaze. She had never started a fire herself and was rather proud of its vigor.

Next came the kitchen floor. After a little rummaging she

found a broom in the scullery and swept the odd orts and leavings of last night's meal into a neat little pile. She couldn't find a dustpan, and didn't want to sweep them outside in case the food scraps attracted hedgehogs, so she guided her pile through the kitchen, past the cook's office, the butler's pantry, and the scullery, and left it just inside the door leading to the patch of lawn connecting the kitchen and the laundry. (A servant's lawn, ill kept, it was cut off from the garden by a tall, thick hedgerow, as the kitchen itself was cut off from the rest of the house by stairs and twisting corridors, so the masters need never see or smell the staff.)

"'Sweep *and* scrub the floor,'" she read with a sigh. The floor looked perfectly clean to her already, but she wearily found a bucket and strong soap, then searched for a mop. There was none, but she did find what looked like a minuscule mop on a hairbrush.

"I don't mind hard work," she told herself for the hundredth time as she sank onto her knees and began to scrub. "Really I don't. But they are doing it to humiliate me, to punish me for my mother's misdeeds, which were not even misdeeds." The mortar ridges between the slate pushed crisscross patterns into her legs, and her thin dress was soaked.

She scrubbed until her fingers were pruned and her hands began to cramp, then used the broom to push as much water as she could down the hall and out the door. The floor was still quite wet, and she considered using some of the stacks of pristine white towels to dry it, but thought this might be frowned upon. Besides, she vaguely remembered it was more sterile to let things air-dry.

She took up the list again with hands that shook and ached, resolutely not feeling sorry for herself, thinking with all her might of where she could be instead. In Buchenwald it would be this and worse. Here there were beds, no rats, no guards, no fists, no whips, no guns. *I am lucky,* she told herself. *Tonight I will get more sleep, and tomorrow this will all be second nature. Then soon it will be over.*

She looked down at the hand that held the list. *And in the meantime,* she thought, *there is that little piece of me there. That place that he kissed.* Feeling foolish, she kissed the scar herself. No trace of his lips remained — her skin was puckered from scrubbing with water and smelled of lye — but the spirit of him lingered there, reminding her of that surprising way life has of being desolate and grand in quick succession and sometimes all at once. Throughout the day she returned to the scar he kissed, like a pilgrim to a shrine, finding comfort in the personal altar of her body. *His lips were there. His lips will return.*

Then she laughed and called herself a fool and went to scrub the front steps and polish the brass on the door, the next things on her list.

SALLY SLEEKED HER GINGER HAIR with water as soon as she entered the kitchen. It was already tied into a tight knot at the back of her head in a most unflattering position, but she needed to make sure that not a single solitary hair entered the food. The kitchen maids had to wear their caps, but when she graduated from under-cook to Cook, uppercase, she threw away all of those ugly white monstrosities. She always thought of them as a sort of combined dunce's cap and slave collar, and though lesser female servants were obliged to wear them, Sally took immediate advantage of her rank and swore she'd never wear one again. She remembered hearing a story about a husband who asked his wife to dress up as a maid to titillate him. She thought at the time that being asked to wear a servant's cap counted as marital cruelty and grounds for divorce.

She was unusually happy that morning. Her world seemed to be falling into place. With three kitchen maids she could do her job properly. Certainly only two of them were trained, but they would direct the new girl, Hannah. Glenda and Judy would have gotten up early enough to guide her. For the first time in weeks, Sally had allowed herself a bit of a lie-in.

It was just as she was meditating on the miraculous emotional benefits of being able to loll in bed for an extra twenty minutes that she noticed that something was drastically amiss. Some many things, in fact.

"Hannah!" she bellowed, then for good measure shouted for Judy and Glenda, too. They rushed in, disheveled, Glenda still in curling papers. Sally glared at them. "The stove's not hot," she said, pounding it with her fist. "And the fire—just look at it!" In the hearth, a tiny crimson rill of flame ate through the last bit of newspaper, gobbling up the headline about Mussolini flexing his muscles at France. Then it died, leaving only ashes. "And what did she use for . . . ?" Fearing the worst, she dashed into the butler's pantry, where each morning the newspapers waited to be ironed. Every one was gone for kindling.

It could not get worse, she thought, yet even as she did so, Hardy the under-gardener came cheerfully in through the back door, bearing a cluster of late chrysanthemums (ostensibly for everyone in the kitchen but really for Hannah) and some sprigs of hothouse tarragon for His Lordship's eggs. Looking up—looking for Hannah—he kicked the pile of crumbs and dust, sending them showering across the still-damp floor.

"Oh, my floor!" Sally cried. Though she was perfectly comfortable with blood and drippings and feathers and flour marring her kitchen as the day progressed, she insisted that her workspace at least begin the day like a sterile surgery.

She threw her hands over her face, not knowing whether to scream or laugh. And to think, not a minute before she'd been thanking her lucky stars Their Lordships had seen fit to authorize the expense of another girl to help her.

"Breakfast is impossible now," she said. "If no one put more coal in the Aga it will never heat enough to so much as boil an egg, and Himself wanted kedgeree and breakfast buns and streaky bacon, none of which can be made in a lukewarm cooker. Hasn't the girl ever used an Aga? Where is she?"

No one knew. They searched the logical places but couldn't find her. Run away, Glenda thought. Drowned herself in the lake after last night's to-do, Judy was sure. Hardy searched the shrubbery, but she was nowhere to be found. Sally stoked the Aga with lumps of coal and prayed it would heat up enough to cook something. (The beautiful part of a coal Aga is that it is always hot. The terrible part is that it takes hours to get hot *enough*.)

Hannah was found at last by an early-morning caller who stopped on his way between Windsor Castle and Buckingham Palace to borrow a book his mother had requested from Lord Liripip. Seeing the little maid asleep on the front step with her cheek against the Brasso rag, he scooped her up, jerked the bell-pull with his teeth, and when Coombe opened the door, carried her in with a proprietary air. "Don't bother the family, I know they're still in bed. I, on the other hand, am still awake. I'll show myself to the library, and in the meantime, where shall I put this?" He looked down at the fetching little face pressed against his lapel, some happy dream curling the corner of her mouth.

"Sir, I . . . I . . ." Coombe began. Had he been of a different nationality he might have ritually opened his veins at the shame.

Behind him, Waltraud (who refused to give up lipstick no matter what Mrs. Wilcox, the housekeeper, said, and who besides had shortened her skirt by two inches and manipulated her cap into something Coco Chanel might covet) gave a little gasp and swore in German before Coombe shooed her away.

"I say," the dashing, disheveled man said delightedly when he glimpsed Waltraud, "old Peregrine picks the prettiest staff. Here, in the parlor?" He set Hannah down gently on a chaise.

Her eyes fluttered open and, hardly awake, she said, "Oh, you're Noel's pretty friend. He showed me your picture when I was a little girl."

The handsome young man flushed and said, "I'll get that book now," and retreated posthaste.

"Young woman," Coombe said with deepest gravity, "do you know whom you have just imposed upon?"

Hannah loosed a deeply satisfying yawn. "When I first woke up I was sure he must be a friend of a friend. Noel, you see, once visited my family in Germany and I remember he had a little picture in a silver filigree frame of a man who looked exactly like that. He let me carry it around all day, and I fell violently in love with that face, though from what Waltraud explained to me later I imagine any man who was deeply admired by Noel would not be likely to succumb to my advances, though perhaps after all his tastes are varied, as so many are. But young girls are always falling for someone unsuitable." She shook her head in faintly maternal exasperation. "I still am, in fact," she added, thinking of Teddy. "Just because we know our proclivities doesn't mean we can control them. That is depressing, but also rather reassuring, don't you think?" She cocked her head at the dignified butler in her pert, birdlike fashion. "It gives us so much latitude." Her inclusive pronouns made Coombe feel quite the conspirator, and he was not happy with what he would have to do next.

"You fell asleep," he pronounced grimly.

"Oh, yes. Another one of those proclivities we can't avoid. You see," she said as if she were giving a quite reasonable explanation of her abominable behavior, "I was so very sleepy."

A great deal of the improving literature Coombe received biweekly by post from the Untangled Ganglions correspondence course dealt with philosophy and logic. He puzzled through her statement. *Sleepiness,* he thought, *is a biologic fact. If I had told her to fetch something from a high shelf and she was too short to reach it, would I fire her for her lack of stature? Then is it fair to punish someone for a fault of nature? The human body, pushed to certain extremes, must sleep.*

But then he remembered the fundamental fact of life in service: servants aren't human.

Then too there was the circumstance of her discovery. If he, or Mrs. Wilcox, or the postman had discovered her asleep at the front door, it might all have been hushed up (after a fitting punishment, perhaps the loss of an afternoon off so she could catch up on her sleep instead of going to a village dance). But to have been found by *him!*

"Hannah, do you have any idea who discovered you asleep like a puppy on the doorstep?" No, *puppy* had been an error—

the comparison made her seem that much more endearing, made what must come next that much more difficult.

"I told you, I thought it was—"

"You were in error," he said with the utmost butlerish severity. "Your rescuer, if I may so style him, was His Royal Highness Prince George Edward Alexander Edmund, Duke of Kent, Earl of St. Andrews and Baron Downpatrick, Royal Knight of the Most Noble Order of the Garter, Order of the Thistle, Order of the . . ."

Almost any other maid would have fainted or—for maids are notoriously archaic in their gesticulation—thrown her apron over her face. But Hannah did not seem at all impressed to have been scooped up by the third in line to the throne. "Then he really must be Noel's Georgie. Funny, I always imagined he was taller."

Something clicked in Coombe's head, a half-remembered bit of gossip. "Noel . . . Coward?"

"Yes, he and my father hit it off right away, though I think he stole some of my father's best jokes for his next play. Still, no hard feelings."

"You know Noel Coward?" he asked.

"Well, I don't know if he'd remember me—it was a while ago."

"Who exactly are you? No, never mind. I'm afraid it won't do. Whoever you were, what you are now is a servant. I am in charge of the smooth running of this household, and I simply cannot permit such disruptions as you have caused. We were prepared to overlook last night's debacle as sheer ignorance, but to fall asleep, in public!"

"Hardly public," she answered, rubbing the last bits of sleep out of her eyes. "A mile from the gate and five miles from a good road."

"Insolence will avail you naught," he said, so theatrically that a giggle burst from Hannah's lips.

She stifled it with her fingers, but her eyes danced. Really, these English were so wonderfully false, always acting every moment of their lives. Sally, who Hannah could plainly see so desperately wanted to be kind and maternal, but who forced herself into sharpness. The Liripips, who had acted their aristocratic parts so long, pretending to be some elevated form of life that transcended such mundane things as servants, that they never broke character. And Coombe, who so obviously wanted to gossip, who understood what it is to be tired, playing the perfect unemotional butler.

And then the humor of it all abruptly vanished.

"I'm afraid I must give you notice," Coombe said.

"Of what?" she asked, tipping her head again in that most beguiling fashion.

"You will be paid for the remainder of the week, certainly, and provided transportation back to London."

"No!" she cried. "You mustn't! You can't!" Since her arrival she'd thought again and again about leaving, to beg for help from the refugee agency, to peddle her voice at the lowest music halls until she could support herself. Her promise to her mother had held her at Starkers. But now she had something else: Teddy's friendship. More than friendship already, she was sure, and she wouldn't give that up. Not until he'd come home again, or at least until she'd gotten his first letter, so she could write back and explain everything.

"Technically, Cook or Mrs. Wilcox should be the one to fire you, but when I have explained the situation I'm sure they will defer to my judgment. No, don't cry. Oh, Lord!"

Hannah tumbled out of the chaise and now knelt melodramatically at his feet, her head bent.

"My dear, ahem, this is most . . ."

"Please do not make me leave."

"Take your hands off my — Oh, my!" She had reached up blindly to clasp him in supplication, and the view that Anna got when she swept into the room was blackmail material if she had ever seen it.

Coombe saw her and stepped back sharply. Hannah, still clutching his midsection, fell forward.

"Miss Morgan, this is not what it appears to be," Coombe sputtered. "Forgive this unfortunate spectacle . . ."

"Of the Unfortunate Fruit," Hannah said, scrambling to her feet. "I quite agree with your disapproving look," she added, regarding the newcomer. It was the stunning blond woman who had taken her place in the car. When Teddy had smiled at her the night before with his world-embracing cheerfulness and good-will, Hannah had been jealous. But it was not this large gold and cream woman he'd talked with for hours, not her gloved fingers he had held. It was not her thumb he had kissed, or she who would get the first dance at the Servants' Ball. She smiled at Anna now; she had nothing to fear.

"I do not make a habit of clutching at men or kissing their feet," Hannah went on. "Begging and abasement are terrible, don't you agree? Yet there are times when they are necessary. I was being cast out, you see, so that is one of the times when one might sink to one's knees—I did it elegantly, don't you think, like a dying swan?—and plead with all one's heart. Do you know, I think Coombe believed I was going to attempt something scandalous, another and much more drastic way of begging, but I am not such a fool as that. To begin with, the parlor is not the proper venue, and then—"

"You will not fire her, Coombe," Anna said, mustering every ounce of pretend authority she had taught herself over the years.

"But, miss, she has absolutely no experience—we were misled. And then she is incorrigible in her behavior: speaking out of turn, sleeping on the job. I'm very much afraid she won't do."

Anna looked at the dark little maid. "You speak German?"

"Yes, of course. I *am* German."

Anna stared evenly at Coombe, until that dignified butler felt like a dickey bird under a cobra's baleful, hypnotic gaze. "I have need of her," Anna said.

Coombe knew the tone. It was the reason he had never married.

He stiffened and made a little bow, then removed himself.

"Freshen yourself up and then come to my room," Anna said, and swirled out in a cloud of rose scent.

Anna and Hannah Discuss
the Slum Disease: Love

〜✖〜

"I AM WITHOUT A LADY'S MAID at the moment," Anna said breezily when Hannah entered her room. Anna was sitting at a florid rococo vanity, idly dusting her nose with powder and blotting it off again to achieve the exactly right artificial naturalness. "Do you have any experience?"

Hannah gave a deep, regretful sigh. "I sometimes feel that I have wasted so many opportunities for experience in my life. There are times when people—young men mostly, but older ones too, and sometimes those who one would think are quite *too* old—make propositions and you say no, because of course you do not care to, and then you think, *Ought I to have?* Because if you are at a nice restaurant and you are served a very small octopus, you eat it, do you not, even if the idea of eating such a perfect little animal who is looking at you and seems to be still alive makes your stomach flutter, because you might not ever have another chance, and then afterward, for all your life, you could say you had—do you see? An experience. Do you think people should sometimes do things they don't think they want to, just for the experience?"

Anna gave her that disjointed look with which so many people regarded Hannah, as if they had fallen too many words behind to ever catch up.

"I would not say such a thing to a man because it would give him ammunition against future women, but to you I can say it. I can tell by the look of you that you must receive many offers of experience, probably more than I, because you really are quite spectacular, almost as frighteningly pretty as Traudl, but then you are an English lady and I think men might not make as many offers to ladies as they do to cabaret singers."

Anna froze mid-powder. An electric sensation coursed through her, sudden and shocking, accompanied, as a real charge might be, by paralysis and a strange overpowering buzzing in her ears. German. Jewish. The stage. A kitchen maid.

How could I have been so stupid? Anna asked herself. *It was there, all of it, right before me.* But there had been so many German and Austrian and Czech girls trickling in over the last year, taking jobs in service, making her father complain bitterly about unemployed English girls being deprived of honest work. There was another one in Starkers—she'd heard her muttering in her foreign lingo as she fluffed the pillows. It was too remarkably obvious: Could she have somehow simply switched places with the girl who was the real step-cousin-in-law? There was not some missing girl waiting to unmask her. The girl was here, in Starkers. But why had she said nothing? Why would a girl who was supposed to be welcomed into the family accept a place as kitchen maid?

With a chill of uncertain dread giving her goose bumps, Anna asked, "What is your name?" Silently, she pleaded, *Let me be wrong*.

"Hannah Morgenstern, and you are? But no, I am not to ask." She gave Anna a sweet smile, without malice. "You see, I hadn't intended to be a maid. I forget sometimes—no, all the time—how I am supposed to behave. I am to be invisible to the family."

For all her small stature, she was perhaps the most visible person Anna had ever seen.

Hannah, she thought. *The name Lady Liripip called me when we first met. Hannah to Anna, not much of a change. Just the thing an integrating foreigner might do. Just as a foreigner might change her name from Morgenstern to Morgan.*

"What had you intended to be?" Anna asked carefully.

"An opera singer, eventually, though truthfully I have nothing against low singing. Comic singing, I should say, or sentimental. I can't get beyond mezzo soprano, so everything I sing is low. Operetta is splendid too, but no one takes you very seriously when you sing Gilbert and Sullivan. And I could only do the harridan parts. Ruth and Buttercup are never kept by marquises, are they?"

"Do you want to be kept by a marquis?"

"Heavens, no. I want to fall in love with one very nice man

whom I will be with all my life, just like my mother did. He can make me expensive presents and buy me pretty little bijou villas if he likes, but it won't be necessary. Love will be enough."

"Love is never even close to enough," Anna said passionately. "Without money, love is like a disease. A slum disease. You must avoid it at all costs, and get rid of it ruthlessly if you catch it."

"You sound as if you know what you're talking about," Hannah said softly. "I'm very sorry."

Anna gulped. "I—" She stopped herself. She could not tell Hannah—she could never tell anyone. Her scheme of personal improvement had not been without a price. One hardship was that there was no one to share her struggle with. And another . . .

There had been boys before, nice boys, who had smiled at her or sent her flowers or affectionate letters. Their fathers had been drapers or clerks, and they themselves had been clever, ambitious, hard-working lads who might have given her a good life, if she'd let them try.

There had been one in particular: He had just inherited his father's flower shop, and he had courted her with all his might. But Anna had never given him a chance. She'd dreamed about him, but she wouldn't encourage him. In her mind she'd built their house together, a snuggery filled with the end-of-day's half-wilted blooms, the rose and jasmine scents deepening as the flowers died. She had decorated that dream house with a grandfather clock that ticked away each happy moment of their long life together. And there had been dream children, too, chubby babies rolling in petals, gleefully tearing flowers apart with their clumsy, imperious hands.

But he had not been good enough for her, and he had married someone else.

Anna had always felt an instinctive attraction to men who worked with flowers. That fellow she'd seen from her window, and later in the garden, for instance. What deity had so little insight into the creation of man that he made gardeners poor and rich men indifferent to flowers? Even now, that glimpse of the fetching laborer with his dirty hands and an armful of blossoms made her breath catch, her heart race, far more than the thought of Teddy. Yet rich, titled—and admittedly just as handsome— Teddy had to be her goal. Why did it ache, that traitorous heart of hers?

"It is hard," Anna said, wondering why she was confessing to this servant. No, she wasn't a servant, she was practically an aristocrat, a relative of the Liripips. *What are our relative positions?* Anna wondered. *Am I higher or lower than she?* It was always the vital question for Anna: Who was superior, and how could she position herself so that she would be perceived as superior?

She went on: "It is hard to be born in one place and then move to another. The old place drags at you. My mother told me stories about Jenny Greenteeth, a fairy who pulls children down into ponds and eats them. People who haven't been in the pond are never afraid. It is those who have felt her claws on their ankles, and then escaped, who know fear."

Hannah looked at her quizzically. "I think, like me, you talk about a great many things at once, and you don't really expect other people to understand everything you say. That's all right, though. Talking helps the talker best." She sighed. "It is another sacrifice of my current position. I am told I must not talk to myself, or speak so much at all. It is very difficult. Perhaps Coombe was right to get rid of me. Still, thank you for saving me. I have a particular reason for wanting to stay. Tell me, is this green-toothed fairy dragging at you now?"

The two girls looked at each other. *This is preposterous,* Anna thought. *I have every reason to fear her, and she has every reason to hate me, if only she knew. But I need help. I need . . . a friend. If only the secret holds!*

Anna was perched so precariously, right at the very pinnacle of success. She might step off that mountaintop into Olympus, or she might tumble off it to her doom.

I could tell her, Anna thought. *She seems kind. Unorthodox, slightly insane, but kind. Maybe if I explained that I just need to be in her place long enough for Teddy to propose, she would allow it.* But Anna could not confess. There was so much she didn't know. Why had Hannah accepted her lowly position? Who was Hannah to this family that a stranger could so easily slip into her place?

I can't do it, Anna thought with despair. *I'll be found out, humili-*

ated. *Have I committed a crime?* It felt as though she had. *The risks are too great, particularly now, with Hannah here. I should confess right away.*

But two forces, one weak, one strong, still held her tongue. There was her unknown mission to ally England and Germany and keep them from going to war against each other, for which it was absolutely necessary to be in Starkers. That, though, was less important by the moment, overshadowed by Teddy. Darling Teddy, who would save her from a life of struggle and pretense. Anna knew she was false now, but he would make her true, a legitimate lady. He loved her, and love levels all ranks. She'd thought she would have weeks of work ahead of her — a good start is much, but far from a proposal — but this morning there had been the note slipped under her door.

> *My darling girl,*
> *Last night was the most incredible of my life. Incredible,*
> *quite literally, because I can hardly believe that I could feel*
> *so much for someone in such a brief time together, with so*
> *few words exchanged. But how deep those words were, deep*
> *and broad, and yet never solemn, but like a wide rippling*
> *river, merry on the surface, dropping down to unknown*
> *profundity.*

Love, Anna was beginning to believe, did strange things to people. She'd worked hard to educate herself, to know a little bit about many things, and where her learning failed, to have a few stock phrases that would make her sound passably intelligent and encourage other people to talk. But even she—who thought so highly of herself—could not describe herself as deep.

> *But there it is. You've stolen my heart like a silver cow creamer. And, I might add, have been remarkably helpful. I'll use what you taught me in the next few weeks, and when I return (one should really say if in this line of work, I suppose, so as not to tempt fate, but really it won't be dangerous this time out) I will claim your hand again.*

My hand! she thought. Breach-of-promise suits had been won with less.

Fortune, she had heard, favors the bold. She would stay. She would keep flying her false colors, and by the time Teddy found out she wasn't who he thought she was, he'd love her so much, he wouldn't care if she were a pirate.

"I need a lady's maid," Anna told Hannah. "Would you be willing to help me?"

"You kept them from forcing me to leave," Hannah said simply, remembering the feel of manly fingers stroking the scar on her thumb. "I would do anything for you."

"Why is it so important that you stay?" Anna asked.

Hannah blushed. "A slum disease, I'm afraid," she confessed, though she knew Teddy would never care if she didn't have money or a title. And she was, after all, the daughter of an aristocrat. A disgraced, impoverished aristocrat who had fled her natal shore and taken up a disreputable profession, but still, the Curzons had been a great family once.

"You're in love? With someone here? Who?" Anna felt a frisson of dread. Not Teddy. Certainly not Teddy.

"Oh . . ." Hannah couldn't tell her. What would be worse, for Teddy to love a servant or the despised Unfortunate Fruit? The family could never know until it was too late.

"Is he here?" Anna pressed. "Have you been meeting him?"

"Yes," Hannah admitted guardedly. "Out in the garden."

Anna, fighting a sharp pang of jealousy, gave her a conspiratorial but slightly superior look. "I bet I know who it is!" She smirked. "It's that black-haired gardener, isn't it? Aha! I see from your blushes that I'm right!" His image rose again in her mind's eye, against her will. He was as fine a piece of manhood as one might find in a month of Sundays, but alas, not a lord who would one day be an earl. Still, good enough for someone else. She had seen him that second time while she took air in the more cultivated section of the garden (most of it was frankly too wild for her, an overtly picturesque mock wilderness). He'd looked at her, long and hard. Though of course she didn't return his look, she'd felt his admiration warm on her skin. She'd glanced sidelong at the play of sinew in his forearms, at the bulge of bicep below his rolled-up sleeve — and liked what she saw, very much. *No, you foolish girl*, she told herself, and pinched her arm where it would not show.

"You must tell me all about it," she said to Hannah. "And you must tell me everything, absolutely everything, about yourself."

If she was to act the part, she'd better study the character.

She ignored the prick of jealousy. She had Teddy. Why should she care if a gardener liked someone else? The fellow was nothing. There was no future in a gardener, any more than there would have been with a florist. A romantic might see a life full of flowers. Anna, who had taught herself to be ruthless and pragmatic about her prospects, saw a life full of dirt.

How funny, she thought, *that the one who should be living with the family is content to slave in the kitchen and fall in love with a servant, while I, daughter of a grocer, bask in Liripip luxury and am a whisker away from being Lady Winkfield.*

There was a phrase that stuck in her head. Where she had heard it she could not remember, but it had resonated deeply—"the will to power." *It is my will*, she thought, *that puts me here. I am a superior being, and so I rise, through sheer force of will and by the natural order of things, to my proper position.*

Why, then, was she deeply afraid of what might happen when her false colors were stripped from her? And why, when Hannah had gone back downstairs and Anna lay on her bed to daydream of future happiness, did her hero have dark hair and dirt under his fingernails?

Because, she snapped to herself, hastily banishing his image, *I shouldn't be daydreaming about happiness. I should be planning for success.*

When Hannah returned to the kitchen and told Sally about her new orders, the cook put her foot down. This time she didn't even have to summon the shade of Trapp. She could muster enough fury in her own right.

"No. Not if Lady Liripip herself demands it. I can scarcely manage this kitchen as it is with such a paltry staff. Oh, I do well enough for family dinners, as the family has about three taste buds collectively among them, but what happens when there are guests? Important guests. Discerning guests. Guests who won't stand for slop dished out lukewarm and underspiced. You, Hannah, are the only thing standing between me and suicide. Coombe can't fire you, and the quality can't steal you. You can't do a thing, you poor waif, but you can learn. Better yet, you can free up Glenda and Judy to do real cooking. If you turn lady's maid with no replacement for me here, I quit."

She made such a show of throwing her apron into the dustbin that Hannah swore she'd do both jobs, scrubbing and cleaning in the morning, leaving the cooks to the easier jobs of breakfast and lunch while she tended Anna, returning to help with dinner preparation, and then going back upstairs to see to Anna's evening toilette.

"I'll speak for you, child, and get you out of it. Ladies can always be cowed by their cooks. If you do both jobs you'll be run ragged, and wind up no good to anyone."

"No, Sally. She kept me from being fired—"

"I told you, I can overrule Coombe. You wouldn't have been sacked."

"All the same, she thought I was, and she saved me. Kindness must be repaid. And then she's . . . I don't quite know how to explain it. She's terribly on edge about something, and talks as if it's her debut in a drawing-room play. As if she's saying her words exactly right, because she's practiced so much, but she's always looking out of the corner of her eye to see if the audience is having the proper reaction. Who is she exactly? Do you know?"

"Anna Morgan is all I know. Some relative. Probably by marriage through one of the daughters. Well, suit yourself, and I only pray she won't stay long. You'll be worn fine as frogs' hair."

Hannah and Anna Reflected in Each Other

～

HANNAH WORKED, AND WHEN SHE SLEPT she hardly knew it. Determined to be better than the Liripips, who had forced her into drudgery, who never by word or look acknowledged her right to more than a roof, she still refused to complain. *Stay here, Mother said, so that they can find me. Stay here,* her heart sang, *for Teddy.* And so she stayed—and scrubbed, and chopped and plucked in the kitchen, and then, patting her pruned hands dry, she would run upstairs to attend Anna Morgan.

Her duties upstairs were certainly lighter, but no less tiring. Anna was serious when she said she wanted to know everything about Hannah. She was reluctant at first, but when after a few subtle questions of her own she discovered that Anna had no intimate connection to the Liripips, she decided it couldn't hurt. She would never have talked about her past with Lady Liripip, but this young woman, sympathetic and near her own age, was a different story.

Hannah never breathed a word about why she was at Starkers. She told Anna the same thing the staff all seemed to believe, that she was a Jewish refugee hired by Trapp, one of the thousands of German and Austrian girls who fled to England. But she hid nothing about her family, her life in the cabaret, or the gradual disintegration the Nazi Party had brought to her happiness and security.

Anna — whose father would take the strap to her if he knew she was talking civilly to a Jewish girl — asked her part-time maid a great many questions, including one her father had never been able to answer to her satisfaction.

"But why do they hate you? Hate the Jews, I mean."

Hannah gave a shrug as she stood behind Anna, combing out her golden hair. "A little boy told me once that I killed God. I laughed and told him that if Jesus hadn't died, then he — the boy, that is — would still be Jewish. I remember he scrunched up his face, had a good hard think, and then spit on me."

Anna gasped. She had been hearing anti-Semitic (and anti-many-other-things) rants from her father for years, but they had always been abstract to her. Like so many children she only half listened to her parents, absorbing a great deal of what they said accidentally, as it were, but for the most part ignoring them as something irrelevant to youth. Banish them, he had said. Tax them, segregate them, put them on leaky boats and launch them to their own fates. Once when a group of East End Jews had come to protest at one of his rallies, her father had spit on one of the demonstrators. Anna had been disgusted, but for the wrong reasons. *A gentleman does not spit,* she remembered thinking.

She had not spared a thought for the person whom he'd spat on.

Now, as she looked at Hannah's reflection in the vanity mirror, she felt a sudden shifting in her world, one of those tectonic upheavals that might raise a mountain or open a rift. *Who is who?* she wondered, staring at both of their images. *I am pretending to be her—I am her, for all practical purposes.* She felt as if that little boy had spit on her. As if her father had spit on her. And it hurt that someone would hate her, the make-believe her, in her fictitious past.

"What did you do?" she whispered.

Hannah gave an impish grin. "You cannot worry too much about what children do. They are always looking for someone to be unkind to, and believe whatever they are told. It only hit my shoes, so I did my best to be philosophical. I had shined my shoes with spit that very morning—they were black patent leather, and nothing makes them gleam more than spit, for some reason—so why worry about more spit? Of course, the problem is not children, it is their parents. Hate is like hunger, I think. When one person feels it and talks about it, suddenly everyone feels it, even if they didn't before."

"And despite that, you stayed in Germany?" Anna asked.

"What, leave because of a foolish child?"

"But there was worse, wasn't there?"

"Ah, not for us. Not until the end. We were *special* Jews, you see," Hannah said sardonically. "Secular Jews with a great many friends in high places. For years, we had entertained the most important people in Berlin within our walls. I had sung to Herr Hitler, back in the early days. It was a song about sheep, of course." She chewed on her lip. "We were lulled by the sheep songs, my family and I."

"But they are getting out?"

"For my mother it will be easy. She is English, you see. But my father may have some difficulty. It is another reason why I must be here, at Starkers. In times of trouble people get lost. I don't know if my parents are still at our home, or in France or Poland. I cannot write to them. So I must be here, until they write to me or show up at the doorstep." Hannah wondered if her mother would deign to use the back door.

Anna quizzed her new lady's maid incessantly. *Tell me what you sang, tell me what you wore. Tell me of the boulevards you strolled upon.* And finally, she asked her to teach her German.

"Just enough to get by," Anna said. "Enough to sprinkle a phrase or two here and there in conversation."

She would keep poor Hannah up till all hours, never caring that Hannah had to rise at five to stoke the Aga and scrub, and scrub, and scrub . . .

But every day at post time, no matter what else she was doing,

Hannah dropped her half-plucked pheasant or her bouquet garni and ran to intercept Coombe with his silver salver.

"Nothing for you, my dear," he'd say with a long face, and Hannah would try to bear it one more day.

In the second week of December, though, she spied a German postmark among the envelopes.

"It's not for you, Hannah," Coombe insisted, but she snatched it off his platter and had it half torn open before she saw the address. It was indeed from Teddy . . . but it was addressed to Anna Morgan.

"Oh," she said, hanging her head and handing it back. "Never mind." When Coombe adjusted the disarranged pile, she saw that there were two more from Teddy, one each to his mother and father.

It is only right that he writes to his parents first, she thought, *and Anna's letter must just be another obligation — hello, how are you, I'm fine, the weather is lovely. My letter will come tomorrow.*

But it didn't. Several times, she was sure she glimpsed Teddy's hand, but Coombe kept the envelopes tucked against his chest and she could never be sure.

Finally, when she had almost despaired of hearing from them, a note came from her mother. Cora had evidently tried to make it cavalier and unworrying, but she'd failed miserably.

> *Dearest Hannah,*
> *We are both alive and well, and most of all happy that*

you are safe and sound at Starkers. I'm sure you're having
a splendid time. Have you learned to ride to the hounds
yet? Give Peregrine a kiss from me, with my thanks. I have
moved from Der Teufel to a charming little apartment,
so much more convenient. I won't give you the address,
though, for I might be moving again soon — to someplace
more charming still — and you know with things as they
are it is better not to draw attention to oneself with foreign
postmarks. Too many people ask questions. Better days are
ahead. They must be.

   Love,

   Cora

Hannah's heart beat in her breast like a trapped bird, flutter-
ing, panicked. So many things were wrong with this letter! *We are*
alive — how dire that reassurance sounded, making her instantly
sure there had been some danger of death. And Benno would
never have made them move from Der Teufel. That simple, big-
hearted boy would never betray his benefactor, never consider
the cabaret as belonging to anyone other than Aaron Morgenstern, no matter what the deed said. Why had she moved? And
where?

   And worse — oh, worst of all — the letter was from her mother alone. There was that *we* in the beginning, then it was all *I. I*
have moved. Not *we* have moved. Always before, when Hannah
had gone on schoolgirl holidays or trips to Austria with her sing-

ing master, her parents had written *ensemble*. Usually her father added a lengthy postscript and jotted amusing notes in the margin of Cora's letters, or at the very least, signed his name and his love. To get a letter signed only by Cora boded ill.

He's alive, she thought. *At least I know that much. She wouldn't lie about that—would she?*

But they weren't living together, and that meant ... what? Was Aaron in hiding? In Buchenwald or Dachau?

Oh, Teddy, please write to me. Tell me you've found them. You promised you'd look.

But he did not write to her.

Despite her mother's warning, she penned a hasty letter to Benno. *Tell me what's happened*, she begged. Then she waited.

The first frost came, and after it light snow, sugaring the garden and the half-tame forest surrounding the house. Sleep came hard for Hannah. When she lay her head on the pillow, her mind raced from worry to worry about her parents. Then when she finally drifted off into fitful slumber, she was plagued with dreams about Teddy that should have been pleasant but seemed a mockery upon waking. She would get up too early, before anyone else in the house was stirring, and go to the entwined yews. Hiding in the cavern, she would ask herself, again and again, *Why does he write to everyone but me?*

"Obviously because his mother would see the letter and it would cause trouble for him," Waltraud said when Hannah repeated the question to her. "Men may feel one thing and wind up doing another, because it is easier. Why do you care so much for him? You knew him for barely a day."

"Have you been in love, Traudl?" Hannah asked.

"Yes, many, many times. Why, just last night I'm sure I was in love with Corcoran—you remember him, the tall, dashing footman with black hair and such very vigorous sideburns that almost amount to muttonchops, so he looks like a Victorian cad. Though that might only have been to annoy Judy, who fancies him. He came tap-tapping at my door, and . . ."

"That is not love," Hannah said with a laugh.

"It felt quite good enough for me. And love is a pretty name for something so nice. Don't they call it *making love*?"

"If you have to make it, like a schoolgirl's papier-mâché craft, bit by bit, it is not love. Love springs fully formed. It is Athena."

"I thought she scorned love," Waltraud quipped.

"Well, Aphrodite too sprang fully formed from the sea foam, which was really you-know-what. Those Greeks!"

"Has there been springing sea foam for you?" Waltraud asked.

Hannah gave her a light, playful slap. "Of course not! We have only talked. But . . . how can I say it? Without sight, almost without touch, with only our minds and words, we have connected. Sitting in the dark, inside that tree, it was like conversing with my own soul, my own self. I love him already. I am sure of it, and sure he feels the same."

"Then you must overcome his fear of what his parents will think."

"How?"

"By seducing him so absolutely in one passionate moment that he cannot live without you."

Hannah shook her head sadly. "I don't know how to seduce, only talk."

"Words, *pff!* Men love with their eyes. They can't help it. He will be here in time for the Servants' Ball, no? On that night, offer him a spectacle—the spectacle of you—and he will be won forever. Give him décolletage. Give him thigh. Lay out the appetizers for the grand banquet you promise him."

"I'm afraid I'm hardly more than an afternoon snack," Hannah said, looking down at her compact form.

Waltraud cupped her friend's cheek in her hand. "Little blossom, I will turn you into a smorgasbord! Now, what shall you wear?" They were in her bedroom, and she sprang for the wardrobe.

"Oh!" Hannah cried when her friend flung open the doors. "You got them all out of Germany!"

Inside were all of Waltraud's glamorous outfits. Other women wanted their admirers to give them jewels. The provocative entertainer insisted her presents be in the form of haute couture.

"You have the Chanels," Hannah gushed. Though she didn't pay much attention to her own fashion, she knew her friend's collection like an often-visited museum. Waltraud's apartment had been next to Der Teufel, and Hannah had often sipped lemonade and nibbled on crackers while the entertainer got ready for one of her many dates.

"And the lime Schiaparelli, and the one she made with Dali, the autumn-colored leaf-skeleton gown."

"You would not believe what I did to get that dress," Waltraud said with a snigger.

"You enjoyed every minute of it, I'm sure," Hannah said, rising to stroke the dresses like old friends. "And the Lanvin blue with those outrageous sleeves. Do you know what these must be worth?"

"I do, but luckily the border guards didn't. I piled them willy-nilly and said they were scraps to make dolls' clothes for poor children." She made her face serenely pious. "I only just got the creases out of them. I'm going to wear this one to the ball, I think."

She pulled out a demure-looking floral on pale pink silk, ruched at the waist, trailing at the hem.

"You, in a floral?" Hannah asked, amazed. She'd been sure her friend planned to shock on her first occasion to dress up. Something daringly low cut, or slit to the hip.

"But see?" Waltraud held it up to the fading winter light. It was entirely see-through.

"Traudl, you couldn't!"

"Don't worry," Waltraud said, hanging it back up. "The plum-colored flowers are the only ones that aren't transparent, and they're strategically placed. At least, they are until I start dancing! Now, for you—"

"I have to run, Traudl. Dinner to get ready, and then Anna to dress for it."

Waltraud made a rude noise. "Why do you have to serve that cow?"

"Be kind, Traudl. She's not so bad."

"Why do you have to serve at all? If you just went down on your knees to Lord Liripip—"

"No!" Hannah drew herself up and flushed. "They want to humiliate me, well, let them. They will see."

"They will see the vixen who will capture their boy and enjoy this pile of rocks when they're dead and buried. Just wait until the ball. Teddy really doesn't know who you are?"

"I'm sure he thinks I'm only a servant."

"I don't care if he thinks you're Lizzie Borden or Typhoid Mary. When I'm through with you, you'll have a proposal."

Hannah as Love's Messenger

CHRISTMAS HAD BEEN MAGICAL at Der Teufel. Hannah's secular father (who would have been atheist had he not considered God almost a relative, a rich absent uncle who might do favors if he was in a benevolent mood, but who was also the butt of many japes) preferred the holiday to Hanukkah, believing the world should proceed as the stage did, with a bang and a punch line, not drawn out interminably. His customers, too, being predominantly Christian, welcomed the holiday décor, wreaths and holly bathed in a diabolical glow, the crimson of flame and blood miraculously imbued with holiday cheer. Whatever the day or days celebrated, the entire month was a holiday of champagne and song. The season itself was comforting, a companionable hunkering-down against the fading year, a tendency to draw near to one another against the encroaching darkest nights. To be in dim, cozy light with friends while all around is dark was somehow better to Hannah than to be alone in the sunshine.

Christmas at Starkers was, at least for the servants, just another day. There was a church service, which Hannah ostentatiously didn't attend (having driven the point further home the week before, telling everyone about the Festival of Lights and begging for candles, though she got muddled and celebrated for only seven days). There were extra birds to pluck, a great ugly pudding to boil, and everyone's hair reeked of Brussels sprouts. ("Which," Hannah told Waltraud later, "taste so nice and smell so horrid when they cook. Is there a metaphor for life there, do you suppose?") Samuels and Corcoran pulled a cracker near Sally's ear and made her drop the chocolate and buttercream yule log she'd concocted for dessert, so she sent Hannah to the hothouse to see if there were any forced strawberries for a makeshift trifle.

It was a treat to leave the house in daylight. Her diurnal life had been confined to the kitchen, the narrow linoleum-covered back stairs, and Anna Morgan's bedroom. If she wanted to breathe real (Brussels sprout–free) air she had to wake up extra early. It was worth it, though, to cat's-paw her way through the dark garden to the edge of the timberline and imagine she was in the Black Forest, listening for the crepuscular hiccup of a cuckoo, the whistling wings of one of the last capercaillies. The Morgensterns would go to Baden in the off-season, to hike beneath the conifers, to giggle at the maidens in their fantastically pompommed hats called *bollenhuts,* to argue about whether to buy a cuckoo clock, weighing their undoubted charm against the annoyance of having something cheep at you on the quarter hour.

But this was not the Black Forest. It smelled different. It sounded different. It *felt* different, creeping over her skin in its unfamiliar way instead of sinking inside her like a second self. *I am German,* she thought each early morning. *But I must become English.* And so she breathed deeply of the English air, and listened intently to English chirps and tweets, and did her best to feel the spirit of the place, to make it her own.

It still seemed acutely foreign to her as she walked to the hothouse. Familiar, as a scene from a book she had imagined so many times, but still foreign. *Yes, that's it,* she thought as she strolled slowly, drawing out her freedom as long as possible. *England is still fiction to me, Wodehouse and W. S. Gilbert.*

She took a slight detour, peering around to the garage. There was Teddy's feline Bugatti, crouching under the chauffeur's chamois. But where was Teddy? Wouldn't he come to her right away?

No, she decided. The English have such rigid codes dividing the classes. *For him to go into the kitchen to seek me out would be nearly as bad as being in love with me in the first place. I must be patient. Tonight he will come to the twin yews. Or tomorrow morning.*

When she unlatched the door to the hothouse she heard singing, something about a flat-foot floozy with a floy-floy.

"I think I know what a floozy is," Hannah called into the lush, junglelike greenery, "but what is a floy-floy?"

"Something Americans catch from floozies, I think," Hardy

said, coming out from behind a potted lemon tree and wiping his hands on a towel. "What, not even a blush? I'm losing my touch. Good to see you, Hannah. I thought for sure you'd be out on your ear by now."

"Not for lack of trying, on my part and nearly everyone else's. My, it's like summer in here!" The air was richly humid and smelled positively green.

"I stay here as much as I can during the winter. You're welcome to visit me whenever you like. Some evening when you're free . . . or very early morning. Oh, now I see a blush! It must have gotten awfully cold in that yew bole, but neither of you seemed to mind. Is it the heat that makes your face so red, Hannah?" He grinned wickedly. "No wonder I pitch the woo at you and it bounces right off. You've been vulcanized by flash Teddy, bane of the maidens."

Hannah tried not to look distraught. Not *feeling* distraught was utterly beyond her. "Is he really so . . ." She could not find the word.

"They claim he's more of a ladies' man than his father was, and that's saying something. The laundry maids all swear he's, er—damn, I can't think of an appropriate euphemism."

"Popped their bubbles?" Hannah suggested, her voice shaking. "Starched their knickers?"

"Oh, Hannah, you aren't serious about him? We might have progressed a bit past the Victorian era, but we keep the fine old tradition of lords knocking up the servant girls and the girls being dismissed without reference. Then it's factory life, the evils of gin, and before you know it you're a flat-foot floozy with a floy-floy, trolling Haymarket."

Hannah couldn't help but laugh. How peculiar life had become, when the most crushing things could be coupled with merriment, a strange gallows humor, hope and despair hand in hand.

"Is he really so bad?" she asked softly when the laughter died away to uncomfortable silence.

"Frankly, I don't know. That's what they say. What the girls say, that is, but you know how they are. But I've never seen any of *them* out with his lordship in the morning starlight. Don't fret. You're clever enough to sniff out a man's real intentions."

"No, I'm not," Hannah admitted.

Which might, Hardy thought, be why Teddy was so interested. But he kept this to himself.

"But look on the bright side," Hardy said. "If he breaks your heart, you always have my open arms to rush to. At least, the way things are going, you will. My love life with the toffs isn't progressing as neatly as yours." He tossed the earth-covered towel over a smug-looking rosebush in full flower. "Can you keep a secret?"

"I don't know. I've never tried."

"Funny," he said dryly. "Though keeping it a secret is probably the problem. She doesn't know I'm smitten."

"Who?"

"You'll laugh."

"Very likely, if it's funny. But it can't be as funny as Teddy and me, which you will keep under your hat, will you not?"

"Trapped beneath my beaver in perpetuity," he said. "Now will you help me?"

"Of course, but how? Who?"

After a great deal of squirming he said, indistinctly and out of the corner of his mouth, "Anna Morgan."

"No! But she's—"

"As much of a swell as your Teddy? But it's different for me, isn't it, because a woman rises—or sinks—to her husband's rank. Fine for you and Lord Ted, he can make a lady out of a guttersnipe. Not so peachy for me and that goddess."

Hannah wondered which goddess Anna might be. Aphrodite was a troublemaker, and ignorant and selfish, but it was probably hard not to like her. Hannah tried to like her part-time mistress, and often she succeeded. But sometimes Anna would say something that made Hannah freeze and gape, because that was the only possible safe alternative to whacking her with the hairbrush.

Once Anna said that poor people should not be pitied, because they evidently chose to be poor. Another time she opined that birds—not just pigeons but songbirds—should be prohibited in cities because of the mess they make. "You can so rarely hear their songs over traffic noise, and then they always seem to sing when I have something interesting to say. Oh, I know: There can be a bounty on their heads, and then the poor people can hunt them and not be poor anymore!" When Hannah, with shades of Swift, muttered that they could just put a bounty on the heads of the poor, Anna looked at her with patient contempt and said, "But they could eat the birds too, and make pretty hats out of them. You can't make anything out of the poor."

But she could be kind, too. Hannah was surprised at how interested Anna was in her life and past, and how eager she was to learn German. She was abysmal, true, but she tried awfully hard, watching her face in the mirror as she wrapped her tongue around difficult words. And she gave Hannah curling papers she didn't want, a scarf she didn't need, and a manicure set for nails that had been broken down to nubbins so there was nothing left to file.

She could see how a man could fall in love with Anna, because as Waltraud said, men seemed to love with their eyes.

"Have you even spoken to her?" Hannah asked Hardy.

"Well . . . no. But she's looked at me."

"That's something," Hannah said, doubtful.

"That's everything, if they look at you right. You can tell, can't you, the second you meet someone, even in the instant you first set eyes on her, if it will be yes or no. It might not ever come to that—you might not have the chance, she might remember Mother and think better of it in the end—but she looks you over and decides all at once if you're a possibility."

"And she looked at you with a yes?"

"With a yes that drooled, Hannah!" Hardy said, sidling closer to her. "She came into the hothouse a few times, and I took pains to be there, nearby, always ready if she had a question. She never talked to me, but she fondled my gardenias like they were my—"

"Hardy!"

"She did, bob's your uncle. And she looked at me sideways-like, out of her eyelashes, and her lips curled and I could see what she was thinking about."

"Hardy, dear, I hate to disappoint you, but Anna Morgan thinks love without money is a sort of disease. She might fancy you, but I don't think she'll let you tickle her fancy in return. Although . . ." She cocked her head in consideration. "Do you think it might be that the lady doth protest too much? Why would she take the trouble to knock love of a poor boy so violently about the head if she had not been inflicted with the symptoms herself? Maybe you have a chance. No, I have changed my mind already. She thinks she is far too much of a lady to fall in love with poor handsome you, though you might come into her bedtime thoughts now and again."

Hardy leaned close and whispered in her ear. "That Anna ain't no lady."

Hannah's eyes flew open wide. "What do you mean?"

"She was looking at these gardenias here. I'd just come in the back, quiet-like, to spy on her a bit, and she didn't have a clue I was there. She smelled the biggest and said . . ."

Hannah held her breath, quivering in anticipation.

"She said, in a shrill voice, 'Cor blimey, ain't that a beaut!'"

"And what's wrong with that? It is a . . . beaut."

"You're a foreigner and haven't got a proper ear, though you do speak far more like a lady than some. *Cor* is straight out of the East End. It's something an eelmonger might say. A lady might pick up slang and use it to be cute when she's talking to her friends, but what a person exclaims when she's alone always goes back to her roots. If she blurted out *cor*, it means she was raised saying *cor*."

"Hardy, I had no idea you were such an etymologist."

"Can't say if I'm that, but my own grandmother sold eels and she said *cor* twelve times a day." His voice suddenly took on a profoundly genteel tone. "My mother, however, was a schoolteacher, and when she's listening, my own elocution is superb." He laughed at himself and slipped back into his careless accent. "Say, I ought to talk like that in front of Anna. She'll think I'm a real swell. What do you know about her, anyway? None of the staff seem to know where she came from or why she's here. Some connection of Lady Liripip's, they think, because she's taken her under her wing, but is she a relative? A friend? A blackmailer?"

Hannah laughed and shrugged. "No one tells me anything. Maybe she's a parasite, like the ancient Greeks had—a poor hanger-on who earned his bread through flattery and a laugh in the right place and occasionally doing clandestine deeds." She thought for a moment. "Whatever she is, I don't think she's very comfortable here. She's always on edge, and trying not to look like she is, and mostly succeeding but not always."

"I'm not rich," Hardy said, drawing himself up to his full—and considerable—height and looking the very picture of yeomanly pride. "But I have a bit put by, and the job comes with a cottage on the grounds. Umbel says I'm ready to be full gardener, so if she's not happy here I could get a place as head gardener at a smaller establishment, and she could keep house and help with the lighter work, herbs and such."

Hannah couldn't quite see Anna mucking about with herbs, but she said only, "You haven't even talked to her, and you're making plans to marry her?"

"Or not, if she'd prefer. I'm not picky about the particulars, long as she came to live with me, let me take care of her."

"What if you aren't compatible?"

"Oh, those things work themselves out, once you're stuck together," Hardy said. "But I guess we ought to chat a time or two before I risk popping the question. So will you help me?"

"How?"

Hardy pulled a pair of shears from his leather apron and began snipping creamy gardenias. "Can you sneak these into her room? With a note?"

AND SO THAT EVENING ANNA found her room redolent with cloying gardenia sweetness. She'd been a little disappointed in Teddy's demeanor earlier. Of course, he'd motored home just in time to dress for dinner, and brought a friend with him, a slender aesthete named Maurice, who had monopolized the conversation by quizzing Lord Liripip about his memoirs. Teddy had been as charming as ever, but not nearly as intimate as his letters from Germany seemed to indicate he ought to be. *Of course he wants to keep it from his mother for now, the sensible man,* she thought, *but can't he even manage a whispered word of love?*

He and his friend talked about Germany in a most depressing way, and much to her consternation kept addressing her in German, so she had to affect an earache and pretend she couldn't hear much of the conversation. Anna was getting into quite a pet when Teddy excused himself early, pleading the rigors of travel. But then as he was wishing everyone good night he whispered to Anna, "Later, my darling, in the delicious darkness," which made her feel like one of those quivering aspics impregnated with strange edibles.

And when she found the blossoms, and read the note — *Meet me where these flowers slumber* — she was certain a proposal was imminent. Or, she thought with some alarm, pondering the references to darkness and slumber, if not a proposal, then some other proposition of increased intimacy, to which, as a cow who most decidedly would not give her milk for free, she would certainly say no. Probably say no. Very likely say no, unless the proposition was accompanied by an engagement ring. Or not.

The moon was new, the stars obscured under a lowering gray nacre of clouds, and Anna stubbed her toe many times in the pursuit of love. But all incidental injuries were forgotten when, the moment she set foot inside the midnight blackness of the sultry hothouse, strong arms encompassed her, pulling her close to a warm chest made hard and muscular, she knew, by vigorous rowing for the Oxford crew team. Any objections she might possibly have were stifled by the beguiling press of very skillful lips.

"But . . ." she managed to gasp at last.

"But nothing," a manly voice murmured in aristocratic tones. "Do you like it?" In the absolute darkness he felt her head nod, brushing him cheek to cheek. "Do you like me?" Another nod, and this time she sought out his lips herself. After that there were very few words.

Hannah on the Road to Damascus

HANNAH HAD DONE EVERYTHING POSSIBLE to see Teddy Christmas evening. Almost—almost she risked another debacle of female-in-the-dining-room, but Sally caught her lingering by the door with a bowl of relish and, smelling danger, sent her to the pantry to fetch an extra fish slice (there being a superabundance of this useless utensil, since every married Liripip couple for the last four hundred years had received no less than twelve of them as wedding gifts). Before dinner she paced in the hall outside of Anna's room, in case he should stroll by. She brought up his name in clumsy and obvious ways, hoping to hear some tidbit about him. Luckily it didn't rouse the other maids' suspicions, because they were all in love with Teddy, though slightly more resigned to the fact that they could not possess him.

Not for himself, she thought. *Not for me, not for love. Only to see if he has word of my parents.*

After that, though, for me. Oh, entirely for me!

Dinner with the other servants was a torment, and afterward Anna kept her up in her room, primping to an extent unusual for one about to sleep. Anna said nothing about the flowers, and Hannah asked no questions, but they exchanged sly, knowing looks. Hannah was surprised to find Anna receptive to Hardy's advances, but she was happy for her friend's success and hoped they'd manage to overcome their differences. If Anna deigned to meet him in the hothouse, it was likely that most of the hurdles were already cleared.

Finally Anna dismissed her with a dreamy look, and Hannah gave herself exactly ten seconds in her room to primp before dashing out into the darkness. She made a beeline for the twin yew trees and curled up in her accustomed cozy nook to wait.

She heard the crunch of gravel on the winding path, and then there he was. She wanted to rush into his arms, to lift her face for him to kiss. She wanted to dispense with the demure offering of herself altogether, stand on tiptoe, grab him by his chestnut hair and *take* the kiss she desired. But she only stretched out her hand, groping until he caught it in his own, and sighed with the simple pleasure of his touch and proximity.

"I'm sorry I didn't write to you more often," he said at once in German. It was their nocturnal language, freeing them from all fear of eavesdroppers.

"Did you write at all?" she asked. Maybe the letter had been lost, or stolen by Lady Liripip.

"Tease! We were frightfully harried, though. Pretending to be students by day, motoring out to the countryside by night to make contact with people who might muck things up for the Nazis if it comes to war, then trying to appear fresh-faced eager students again come morning, after two hours of sleep. Maurice took it rather better than I — he amuses himself at those private dance halls that never seem to shut down, and then sneaks back into Oxford and blooms fresh as a dandelion by matins. We think he's going to dissolve at thirty, but for now he holds up amazingly. I, on the other hand . . ." He gave a prodigious yawn.

"Did you find my parents?" she asked, unable to control herself any longer.

He was silent for a long time, and she braced herself for tragedy. "It's very . . . disorganized in Berlin right now," he said at last. "Among your people, I mean, or your father's people."

"But you looked for them? You remembered their names?"

"I asked wherever I could, sweetheart," he said gently. "Rabbis, musicians, actors, anyone I thought might know of them. Anyone I could ask without arousing suspicion, that is. I couldn't draw attention to myself by going through official channels. I might well be back there under cloak, with dagger, so the fewer people in power who know my face, the less likely Hans the precocious farm boy is to be unmasked as a British spy."

Hannah pulled his hand to her breast.

"All those people you asked, they knew nothing?"

"They seemed never to have heard of your father."

"But that is impossible! Everyone in Berlin knows the name of —"

Before she could say her father's name, they heard a low thump and a sharp muttered curse in fishwife patois. They both froze until the person passed.

"Someone is in love with Hardy the under-gardener," Hannah said. They heard the distant hothouse door open and close.

"I did my best to find them, darling," he said when the danger of discovery had passed. "People have become suspicious and close-lipped, and understandably so. They might just be refusing to speak of him for some reason. Maybe they don't trust me. Maybe he's gone underground, doing secret work."

"Maybe he's being tortured in Buchenwald. Maybe he's being interrogated by the Gestapo. Maybe he's dead." Her tears fell onto their clasped hands.

"I'll be going back soon. I graduate in May. I'll be able to come to Starkers for a day or two and then fly to Germany again . . . presuming things remain as they are. I'll look for them again, I promise."

"And my mother, you heard nothing of her either?" She told him about her mother's troubling letter with its muted undercurrents of disaster.

"Nothing. She's in no danger, though, I'm sure. It was mostly men being taken, it seemed. Unless there's reason to think she's working as a spy or saboteur?"

"Mother? Good Lord, no. Unless, of course, my father was

in danger. She'd sink the entire German fleet to save him. Oh, Teddy, you should see how they love each other. No force on this earth could keep them apart. Not war, not death, I think. Do you know they changed their religion so they could imagine themselves together after death?"

"She converted?" he asked.

"Ah, no. They were both essentially atheists, you see, though he was brought up Jewish and of course she had the Church of England thrust on her as a child. As atheists they couldn't believe in an afterlife, and though they knew their molecules would mingle for all eternity—you know how they say we're breathing bits of Marc Antony every day—it wasn't quite as satisfying as getting to hold hands in paradise. So they became agnostics. Not believing, not *not* believing. This way they thought that if there was someone in charge, perhaps he wouldn't be offended and would let them into whatever good place he had available. And of course my father donated to the synagogue, which might be like slipping money to the maitre d'—you get a seat in heaven even if you don't have a reservation." She added solemnly, "It is quite a big thing to change one's religion for a beloved."

Teddy laughed. "I'm not sure our bishop would see a switch from atheism to agnosticism as a conversion."

"It was! A veritable road to Damascus. It is as much a comfort to them as an actual religion is to most people. They do not need liturgy and law, only a little wiggle room on the matter of an afterlife."

"And what do you believe?" Teddy asked.

She stroked the back of his hand. "In this. I stepped on the road to Damascus when you pulled up in your car, though I didn't know it."

"And when did you love me?"

"Did I ever say I love you?" she asked archly.

"With every word."

"I love you," she whispered.

"I love you," he echoed. "Come out so I can see you."

"You can't see in the dark, darling *Dummkopf.*"

"But I can feel you. Let me hold you. I won't do anything more, I promise."

"Ha! And what if I do the more, eh? You might be able to control the fiery passions of youth, but I cannot. If I leave this yew bole I am lost, a fallen woman." She spoke with levity, but she was serious, too. She didn't know if she could control herself, and it wouldn't be right to give in to desire when her parents' whereabouts were unknown. It felt almost wrong to be in love when they were in danger . . . but there was nothing she could do about that.

Another thing held her in check, kept her hidden inside her cave so that all he could possess was her hand. *Men love with their eyes,* Waltraud had said, and when it came to men, she trusted Waltraud's judgment absolutely. In all the time they'd spent together—and it was little enough, though it felt like so much more—Teddy had been looking at her for only a fraction of the time. *I can charm him with my words, with my voice and wit,* she thought, but she didn't know if she could charm him with her body and face. She liked this utter darkness, where they were just two souls in their own paradise, unencumbered by physical form.

She compared herself to the brazen, buxom laundry maids of whom Teddy was said to be so fond, and to the statuesque goddess Anna, whom she had feared once but no longer, thanks to Hardy's cocky presumption. *If Teddy holds me in his arms, he'll remember I'm not like those girls. He'll hold a sharp little stick of a creature and wonder what he ever saw in me.*

"No matter," he said, caressing the little scar on her thumb, which had become his favorite square inch of skin in all the universe. "Tomorrow I'll claim the first dance with you, and then you won't be able to escape my embrace."

"Will it be a waltz?" she asked.

"Of course."

"Do you know the waltz was once considered the most degenerate, corrupting dance? It was banned for ages, simply because the couples touched at more than the fingertip."

"Fingertips aren't nearly enough," Teddy said, tracing each one of hers.

"They must be, for now." And then, like the painful debriding and cleansing of a wound, she made him tell her about her beloved Berlin.

"It is both a reassurance and a kind of betrayal to know that the river Spree still flows despite what is happening in my natal land," she said afterward. "You would think it would stop itself in protest. Did you go to the Neues Museum? Did you see Queen Nefertiti? When I was a child I used to stare at her for hours, wishing that one day I might be as elegant as she. Alas, I'm not the right height. She always struck me as being sublimely good and just. If she had legs and was not a mere bust, she would storm out of the museum and out of Berlin and out of Germany until it came to its senses."

"Where would she go?"

"I don't know. She needs some new world to rule." A spirit of mischief took her and she said, "Perhaps she could come here and be the next Lady Liripip. She looks like one who could keep the servants in their proper place."

Very softly, so she had to strain to hear, Teddy murmured, "I rather have someone else in mind for the job." He drew her hand out of the bole and kissed her knuckles, her scar, the tip of her pinky.

"You must not wear gloves to the ball tomorrow," Teddy insisted. To which Hannah readily agreed, for she had none.

They talked until the owls hushed and the song thrush started its morning melody. When Venus began to brighten the sky, peeping through the overcast haze to warn the world that sunrise was nigh, Hannah said, "I've done it now. I'll be too tired to dance tomorrow night."

"Tonight, you mean. Go to bed straightaway and sleep all day. I'll do the same, and we'll both be daisies by evening."

"I doubt Cook will be so understanding."

"Let my mother worry about our menu," he said, thinking Lady Liripip had co-opted her for household management chores. "I want you gay and chipper when we dance, not yawning in my face. Though your tonsils are one part of you I'm longing to see. I bet yours are the most appealing pink."

Hannah chuckled. "Another intimacy that must wait for another day. Good night, my own Teddy."

"I am your own," he said. "Your very own, forever. Let me walk you inside."

But Hannah, who was feeling a little faint with giddiness over his last remark, said, "No, you go. I believe I'll stay here and sing before the household rises. They really don't like me to sing indoors. Apparently the walls of Starkers reverberate in a most distressing way when they hear a contralto."

"My family's musical tastes run more toward the hey-nonny-nonny faux country ballad. Shrill virgins and all that. But I love opera, and if I didn't, I still love you, so the house will ring with arias. Will you sing for everyone tomorrow at the Servants' Ball?"

"I just might," she said coyly, "if your mother doesn't object."

"If she does," he said, "I'll tell her she can stuff a sock in it."

He listened to her serenade him as he walked off, dreaming of the moment he could take the tall, luscious blond woman he adored into his arms and kiss her sweet mouth.

Hannah's Boxing Day Dismay

~∽~

"THERE YOU ARE," WALTRAUD HUFFED when Hannah dragged herself into her bedroom in the rosy pinkness of morning. Hannah had gone straight from the garden to the kitchen, doing her early chores before running up to her room to bathe her tired eyes.

Waltraud was immaculate in her starched black uniform, which she wore against orders (blue was for morning, black for evening), claiming chicness as her defense. "And whose bed were you sleeping in, if not your own, as if I didn't know, or presume, or hope. If you have stolen Corcoran from me I will never forgive you until after lunch, because frankly he is becoming a bit of a bore, and his formidable whiskers are giving me an irritation just here." She caressed a place that women would not generally expose in public for another fifty years, and even then . . .

"I was in no one's bed," Hannah said a bit primly.

"Oh, Hannah, why did I not take pains to instruct you better? Never, positively never do it out of doors. It sounds so romantic, but you'll end up with bites and scratches—not the good kind—and a sore body—though not in the right places. Never become attached to a man who cannot provide a comfortable bed. Even the lowest prostitutes manage to get a bed for an hour."

"Traudl!" was all she could manage.

"Let me guess," her friend went on. "You talked. All night."

"In fact we did."

"Well, I hope it was worth it . . ."

"It was."

" . . . because you missed your Christmas present. You missed your Hanukkah present too, for that matter, but since you're neither this nor that, I'm sure you don't mind in the least if I give your present to the deserving poor. And that is me. But alas, it would not do for me, not anymore."

"I have nothing good to give you," Hannah admitted as she went to her chest of drawers and took out the little parcel for Waltraud. "I would like to give you a strand of pearls, but they are my mother's, and when my parents come to England we might need them."

"You will," Waltraud said. "There is an exit tax now, you know. One percent."

"Oh, that's not too bad."

"One percent is what a Jew is allowed to keep when she leaves Germany, that is, if she can hide it well enough." She hugged away Hannah's worried look. "They were probably whooping it up in Paris last night, kissing under the mistletoe at the Ritz. You'll get word soon enough. Keep your pearls, *Liebchen*. I'm quite happy with these violet mints and the toffee," she said as she tore open the package. "Though what I got you is slightly, just ever so slightly better, I'm afraid. But because you were a naughty girl who stayed out all night with a most unsuitable boy, you may not see it now. Ah, but wait until it is time to dress for the ball tonight, and you will see! My gift is my seamstress skills. I've altered the . . . No, I won't tell you which one, after all. It must be a surprise. And the dress is yours now, for I had to take four inches off the bottom."

"Oh, Traudl, you shouldn't have!"

"Don't fret. It never suited me. I only kept it for sentimental reasons. It was given to me by a man who reminded me of a pug I had as a child. Did your handsome young lord propose yet, by any chance?"

Had he? He'd said so many things that seemed to point to a life together. *I love you.* They'd both said it. That, to her, was bended knee and diamond ring in itself. *I am your very own, forever.* Waltraud might have explained to her that funny way some men have of saying *forever* when they really mean *for now*, a linguistic quibble they never seem to be clear on. But to Hannah, forever was simply forever.

"He prefers me to Nefertiti," she said at last. "But I think he's still afraid of his mother."

Waltraud gave an exasperated shake of her head. "The idiot. Well, when he sees you at the ball tonight he'll defy an entire army of mothers to have you."

"That must be some dress you have for me."

"Darling, you'd set the Rhine on fire in this gown. Now, I'm afraid we must go and receive our Christmas presents from our employers. Brace yourself."

"Why?" Hannah asked.

"You'll see."

They ran downstairs and were lined up in the servants' parlor (really an odd-job room with a few chairs and an old print of Queen Victoria on the wall) with their hands folded demurely, waiting to receive their Christmas bounty.

"Corcoran explained it all to me last night. In a bed, I might add." Waltraud gave her friend a pointed dig with her elbow. "You see, Christmas is the day when equals exchange presents. The Liripips gave each other, oh, Rolls-Royces and pearl chokers yesterday. But today is the day for giving presents to your under-lings. Boxing Day, they call it, though I've no idea why. Wouldn't it be nice to have underlings? As an aside, I wish Lady Liripip would choke on her choker, and all of her silly old ropes of dingy pearls. She was in a tizzy last night, insisting they be cleaned, and had Tilly and me going at them with toothbrushes. They're still grubby, and since some of the royals are coming she insists on wearing them. No amount of pearls will make her look like anything other than an old harridan. Pearls are for young skin, not her wrinkled, yellow old wattle."

"That's not kind," Hannah said. "If we're lucky, we'll all grow old and get wrinkles."

"But we won't grow mean, no matter what sorts of hardships the world throws at us. She's been thrown nothing but cream, and look at her. She deserves every bit of chicken skin. Diamonds—now, they might help her. Enough of them twinkling under bright light and they might make so much of a glare that no one can see her face, or her soul. But not pearls. Oh! You must wear your pearls tonight!"

"But I'm a servant," she protested.

"You're serving. There's a difference. Cora's pearls are better than old Lady Liripoop's by a mile. Please wear them. They will be quite the epitome of chic with the dress I've picked out for you. And it is a day to honor the underclass—us. We have to be at our best. Clean aprons and starched caps, and miles and miles of Europe's best pearls."

"The dress isn't something scandalous, is it?"

"Heavens, no," Waltraud said, crossing her fingers behind her back. "Would I do that to you?"

They waited for Lady Liripip to come down, while their chores waited for them, undone. She would be cross if anything in the household schedule was delayed or unfinished, but she would also be cross if the servants weren't waiting for her in their orderly rows, standing at attention, primed to bow and scrape and curtsy and tug their forelocks the moment she appeared.

She came down the stairs, those symbolic steps that had divided the classes as a rift or ocean divides species, forcing them into polar evolution. Her hands were empty, for a lady's hands are always empty. Even purses are a sign of the middle class. The nobility has people to do the carrying of even dainty objects—a *mouchoir*, a coin. Though of course a coin would not be needed, as the nobility buy on credit, having their purchases delivered without question, the bill sent and settled by some other minion.

A great many things had changed in England over the course of the last few centuries. But in the best families, things did not change quite so quickly.

Lady Liripip's stepdaughters trailed behind her, picking their way uncertainly down the stairs like amateur mountaineers. They were more hampered than their stepmother, because they could not hold on to the rickety railing. Their arms were filled with soft, paper-wrapped bundles tied up with string, piled to their chins. Behind them, humming strains of a wassailing carol, came Teddy.

Hannah's heart leaped, then crashed, then leaped again. She met his gaze with open, radiant joy. Teddy's delighted, delightful smile rested on her for a moment, then passed, with equal charm and sincerity, to Waltraud, and Glenda, and all of the others in succession. *It's as if he doesn't know me,* she thought. *As if I'm just* another servant in his house for whom he feels a vague benevolence but nothing more.

Then she caught Lady Liripip's stern, unforgiving visage. *Of course he can't look at me with the love he poured out upon me last night. I am still a secret.* She resented being swept under the rug like a stray bit of fluff. *Is that all I am to him, his bit of fluff? No. If I had been in his bed last night I might believe that. But no man spends a freezing night in a December garden with a bit of fluff. He is sincere, in what he said and what he feels. He will tell his mother soon.*

An amusing, wicked thought struck her. *If he doesn't, I will. Just to see her face.*

But a not-so-amusing thought followed: *What if he is not strong enough to resist her orders? He has known me for a few hours, all told. She is his mother.*

Then that hard woman celebrated the brotherhood of mankind, peace, and goodwill by dispensing charity.

Charity had always been a good word, for Hannah. To her it meant kindness, compassion, understanding. Her father gave to charitable causes because he saw a need and wanted to answer it. He brought a homeless man off the street and fed him on oysters and veal and the little marzipan and rosewater treats called *Bethmännchen*. He gave with love. His gifts were Christmas gifts, all year long, given in the spirit of equal to equal.

Lady Liripip's gifts were Boxing Day in the extreme — gifts for inferiors. She made *charity* an ugly word.

She directed her stepdaughters and Teddy to deliver the packages. Without thanks for a year of service, she said, "Here you will find goods sufficient to make yourselves a new uniform for the coming year . . . if you are conservative with your patterns. Full skirts, as you know, are an impediment to domestic efficiency. Those of you who are thin and find yourselves with extra material may feel free to keep the scraps for your own use," she added in a paroxysm of benevolence. "Though you may wish to donate them to the plumper members of the staff." She gave Glenda a significant look that made Hannah want to slap her. She thought about having Lady Liripip for an in-law. Was Teddy worth the price of his mother? Yes, but only just.

Teddy carried Hannah's package to her, and again her eyes silently begged him for just one look of acknowledgment. He grinned at her. He winked at her! His mother said, "Those of you who joined Starkers after the summer are not really entitled to a new uniform yet, but I believe in seeing my staff well turned out. Please remember, though, that if your employment here should cease for any reason before Boxing Day next, any new uniforms acquired during the year must be promptly returned or their cost shall be deducted from your salary and your letter of reference withheld."

Teddy flinched and gave a little sigh. Hannah felt her lip twitch in an almost smile.

The housekeeper got a pair of gloves that did not fit her meaty hands; the butler received a box of handkerchiefs with the letter *L* embroidered on the corner, allowing him to maintain the illusion that the *L* was for his first name, Laurence, and not that they were an old box of Liripip-monogrammed hankies that no one had ever bothered to open.

"For you, Cook," Lady Liripip continued, directing one of the stepdaughters to hand her a little box. "Though I trust that if Trapp should return from the sanatorium before the end of the year, you will submit this gift to her, as it properly belongs to the head cook, whoever she might be."

Lady Liripip gave a little jerk of her head that might have passed for a bow of thanks, and on that cue all of the staff descended once more into their assorted obeisances.

Teddy left last of all, and Hannah's eyes tugged at him with all their might. *Just look back,* she pleaded, feeling foolish but longing for it all the same, that final cast crumb.

He didn't look back, and she slumped, telling herself that it didn't matter, that she would see him at the Servants' Ball and touch him and look at his wonderful face as they glided and spun under every eye, even his mother's. But it still mattered.

Then she heard feet on the stair. He was back! He would take her in his arms and say he couldn't stay away from her. He would kiss her for all to see, unashamed.

He sought her out, looked at her with those eyes so earnest and frank. She might name them that, the left eye Ernest, the right one Frank, she thought giddily as he stood even closer than when she had mistakenly thought he was going to blackmail his way into her favors. What a silly notion that had been. She tilted her head to him, parted her lips.

"I forgot to tell you," he said affably, "I won't need you to help me with my German after all. I've found another tutor." He gave a little smile of conspiracy. "I couldn't find a trace of your parents, though. Everyone has someone missing in Germany. I'm very sorry. I'll be going back soon, though, so buck up." He chucked her under the chin and ran up the stairs, back to his own world.

She did not know whether to be pleased or disappointed. What was that?

"An excuse to touch you," Waltraud whispered.

The servants took a moment to unwrap their presents, though there was neither anticipation nor enthusiasm. Black or blue material for the house staff, dim florals straight from the remainder racks for the kitchen staff. Hannah received a bundle of calico with a field of sickly yellow asters.

Sally opened her present (or Trapp's present, depending) with a resigned sigh.

"What is it?" Hannah asked, peering over her shoulder.

"A fish slice," Sally answered wearily. "A used fish slice."

"I now know why it is called Boxing Day," Waltraud said, her arched, penciled eyebrows descending in a fierce frown. "Because at this moment I should like to box every one of their aristocratic ears."

Lord Liripip Knows Exactly What Hannah Is

~⌣~

HANNAH GOT THROUGH HER MORNING as best she could with an interminable series of jaw-cracking yawns and long, heavy blinks, during which she seemed to actually fall asleep for a matter of seconds before jerking awake. It might have been the day of the Servants' Ball, but, if anything, their work was increased. The house staff had to have everything impeccably clean and lay out all of the decorations that were supposed to be for their enjoyment but were, of course, to impress the titled guests who would be attending the fete. Servants' balls, with their Saturnalian reputations (for what else but a period of utter riot could induce the classes to mingle?), often attracted the faster kind of aristocrat — younger sons and new money with purchased titles.

The kitchen staff too were kept on their toes. True, they would get to eat with the others before the dancing began, but they also had to prepare the food for their own consumption. It was laid out buffet style, so in theory, once it was prepared, the cook and her minions could relax and partake, but in reality there would be last-minute things to peel and arrange, and if anything ran out, they were the ones who would have to replenish it, recruiting some disgruntled footman in his Sunday best to carry it out. (Things might be topsy-turvy at a servants' ball, but they were not so topsy-turvy as that.)

So on her special day, the day honoring servants and all their hard work, Hannah had no time to rest. In between chores, at the hours when she usually attended Anna, she would creep up to Anna's room and see if she'd woken up. Each time she found the girl with her head buried in her soft down pillow, the blankets pulled up over her ear like a quilted carapace, gently snoring. Hannah would have liked to resent her this comfort—and she did, a little—but mostly she was glad that Anna evidently had had as good a night as she herself. *Love is such a surprising thing,* she thought. *It really is, as Anna said, like a disease, springing unseen, infecting with the most minuscule microbe and proliferating in the unsuspecting body.* She was glad that Anna wasn't as immune as she'd thought. Hardy was certainly a fine fellow.

The one concession to the special day was that the servants (assuming Starkers was spotless and the food prepared) could have an hour of free time to make themselves presentable. Lady Liripip had put forth the idea that it would somehow be more picturesque for the servants to appear at the dance in uniform, but her son and stepdaughters convinced her this might arouse a certain ire in the people who could so easily poison their food or stick pins in them while dressing them, and she reluctantly capitulated. No amount of persuasion, however, could keep her from deducting the hour from the servants' next afternoon off.

Hannah wondered if she could sleep for fifty minutes and manage to dress in ten. It was tempting . . . but no, she still had to snip the strands of pearls out of their hem-and-seam hiding places, and if she didn't want to ruin her one remaining nonservice outfit, she'd have to work slowly and carefully.

Ah, well, she thought, not bothering to stifle the next yawn. *I can sleep when I'm married. Mmm . . .*

She was alone in the kitchen as she indulged in this pleasant thought. Just then one of the bells rang.

In the hall beyond the kitchen was a miniature carillon. Bells of every size, tone, and timbre were mounted on the wall, each with a name or location written in precise copperplate script. Whenever a bell rang, it was the job of whoever was closest (or if several servants were present, whoever was lowest on the social totem pole) to make a mad dash to see who had been summoned, and where. They were supposed to recognize the caller or room by its pitch, but only Coombe and Mrs. Wilcox could do that. For the others, it was a matter of reaching the bell before it stopped pealing, or, failing that, before it stopped trembling. The smaller, lighter bells might quiver for several seconds after they fell dumb, but the largest—which were for the most important people—gave two rings at most and were then utterly still.

A terrible system, Hannah thought, because a lesser guest, with his faint, tinny ring and long, silent shuddering, would forgive the necessity of a second ring. Lord or Lady Liripip, never, and don't bother explaining that the only servant in the vicinity had been making a béchamel that simply would not tolerate abandonment. White sauce lumps be damned — she'd better drop everything if she liked (or at least wanted to keep) her job.

The bell that rang now was the largest, the deepest, a veritable church bell. Hannah had only been smashing almonds with a satisfying ferocity, so she could drop her mallet and see who had called. It was Lord Liripip.

The problem was, who could attend him?

Usually when he rang, it was for his valet, his gentleman's personal gentleman, Brigand. Hannah had heard the name of this elusive man for days before she finally saw him, and had been expecting something considerably more piratical than the lean, long-shanked cadaver who attended to Lord Liripip's intimate wants. He looked as if he should be even more of an invalid than his master, but in his slow, spiderlike way he seemed to get His Lordship dressed and groomed and Macassared. (Hannah clearly remembered the frisson of terror she felt when she intercepted a note stating that Brigand was ready for the massacre. She'd never dreamed of an infusion of *Treasure Island* in her Wodehousean idyll. But it turned out that the servants weren't very good spellers, and the valet was only ready for the Macassar oil he used on Lord Liripip's hair.)

Very likely, Lord Liripip was calling Brigand to double as nursemaid and bathe and swaddle his gouty foot. Unluckily, Brigand had been sent into town to fetch the only sort of shoe polish His Lordship could tolerate, and he wouldn't be back for another hour.

But someone had to attend him, and as Hannah had learned, there was an accepted order to everything, to violate which could spell disaster. Perhaps not to quite the same extent as a female serving in the dining hall (which practically heralded an apocalypse), but it could still make the masters gape in disbelief and very likely talk of termination.

The butler would be the next best choice to send up to Liripip's library — he was quite gravid and male enough to suit. But he had been dispatched to London to get the various kinds of cigars and cigarettes their assorted Royal Highnesses preferred, in case any of them should show. (They were notoriously lax in their RSVPs, and at best their social secretaries might manage to call when they were en route.)

Everyone else was occupied too. The housekeeper, the parlor maids, the ladies' maids, all so far above her on the social hierarchy and far more suited to attend His Lordship in his hour of need.

But there was only she, and heaven forbid he ring the bell a second time.

There was nothing for it but to go and chance the consequences. Giggling at her own temerity, and more at the thought that there was anything to fear—imagine, her, Hannah Morgenstern, being afraid of a gouty old man—she picked the last bits of almonds out of her ragged, short nails and dashed upstairs.

She gave a soft rap at his door.

She didn't see Lord Liripip's head shoot up in alarm, didn't have a clue that her gentle tapping reminded him of the deathwatch beetles he'd heard in his youth. His grandmother had told him the story, and ever after he'd lie awake listening to the minuscule animal noises found in even the best houses. The skitter of mice in the walls. The insidious chewing of woodworm. And sometimes, rarely enough to make it seem more like an omen, the tip-tip-tap of a deathwatch warning of someone's imminent demise.

And so when Hannah poked her small dark head through the door, Lord Liripip was feeling particularly . . . mortal.

"You rang?"

How, he wondered, *are all the ages of man contained in one moment? How am I a timorous child in my bed and a lusty young man and a love-struck middle-aged man and at the same time this rusted-out old hulk that can do none of the things those other selves could do?* Seeing Hannah, that peculiar servant girl who had spoken to him so flippantly of *droît du seigneur,* who had bearded them all in their lairs, he wanted his flesh to be firm and strong once again, filled to the brim with vital juices like a ripe peach toasting in the sun.

Foolish old man, to be rutting after the skivvies, he chided himself. *Just what they would expect of you, though. As if you had the heart or lungs for it . . . or any other body part, for that matter.*

"What are you doing here?" he asked, his voice querulous with the sense of his own inadequacies.

"Everyone else is busy preparing for the ball tonight."

"And you were lounging around eating bonbons, what? What do I pay you for if all you do is sit on your bum taking your ease?"

"I have never had a bonbon, I think, though I have danced to Strauss's *Wiener Bonbons* waltz. Do you know it? With the terse little pizzicado opening and then those long, grand sweeps? But no, I do not take my ease, and neither have I taken my ease in all the days I have been here. I sleep, you will say, but not so often, or for so long, and the bed is simply abominable. True, it doesn't have bedbugs like the beds at the refugee center, but that was not their fault. The poor people who stayed there had come from the most *horrid* conditions. But bedbugs are not the only things that can disrupt a good night's sleep. Lumps are nearly as bad, and thin blankets. Worries and cares, also, but for those I cannot entirely blame you. Do you think they will play *Wiener Bonbons* tonight?"

Lord Liripip got that slightly dizzy sensation people tended to have when Hannah got a good head of conversational steam going.

"Where is Brigand?"

"In the village. Do you need someone to tend to your buttons?

I can fetch Waltraud, one of the parlor maids, who happens to be my particular friend. She has great skill in the removal of male attire."

Liripip grunted. "Women valets? Continental effete buffoonery."

"Oh, no, her experience is strictly of the amateur kind. I assume she can reverse the process and help you dress, though."

"Harrumph. I don't want to dress yet," he said. "I've finished another chapter of my memoirs and I need to try them out on someone. What I need is Brigand to give me his ear."

"Ah, like friends, Romans, and countrymen? Well, I am none of those things, but perhaps you could read them to me?"

What a peculiar specimen, he thought, *chatting with me in her magpie way, with her faint and pleasing accent, just as if she were a favorite daughter.* He thought of his own two daughters, plain and lumpen things who took after their mother. Since infancy they seemed to be delicately offended by everything about him except his title and money. When their mother—his first, unlamented wife—died, he left them largely to the care of governesses and later shipped them away to finishing school. Age and motherhood had not improved them. If only he'd had a bright, lively little thing like this servant to entertain him.

"Wouldn't be suitable," Liripip said. "What I do is read them to Brigand, and if I can make his cheeks turn pink I know they're salacious enough. If he refuses to blush, I go back and add some more dirty bits."

"I never blush," Hannah said. "But I should like to hear the dirty bits all the same. Are your memoirs true?"

"*Ahem.* They are as I remember them. True enough. No, you must have work to do. I can't trouble you. Fetch Anna Morgan for me."

Still harboring thoughts of anchoring his only son by a marriage, he'd been making an effort to cultivate Anna. And what an effort it was! She was chatty enough, but the things she said! Like conversing with a peacock, all squawk and feathers. Still, he could not escape the glamour of the idea. She was the child of his lost love. He did not know how Caroline Curzon had produced this big, brash, blond thing, but he supposed after Teddy married her, he'd get used to her. The important thing was to keep Teddy out of spy work. No newly married man volunteered for a dangerous assignment.

"I will not do that," Hannah said, folding her arms decidedly.

"What!" No one, noble or humble, had ever said no to him. Well, some of those girls in the carriages, but they had said yes with their eyes and that was what counted. This servant's eyes held a world of refusal.

"She is deeply asleep. I do not believe in waking people who are asleep. It is bad for the constitution, and for the soul. Plus, they often throw things at one's head."

"Do you mean to say that you will not wake her?"

Hannah nodded, the immovable object.

Liripip blinked heavily, owlishly. "You really want to hear my memoirs? Very likely your ears will fall off. Don't say I didn't warn you. Have a seat right here." He patted a chair close to his own.

"Perhaps I will sit over here instead." She took up a position on a chaise. "Out of arm's reach, in case your youth springs upon you again."

The look they exchanged made his heart do roebuck leaps. He was beyond desire (or at least the capacity to fulfill it), but no one is ever beyond memory, and the servant girl's conspiratorial smile, like a wicked little seraph, made him flush in unaccustomed places, near what might be the cockles of his heart. He wanted to take her out on the town. He wanted to buy her dresses and jewels, as he used to do for women of every stamp. Only, he wanted nothing from her in return except that mischievous grin, that effervescent spark of life she shared with him so freely.

"*Hrrum.*" He cleared his throat with one of his eloquent grunts that was part articulation, part protest against the aches and creaks of age. "Would you like to hear what I wrote yesterday, which is bad, or what I scribbled today, which is far worse?"

"The worse, please," she said. "Then afterward, when I'm flushed, the merely bad will be soothing."

He shuffled through his papers and commenced a story involving him and the late King Edward VII, about whom his own mother, Queen Victoria, once wrote, "I never can, or shall, look at him without a shudder."

"And that," he said when he finished reading, "is the real reason Bertie collapsed back in March of 1910 at Biarritz. The papers put it out that it was bronchitis. Balderdash and stuff, I say. The man had lungs of iron. It was really that Fifi who wore him out, and of course I had taught her all the tricks I'd learned from that whore from Bayonne, so I suppose his demise was all my fault after all. Har! Think I'll be tried for regicide once these memoirs are published?"

Hannah pulled a face. "Someone's really going to publish this?"

"Are you kidding? They're fighting over it, and the Americans, too. I can do it, you see, because everyone I talk about is already dead."

She rose to stand and peered over his shoulder, flipping through page after page of the most salacious scandal written in the very purplest prose. "And if not, they will be when they read this."

"But you didn't bat an eyelash, girl. What were you back in Germany, eh?"

She gaped at him. Didn't he know? But he must.

"Lady Ascot says she has a doctor polishing her boots, and that upstart Psmith's children are being tucked into bed by a female professor of mathematics. All kinds of interesting people are going into service—lucky us, poor them. We're like the Romans with their learned Greek slaves, so much smarter than their masters. Let me see: What could you be? What sort of girl can't muster up a gasp for a story like that?"

"You know what kind of girl I am," Hannah said archly. And then, because a person can only control herself so far, she added, "Not the kind of girl who belongs in your kitchen." Deep as her resentment might be, she found herself warming to this ribald old gentleman. Very likely keeping her in the kitchen, humiliating her as a servant, was all Lady Liripip's doing, and he went along with it for the sake of a peaceful household. Hannah imagined Lady Liripip might be capable of making a household very unpleasant indeed. Still, Hannah would forgive him. It is easy to forgive when you're in love. When he was her father-in-law, they would probably laugh about this. *It is a lover's trial,* she thought, *as princesses have to do in fairy tales. Psyche had to separate grains, I have to pluck high pheasants. And when Lady Liripip is a dowager and I am Lady Liripip myself, I will only occasionally rub her ill treatment of me in her face, and always send game and fruit to her dower house. Though she will not eat dinner with us more than twice a year.* On that, she was adamant.

Lord Liripip got a much different impression than she had intended. Lost in the delightful fug of his licentious youth (and middle age), his mind on a certain kind of woman who had given him so much pleasure, for such a great price, he immediately decided what kind of girl Hannah must have been in Germany. *Yes,* he thought, stroking his whiskers in meditative luxury, *I know your sort intimately.* Not a whore, exactly, but a hussy all the same. Clever, witty, pretty, unashamed, with that bit of outward primness they so often used as their cloak . . . She must be a courtesan.

It was an old-fashioned word, but he was an old-fashioned man. And she was so fresh, so young — she looked no more than seventeen or eighteen, though he guessed she must be in her twenties, and her apparent youth was the result of special care. She'd probably been kept in style for several years, accustomed to luxury and ease, to champagne and nightclubs. Had her lover grown tired of her? No, no one could do that. It must be because she was Jewish. Lord Liripip was neither political nor philosophical, but he could not abide a country where a beautiful girl was discriminated against. Pretty young fillies must always be nurtured.

"I know exactly what kind of girl you are," Liripip said with fervent approval. "And you don't belong in the kitchen. Just look at your poor hands!" He caught them in his own and felt vague priapic stirrings, but more than that, an avuncular desire to offer protection for its own sake. "How lovely they must have been when you were, *ahem,* practicing your former profession. They will be again, my dear — never fear."

"Oh, I don't mind about my hands so much," Hannah said

lightly. "The work is hard, but after all, it does nothing to my mouth, and so long as I have my mouth I can make my living."

At this, even the jaded old roué blushed along his sinewy turkey neck.

"Not that I have much of a chance to practice my trade," Hannah went on. "No one seems to approve. I certainly can't do it in the kitchen, though I have seized a few opportunities in the garden."

"Oh, the lucky fellow," Liripip murmured under his breath.

"Pardon? Shall I entertain you someday?" she asked in all innocence, and had no idea why he gulped and sputtered.

"No, my dear, best not," he finally managed to choke out. "My wife . . ."

"Say no more," Hannah said, extricating herself and giving his liver-spotted hands a sympathetic pat. "I understand completely. Perhaps one day things will be otherwise, and then I shall be at your absolute disposal."

When Liripip had regained a measure of his self-possession, he said, "You are a credit to your profession. If I were a younger man . . . but no, it would be folly. Stay here for a time, my dear, and you may find it lucrative after all. It is a shame I cannot take you into the household proper, but, *har*, wouldn't do, wouldn't do. Still, if you aren't in a position to settle yourself elsewhere, perhaps I can look out for, *hmm*, patrons. Introductions can be made . . . who knows what might follow."

"Oh, sir!" she cried, and flung her arms around him so that his face settled pleasantly in her softness.

"Nonsense," he said, his voice obscured. "I take an interest in you. Old habits, you see. Can't do much for you myself, not in this state, but you'd be surprised who might be interested in your talents. Why, at tonight's ball there will be several whose own equerries don't know the half of what they get up to. Are you, *haw*, versatile? Can you cater to unusual tastes?"

"My preference is for the standards, but I would gladly take on the strange or the avant-garde, though I might need a little guidance from whoever engages me. I am willing to do anything!"

"Capital, my gallant girl! What spirit! What spunk! England should be proud to have you! Just for that I will read you another chapter. This one is about my adventures with a lovely pair of Andalusian conjoined twins I met on my travels."

It was a thrilling tale indeed, but even the bluest of language cannot stimulate a girl who has been up all night and put to work first thing in the morning. Hannah had perched once more on the chaise to listen, then slowly her head sank down — just for a minute, she swore with her last bit of consciousness. Then her breath settled into heavy regularity and she was thoroughly asleep.

Lord Liripip looked at the dark lashes resting on the high curve of her cheek, at the gently parted lips, and thought, *Oh, but for a few decades, what danger she would be in*. Now, though, he was content first to watch her sleep, and when that palled, to let her rhythmic breathing lull him as he began on a chapter about a pretty little equestrienne who wore a riding habit so tight, she had to be sewn into it.

When, several hours later, Brigand returned and discovered her, still snoozing as his master scribbled, both men pretended she did not exist. But he reported his discovery to Mrs. Wilcox, who charged upstairs, determined to fire Hannah on the spot. She liked the girl, but such things could not be tolerated at Starkers.

"Naughty girl!" she cried when she burst in and found Hannah curled in her cozy ball.

Lord Liripip looked blandly at the interloper as Hannah started awake. "No, alas, I could not convince her to be naughty, madam. But I am indeed a naughty old man, as well you know."

Doing her best to ignore the notoriously eccentric Liripip — as she'd often been instructed to do by his lady — she took Hannah by the ear. "Forgive me for allowing this to happen, sir. I promise you, she'll be out of the house within the hour."

"Nonsense," Liripip said. "Unhand her at once. The fault is all mine. I think many of the mechanisms of pleasure are mysteries to you, my good woman. Perhaps you do not know what intense stimulation I can find simply from watching a fetching young nubile such as this sleep."

The housekeeper gasped.

"I am a dirty old man," he admitted, "and she but a lowly servant with no choice but to obey my prurient commands. Do you think she *wanted* to fall asleep under my lascivious gaze? No, but I am the master, and when I gave her an order to sleep she had no choice. She trembled, she pleaded, to no avail. Forgive her, poor victim that she is." He gave Hannah a broad wink. "Don't bother to forgive me, though. I'm quite beyond redemption."

Teddy Figures It Out

SO BY THE TIME HANNAH was released from her duties to dress for the Servants' Ball, she was slightly more refreshed than she would otherwise have been.

"You poor, poor girl," Mrs. Wilcox gushed as soon as she got Hannah safely out of the monster's clutches. "How frightened you must have been. Didn't anyone warn you never to allow yourself to be caught alone with him? Watching a girl sleep! How peculiar. Though I must say, you got off lucky. I have heard stories . . . oh, not for years and years now, not since that wild Curzon girl disappointed him. But before my time it was quite a common thing for pretty servants to be . . . Well, I won't shock you. I'm just glad he left something in you to be shocked, you poor, dear innocent."

Word spread quickly below stairs, and by the time they ran off arm in arm to dress, Waltraud had heard. "What's the going rate for an hour of slumber? I've always had a suspicion that fetishes — the gentler kind, mind you — might be my future. There was a gentleman once who so admired my feet. Do you think Liripip would let me sleep for him?"

"It was nothing like that," Hannah insisted. "He made that up to protect me."

"I know, you ninny. Still, I bet I could come up with a few other things to entertain the old gentleman. But no, he will be your father-in-law soon enough, and it would embarrass you to have me sitting on his lap at your wedding. I will search for other prey. There will be some interesting prospects tonight, if only I can make it quite clear that I am not really a servant. People never make proper presents to servants, have you noticed? It is a very sad world. Come, let me fix your hair first."

"I want to see my dress!" Hannah begged like a child pleading for sweets.

"No, not until it is too late. It is so daring that if you saw it now you would flee. I must slip it on you like a horse in harness, and once you're in your traces you'll trot along happily enough."

"Oh, Traudl, I hope it's not too—"

"It is the most *too* you have ever seen. But also quite modest in its own saucy way. You will see. Here, let me have your head. Ah, such soft dark waves, like a buzzard's wing."

"That's not very flattering," Hannah said with a sigh. "Men don't like to stroke buzzards' wings."

"Well then, a starling, or a dove, or a spaniel's ear. Let *him* murmur soft comparisons while he kisses you. I will worry myself with setting it stylishly. I have spray lacquer here, and a little diamond clip. Well, not a diamond, only a diamante, but your pearls are so very real that people will assume. Isn't it sweet? It will glitter in your night-sky hair like the morning star. Is that a better blandishment? I will corner your Teddy before the dance and teach him what to say. Here, sit still while I brush."

"Shouldn't you be doing your own hair?"

"No, I have it in a mass of little braids so all I have to do is unbind it and I will look like one of Wagner's Rhinemaidens, only not so damp and troublesome."

"We don't have much time," Hannah said. "He promised me the first dance."

"You can't have the very first dance," Waltraud said. "Corcoran explained it all to me. There is a tradition for the first dance, and everyone would melt into a jelly of discomfiture if anyone dared break it. To open the ball, the lord dances with the housekeeper, the lady dances with the butler, the eldest daughter partners with the valet, and the eldest son squires the cook. It is all to appease the ancient gods of Britain, I think, a sort of sacrifice of dignity on behalf of the masters that makes the crops grow next year, if I remember my Fraser right. He must have meant the first dance after that, so you have plenty of time to make yourself perfect. He will drop to his knees at the first sight of you, as will every man in the room. The women will hate you, of course, but there is no alternative to that. Even I will hate you in this dress."

TEDDY HAD NEVER BEHELD ANYTHING more lovely than the woman he adored. She stood as tall as an Amazon in heels and high-piled golden curls, and her dress was made of some pale shimmering material like starlight. She paused at the head of the stairs, calculating her dramatic effect, until all eyes were on her. Everyone, from the Duke of Kent down to the giggling, slatternly laundry girls, stared at her glorious beauty in open, utter amazement. The swell of her bosom was like a ship's figurehead, breasting any wave. The curve of her hip made men who had been to India think of the temples they had seen, of those ecstatic dancing nymphs, so sacred and so profane. She held herself like a queen or madonna or imbecile, her face utterly placid and devoid of lines, blinking as though her eyelashes were almost too heavy to lift.

I would like to place her on a pedestal, Teddy thought, *and run my hands along all of those lovely curves like a sculptor, creating her under my touch.*

This certainly was a pleasant idea, but it left him feeling a little hollow, superficial. He knew there were such magnificent depths to Anna. He had learned them in their night talks, those soaring discourses in German of profundity and wit and sheer silliness that had revealed to him a person of great intelligence, kindness, value. But looking at her—the outside of her, the skin of her—

he had a flash of nightmarish fantasy that this might be all there was to her: a shell. It was absurd, of course. A person can be beautiful inside and out. Still, to look on all that external loveliness, it seemed there could be no room for anything else.

And then, he had noticed something a little disturbing about their very few, very brief daytime relations.

Anna was descending slowly now, pausing at each step with a little sway and bob that drew the eye to all the right places. She did not make a beeline to Teddy, but seemed to hover in an indefinite state, nodding here, smiling there, bestowing the glory of herself on all of the guests and servants before drifting in a direction that happened to bring her to Teddy's side. It was masterfully done. Even Lady Liripip, had she been scrutinizing her, wouldn't have said that she sought Teddy out. Still, there she was with her hand resting on his arm.

"Tell me who all of these thrilling people are," she said. At night, in German, she would have said it in another tone, a little playful, as if the guests, however important they might be, were no more than a corollary to their perfect happiness together. By daylight, in English, Anna seemed genuinely impressed with the stellar cast of visitors. He saw little paroxysms of something like starstruck envy when he pointed out Their Highnesses.

"And who is that old cow in the mud-colored velvet?" she asked, making a mocking little frown behind the back of a dowdy woman with very kind, overly made-up eyes.

"She was my nurse when I was a boy," he said, looking at Anna strangely.

"Oh, forgive me," Anna said, and he did, instantly, because her bright blue eyes sparkled at him so guilelessly. "And that one," she said, hurriedly turning to another older woman whose moth-eaten fox collar looked more like ferret or cat. "Was she your governess?"

"Ah, no, she's . . ." And here he named a name so renowned for wealth that even though she didn't have a title, one felt inclined to curtsy or perhaps grovel before so august a personage.

Immediately the disdainful curl of Anna's mouth unfurled like a burgeoning fern. "Will you introduce me?" she begged.

"Later, my sweet. Now it's time to open the ball." He peeled her fingers from his arm and made a little bow.

"Where are you going?" Anna asked. "Surely the first dance is for me."

"I know I promised it," he said. (Had he? Anna tried to recall.) "But tonight we honor the servants. I always partner Cook for the first dance. Of course, it used to be Trapp, who moved like a furious marionette and smelled stale, but that isn't very charitable of me, is it? Excellent cook, but a truly horrid woman. It was only my father's digestion that kept her around so long. Now her gall has caught up with her and she has to live in the seaside sanatorium and boss nurses. The new one, Sally Mayweather, is quite a different story." He smiled across the room at the merry little cook in her neat burgundy suit dress with a hothouse orchid pinned to the lapel.

Anna felt an unaccountable stab of jealousy and was suddenly determined that no force on earth would keep her from having the first dance with Teddy. She caught his arm again and almost dragged him to the floor.

"Really, I can't," Teddy protested. "She's expecting it — it's tradition. If you were slaving away in a kitchen all day to feed other people, wouldn't you be pleased to be singled out one night of the year?"

From somewhere came the idea that she *had* almost been a kitchen servant, that she might have worked hard all these weeks and had nothing to look forward to but the chance to dress up and dance with the young lord before everyone's eyes. She quickly hushed that rebel thought. *I contrived that it should not happen that way. I put myself here, and I deserve to reap the rewards. Didn't I give him everything last night? And still I wait for those magic words:* Marry me.

She searched his eyes for some secret conspiracy of memory, some gratitude for the gift she'd given him in the hothouse. But though he looked at her with admiration, devotion, she saw only someone in love with her, not a lover. Did it mean nothing to him?

Teddy's brow was puckered in faint puzzlement, and then he caught his mother's disapproving stare over Anna's shoulder. Of course! He was so relieved, he raised his hand to the orchestra and swept his love into the opening waltz.

She was so different by daylight, speaking English with such a prim, controlled, artificial voice, that deliberate aristocratic accent that seemed to demand such effort — how far removed from her poetically beautiful German, which soared to Goethe and stooped to the gutter from word to word, language that played like a precocious child. Diurnal Anna was stiff and stilted, slightly uncomfortable. It was as if she was an entirely different person by day, and it troubled him.

But when he saw his mother's disapproving gaze, he realized — it was all an act. She was simply afraid of his mother, and while there was any chance the woman could observe her, Anna was desperate to paint herself as a model Englishwoman. She did things — said things — that his mother must approve of. Even when there was no danger of being overheard, she criticized servants, maintained a superior attitude that echoed Lady Liripip's, kept her manners above reproach. Why, even though she'd promised to go gloveless, she wore them now, no doubt at his mother's insistence.

Those hurtful little things she said, they were just hangovers from trying to placate his mother. How scared she must be, separated from her home, her country going haywire, her parents far away and in danger, with only his own unkind mother to lean upon. She must be in constant terror of being cast out on the streets, the poor girl! He knew that his mother — horrible as he admitted her to be—would not stoop so low. But Anna did not know it, and even if Lady Liripip let her stay, she could make Anna's life a torment.

Now that he thought about it, Anna was a spy. He himself was learning how to mask his feelings and alter his words to blend in. Burroughs and his fellow spymasters had rigorously drilled him in remaining impassive while disgusting things were said about all the many people the Nazis hated, because when he was there, he would have to pretend to agree with them all. He had listened to the filth and learned not to give away his real thoughts by so much as a twitch. He could pass as a Nazi, the thing most antithetical to his nature. Anna was doing her best to pass as the shallow, bigoted, selfish, narrow sort of woman his mother favored. And in the way of a real spy, it was necessary to keep up the act even when unobserved. He would never have fallen in love with the Anna he saw in daytime. Oh, he might have lusted after her, but never in a million years would he marry her.

What a beast I've been, Teddy thought as he glided and whirled with that divine woman. He'd acted as if they had all the time in the world. Yet they'd only known each other, all told, for a few days. And tomorrow he must leave again. But he knew, absolutely and unequivocally, that he loved her. The nighttime her, the real her, not this daytime sham. Why wait? She should know how he felt and what he meant to do. He would propose tonight. He'd make his intentions absolutely clear so she didn't have to torture herself acting in that hateful way. His mother must have told her to dance with him first. She had always despised the Servants' Ball. Anna was afraid to defy her, and dragged Teddy onto the floor. He'd have to explain it to Sally, but she would understand. She could have the next two dances.

Once Anna knew that she was safe forever, she'd be herself again. Once she knew he meant to marry her, she could be her true self day and night. She could prattle in German, sing her glorious opera, say all of those things that would shock his mother, and no one could do a thing about it!

Tonight when they met at the yew, he would propose. Then in the morning, before he left again, he'd tell his mother.

He looked over at that formidable woman, mincing through the waltz with Coombe. He could not tell which of the two dancers looked the most uncomfortable. His mother's face was held in a strange, sour smile, that stiff one she plastered on for those she condescended to. The sapphires around her neck gave her an artificial sparkle that seemed as false as her smile. She was cross about that, too, he knew, the mysterious disappearance of her heirloom pearls that she'd told the ladies' maids to clean.

Looking at the fearsome face of the woman who bore him, the woman he had long since given up trying to love and never respected but still half feared, Teddy thought: *Maybe I'll tell her when I return to Starkers next time.* That would be in May, when he finished at Oxford. After that, he'd continue his spy training, and then if things went as planned, he'd be in Germany. Yes, right before he left the country would be a perfect time to tell his mother he was marrying Anna.

HANNAH CRANED HER NECK over her shoulder, trying to see how very bad it was.

"I can't," she said. "I simply can't!"

"You wear this or you wear your kitchen dress," Waltraud said sternly, adjusting the fabric on Hannah's slight curves.

"I could wear my traveling suit."

"No, you can't, because prophetess that I am, I snipped the buttons off to prevent that very thing. I knew you'd be a coward at the last minute. You've done the talking—now you have to put your body to work."

"Such as it is," Hannah said, looking at her rather flat front.

"Fried eggs are as delicious as melons," Waltraud insisted. "You want a proposal? You'll get it in this dress."

"I don't need a proposal. He loves me; that is enough."

"It's not the right kind of love if you're his secret. A boy who feeds a hedgehog in the garden doesn't have a pet. Do you want to be Teddy's wife or his mistress?"

"I just want to talk with him, and laugh with him, and *know* him—forever."

"A mistress isn't forever, *Liebchen*. Thank goodness, for me, because I get bored in about ten minutes and then I get my farewell dress and go on the prowl again. That suits me. But you are not a mistress, love. You are a wife. A dear little *Hausfrau* with a herd of children and the ability to tell your mother-in-law to go to hell. Now be a man and go out there. The first dance is ending, and he'll be waiting for you."

Waltraud settled the ropes and ropes of pearls and gave her a little shove.

"Opening night at Cabaret Starkers," she said. "You're on."

Hannah Is Propositioned and
Almost Proposes

⌒⌒

HANNAH DID NOT MAKE AN ENTRANCE. She appeared with
stealthy suddenness, like a ghost, or a fox, and was with the rest
before they knew it. Servants, of course, come in through the
back stairs.

When walking in the gloaming, one does not immediately
notice the first star. So Hannah came among them, unremarked
at first, but before long eliciting whispers and gasps. Lord Liripip, limping his way through a mockery of a dance with Mrs.
Wilcox, stopped dead still and thought, *If that girl does not find a
royal keeper tonight I'll eat my hat.* His Royal Highness the Duke of
Kent, known to Hannah as Georgie, downed his cocktail and began to weave his way toward her, his eyes bright. His tastes were
as varied as Waltraud's, but at that very moment he could think
of no man or woman more exciting than this girl of night and
moonlight.

"Who is she?" voices asked, and no one had the answer. Was she an actress, with those expressive brows, that Lilith look, that serpent grace? Was she one of those royals no one seems to remember, a Greek or a Swede? An upstart jeweler's daughter with those yards and yards of pearls?

Teddy stepped on Anna's toe and stopped dancing. He did not mean to stare. He was with the woman he adored, and if he recognized the transformed creature as the little German kitchen waif who had briefly amused him before, that was no reason to utterly forget—for the space of only a few seconds, mind you—about the woman whom he planned to make his fiancée very soon. But he simply could not help himself. If it was put to a poll, Anna would be voted the most beautiful woman in the room by a landslide. But the kitchen maid in her remarkable dress and those pearls was by far the most interesting.

When Waltraud had worn the dress, once, to privately entertain a visiting diplomat, she wore it right way around, so the Grecian draping plunged daringly down below her navel, requiring perfect posture or absolute indifference as to who might see one's bosom, both of which Waltraud had in abundance. But she knew her little friend did not possess such aplomb, so after pondering the dilemma awhile, she simply reversed the garment, lopped off the bottom, took a few stitches, *et voilà!*

It was a Vionnet dress, deeply black, bias cut, draped in supple waves. In the front it was virginal, showing no more than a glimpse of those delicate hollows above the collarbones, and from there descending to the floor. But in the back . . .

The flowing wavelike folds skimmed Hannah's shoulder blades and dropped to the first curve of her buttocks so enticingly that every man pleaded for one more inch of flesh — just one! But the bare expanse of creamy back wasn't stark against the black material. She wore three long strands of pearls reversed, so that in front they looked like a choker, while in back they rolled across her naked skin in a precious veil, concealing, revealing, and concealing again. Two heavy ropes were wrapped around her forearms, and another, more delicate, made a headband on her short dark hair.

Hannah did not see the way the entire room looked at her. She saw only Teddy.

She was confused when she saw who was in his arms, because Waltraud had been adamant that Teddy would dance first with the cook. She had heard the waltz begin, and only now was it ending. Sally was standing morosely against the wall. Why was Teddy with Anna?

She called out to him wordlessly across the crowded ballroom, and for a moment he answered with a yearning look of his own. But then the golden woman in his arms said something and he turned his gaze away from Hannah. He didn't look back, not for a wink or a smile.

You were wrong, Traudl, Hannah thought. *Even this dress is not enough to make him run to me before his mother and all the world.*

She wanted to flee, to cover her exposed flesh and take off the ridiculous, glorious dress that was not her at all. But the second dance? *Surely he will come to me for the second dance.*

No. He didn't look at her at all, but left Anna in the care of his friend Maurice and then pulled Sally into the Sir Roger de Coverley. Hannah watched the sprightly country dance and wondered when her turn would come.

"You are not accustomed to being against the wall," said an insinuating growl from behind her ear. "Or . . . perhaps you are?"

She turned and found the handsome Duke of Kent lurking at her side.

"Forgive my coarseness. Liripip has been stimulating my imagination with his memoirs. Are you really the sleepy little kitchen wench who knew Noel? What hidden . . . depths." He peered down her back to see them. "Liripip says, in his usual brusque way, that you are in want of a patron. Shall we dance and talk? I require conversation, intelligent and incessant, during even the most arduous activities, so this will be a test. Not a reel, though. Something more intimate. Stay here, and if anyone tries to steal you away while I'm gone, I'll consider it treason."

He had a word with the conductor of the small, versatile orchestra, and when Roger de Coverley spun to a close, the horns immediately struck up a swinging jazz tune.

It was impossible to worry when dancing. In the first number, an easy shag, Hannah was able to keep up a panting conversation of double entendres.

"My wife, Marina, won't object too strongly," he said after sufficient repartee, thinking he'd made himself abundantly clear. "We have an understanding, and get along swimmingly."

"She doesn't like opera singers?" Hannah asked.

"Or chorus girls, or chorus boys, but as long as we keep our peccadilloes discreet we are all happy."

Hannah smiled up at him. "Is opera a peccadillo in this country?"

"No, but the singers are, if they're kept in secret apartments and drive little coupes. Or would you prefer a Rolls and chauffeur? The royal treasury can support it, and if not, last season all of my horses placed, so I'm flush."

Still not understanding, she said, "Are you always so kind to your protégés? You haven't even seen me perform."

"What you don't know I can teach you. My tastes are simple. Well, broad but shallow, I should say." He let his hand run down to the small of her back.

"You can teach me opera?" Hannah asked, incredulous. "I never knew you sang."

"Teach you . . . oh, good lord, have I put my foot in it?"

"I don't know. What were you talking about?"

"Liripip claims you're a notorious courtesan. He might have been demobbed eons ago, but I trust his judgment where women are concerned, and if he says you're worth it, I figured I'd get in before some other fellow does. I take it he was, er, mistaken?"

"Rather. I'm an opera singer. Well, cabaret-*cum*-opera. I want to start singing here in England, but of course I know no one, and a girl who works in the kitchen all day can't exactly go out and audition. I thought you meant to hear me sing and mention my name around. I'm really rather good. I was supposed to join the Vienna Opera soon, but . . ." She cocked her head up at him. "If you have an apartment and a coupe free and are looking for a notorious German courtesan, I know someone who would require absolutely no training whatsoever. Do you spy that Rhinemaiden in the see-through dress?"

She promised to introduce them, but Georgie wanted one more dance. "There's no sham with you, is there, and no shame. How very unusual. My wife would like you after all, I think, particularly if we're not to be lovers." He added wistfully, "We're not, are we?"

She glanced unconsciously toward Teddy, who had partnered Sally for the shag and now sought out Anna again. Everyone was surreptitiously watching the lovely little night-and-starlight girl charm His Highness; everyone except Teddy, who was looking like a mooncalf into Anna's eyes, full of his new understanding of her, thinking of exactly how he would propose.

"Ah," Georgie said. "You *do* know that the best cure for unrequited love is a good—" But what exactly his prescription was, Hannah never learned, for the shag transitioned into a Lindy that was as improvisational as the music itself, and she had to give herself over entirely to the sudden dips and air steps and, dramatically at the end, a flip that made all the other guests gasp. She was in Berlin again, in the dance clubs she knew so well, with her family and friends and cabaret coworkers all around her. For a moment her body freed her mind and she was passionately happy.

Then the music stopped, and she remembered.

Her friends were back in Germany, dead, fled—who knew? Her family . . .

She panted in the middle of the mostly cleared floor. Only the youngest guests had remained for the modern "rude American dances." Another waltz was beginning, and Hannah recognized the opening measures of the *Wiener Bonbons*. Lord Liripip must have ordered it specifically for her. Had he really thought her a prostitute? No, what had Georgie said, a courtesan? Did he really not know who she was, or had that wicked Lady Liripip lied to him, telling him the daughter of his former love was a prostitute?

It is not right that the world is so full of wicked people, Hannah thought. No, she amended almost immediately, looking at Lord Liripip lounging in a chair, looking inordinately pleased with himself. *There are vastly more kind people than evil people. It's only that they let the wicked people get away with so much. A great wonderful world, and what does it do about Hitler? A family of decent people, and what do they do about Lady Liripip? Nothing.*

Hannah was tired of waiting for the rest of the world to do something. There wasn't much she could personally do about

Nazis, she had no real idea how to help her parents, but she could defy Lady Liripip. Then Teddy would have to defy her too . . . or lose Hannah.

She led Georgie to Waltraud and made a quick introduction. They took to each other right away, each with a frank understanding of what they could do for, and get from, the other. Waltraud hooked her pinky in His Highness's and pulled him toward a curtained alcove.

"Have fun," Hannah said. "I'll be back in a moment." She gave Georgie a peck on the cheek, which would appear, in anonymous form, in the next day's society column.

Hannah weaved through the dancers, stopping directly before Teddy, who clasped Anna by the hand and hip. She didn't know what she would say, but she had to speak now, while her courage was strong. *I love you* might be a good way to start. *I love you, and you said you love me, and you have to tell your mother now. I do not wish to make a scene, but love is a spectacle; not a secret but a thing for the world.*

It sounded very good in her head, but all she managed, under Teddy's perplexed half smile and Anna's look of outright hostility (for Teddy had been murmuring something promising in her ear), was, "Teddy, I—"

Then came the strident voice Hannah had rather suspected would be doing quite a bit of shouting . . . only not so soon.

"Ingrate!" Lady Liripip screeched, pointing a *j'accuse* finger at Hannah from across the room. "Criminal! Call the police at once!"

Hannah looked at Lady Liripip in alarm. Was the woman not only unkind, but positively mad? She had hiked up her mauve beaded gown and was charging at Hannah, her finger still jabbing the air in her direction.

"She is a kitchen maid, an insolent trull who should have been fired weeks ago. I let her stay out of the kindness of my heart" — here Hannah could not suppress a little snort — "and she repays me with base treachery and theft!"

"Lady Liripip," Hannah began, thinking she might explain that she was not stealing a son but giving a daughter-in law. But she was not allowed to continue.

"That wretched creature has stolen my pearls!"

Hannah Learns That Pearls Mean Tears

SINCE THERE WERE MEMBERS of the royal family in attendance, there were several unobtrusive muscular types who lingered on the fringes waiting to tackle anyone who threatened the line of succession. Hearing the alarm raised, these moved in like sharks scenting blood, surrounding Hannah, who stood alone.

"These are my pearls," she said, doing her best to sound calm and reasonable, though she was both frightened and furious. "At least, not *exactly* mine, although . . ."

"You see, she admits she has stolen them. Police!"

Constable Bates, who had been hired to keep the village riff-raff out, heard the call and asked what seemed to be the trouble.

"I told the maids to clean my pearls — an heirloom set, you see how perfect they are. Then afterward no one could find them."

"They *are* mine!" Hannah said, trembling, outraged.

"She says they're hers," the constable said with a shrug. He'd been the object of too much condescension and even outright rudeness from Lady Liripip to take her side readily. Besides, the girl she was accusing looked like a princess.

"How could they be hers, you dimwit! She's a *kitchen* maid. Kitchen maids don't own pearls. Get them off her before they get filthy." She made a snatch at them, and Hannah backed out of reach, right into Teddy's arms.

"Help me," she whispered to him, but he only gave her an uncomfortable smile and gestured to the constable. Hannah felt her throat tighten, and for a moment she was sure she'd never breathe again. She felt the tears begin to burn behind her eyelids, but she caught Lady Liripip's malevolent glare and swore she'd die before she shed them in front of that woman.

"Let's take them off now, shall we, missy?" the constable said coaxingly. "Don't worry—we'll get to the bottom of it." He reached for the dangling strands, but she jerked away.

"They're my mother's!" she shouted. "*She* knows that!" She pointed her own accusing finger at Lady Liripip, who rounded on her in fury.

"If you won't do your duty, Constable, I will," she said, and snaked her gaunt, clawlike hand out, catching one of the magnificent strands. She pulled at it, ripping it free and tearing Hannah's dress half off her shoulder. The rope broke and pearls scattered and fell, bouncing and rolling across the ballroom.

"No!" Hannah cried. The pearls were so connected to her mother, it felt as if she had been violently ripped from a maternal embrace. She fell to her knees, slithering among legs, hunting them down one by one, while Lady Liripip continued to screech and the gossip columnists filed away every thrilling detail for their papers.

Above her, Hannah heard Teddy say, "Come away from all this fuss, Anna."

After that, even pride couldn't burn away her tears. Constable Bates took her by the shoulders and helped her up, only to have her fall weeping against his chest.

He patted her back soothingly, which was not at all how he had been trained to deal with dangerous jewel thieves. "Don't cry, my dear. Prison ain't such a bad place. They feed you well, at least, and teach you a useful trade." Unable to quiet Hannah's increasing hysterics, he requisitioned a room in which to question her, and then pointedly slammed the door in Lady Liripip's face.

"He didn't even care!" Hannah moaned when they were alone, much to Bates's confusion and consternation. "I am nothing to him." She buried her face in her hands. "He said so many pretty words, and they are lies—all lies!"

"Who's that now, your partner in crime? If you were coerced, you can make a plea and the scoundrel will do the time. Now then, tell me everything and it will go better for you."

She did, treating him like a confessor. As the tears gave way to hiccups, she told him of Germany, of her lovely mother and gallant father, of her love for Teddy. By the time she was done, the grizzled old constable's eyes were positively dewy.

"The blighter," he whispered. "The absolute rotter. Forget about the toffs, miss. I have a son, now, would be proud to know such a girl as you. At least, if you really aren't a thief. Tell me how you came by these pearls."

Before she could speak, there was a sharp rap at the door, and Lady Liripip stuck her beak in. "What's taking you so long? I demand my pearls back!"

Bates excused himself and left one of the royal bodyguards to watch over Hannah (and the pearls).

"Can you describe the pearls in question, ma'am?" he asked Lady Liripip when they were alone, deliberately neglecting the "Lady" as she so deliberately had left off "Constable."

"They are . . . pearls," she snipped. "Surely you've seen pearls before, if only the costume variety. These are similar, though better, and worth more than you'd make in twenty years. They have been in the family for six generations."

"Then I must say it was rather careless of you to mislay them," he said blandly. "Can you identify them with any more precision? Length, perhaps, or number? Type of clasp? Size?"

"They are pearls, you imbecile," she shouted. "Lots and lots of pearls, and they're mine! I want her taken into custody. What do I pay you for, if not to arrest a criminal from under my own roof?" She stomped her foot.

"The county pays me, ma'am, to uphold the law." With that he excused himself, smirking, as she sputtered behind him. He sincerely hoped the girl had not stolen the pearls.

When he rejoined Hannah he asked her again, very gently, to take off her pearls. She handed over the two remaining strands around her neck, but when she reached up to uncoil the pearls gleaming like stars in her hair, he shook his head and said, "Not just yet. There may be dancing left in your night, and you don't want to be mussed."

Constable Bates examined the pearls closely.

"Your mother, what is her name?"

"Caroline Morgenstern, née Curzon."

"I remember her. A bonny girl."

"Onstage she goes by the name Cora Pearl. Like the, um . . ." There had been too much talk of courtesans that day.

"Exactly." He held one of the clasps very close to his eye. Engraved in minuscule script were the initials CP inside a heart. On another necklace he found the name Cora.

"These are very fine pearls, my dear," he said, carefully draping them over her head and settling them, with paternal disinterest, against the soft, creamy skin of her bare back. He gathered up all of the loose pearls and broken segments and put them in one of the evidence bags he kept in his pocket. "You should take great care of them. Particularly in a house where valuable things seem to vanish."

He gave her a little pat on her upturned head.

"I'm free to go?" she asked.

"Unless you'd care to give me the next dance. But no, I'm on duty, and I must go break the happy news to Her Ladyship that she does not harbor thieves under her roof."

"You won't tell them, will you? About . . ." She gulped. "About Teddy?"

"Not a word, miss. Now go back to your party. There are plenty of young men for you there. Men who will stand by you."

But Hannah did not return to the ball. How could she, when the man who said he loved her, who swore that he was hers, forever, did not so much as lift a finger to come to her rescue when she was being dragged away by the police?

"He looked at me as if I were nothing," she fumed to herself in her room, weeping and raging all at once. She flung the pearls onto her narrow bed. "There he was, a toff among toffs, hanging on Anna because she is blond and English and Aryan. Yes, Aryan! That's what it comes down to. I'm foreign, poor, a Jew. That makes me good enough to talk to when no one can see, but to acknowledge me in front of his family and friends—impossible. *Scheisse!*"

She slipped out of the dress—carefully, because she would give it back to Waltraud, who might be able to use it as a cocktail dress now that it was too short for an evening gown.

"Stupid, *stupid* me," she wailed as she stomped around her room, fury winning for a moment. "And stupid, *stupid* him. I cannot stay here any longer. What a fool I was to think that I could possibly be accepted here. Though my mother warned me, and

Lady Liripip wrote that horrible letter, I was convinced it was a Wodehouse comedy, so very amusing and English, full of obstacles easily overcome. But she is a witch, and Teddy is an invertebrate, and I do not belong here."

Yet where did she belong? *In Germany as it once was, but not as it is,* she thought.

What a shame that Georgie, as she could not help calling the Duke of Kent, only wanted her as a mistress and not as a singer. She wondered how he and Waltraud were getting along. Perhaps if things worked out well, her friend would let her use her apartment in Mayfair, her smart little coupe, while she looked for a job. Hannah was hesitant to leave, because Starkers was the only contact information her parents had, and she had surreal visions of them all wandering around foggy London for an eternity, searching for and never finding one another.

That's nonsense, she told herself. *Sally or Coombe will keep any letters for me if I ask them, and forward them. I go tomorrow.*

Resolutely, she packed her bags, a task that was completed in the space of one minute. While the bànd played in the great hall below her attic chamber, she sat shivering in her slip and painstakingly sewed her mother's pearls back into her traveling suit and stitched the buttons on again. She left her Boxing Day parcel on her dresser. Then she curled up under her paltry blankets and slept, more or less, on a tear-damp pillow.

IN THE GARDEN, beneath the twin yews that grew so closely entwined they were almost one, Teddy waited. He did not wait patiently. The ball had ended at one (earlier than most successful balls, out of consideration for the servants it honored, for they had to be up again by five or six), and after bidding Anna a formal good night under his mother's eye, he retired to his room, waited until the house was quiet, then crept down to find his love. "Meet me in our special place," he'd murmured as they danced.

He was there; she was not.

He paced, thinking of Anna's transcendent beauty as he held her in his arms. She was like a benediction, and he was grateful for the privilege of being allowed to look at her. It was like a spell, he thought, or perhaps more like a drug. For the first hour of waiting, he was consumed with the visual and tactile appeal.

Then, as his glances toward Starkers became more frequent, as the cold began to seep into his bones, as the proposal speech he'd prepared began to sound trite on the twenty-fifth rehearsal, he forgot to think of her beauty. Instead, he thought of her.

Of her lovely low voice . . .

No, it was a lovely voice, but not so low. If anything, as he'd noticed when they were dancing that evening, it sometimes squeaked. Trilled like a bird would be kinder, though less accurate. It was a changeable voice, rising and falling in pitch. Was it night that softened it, or only memory? For surely when she spoke in their hushed secret nighttime German, her voice was dulcet. And her singing voice! He would beg her to sing tonight. Perhaps he'd even invade her private concert hall in the yew bole.

But her occasionally squeaking voice didn't matter, not in the least. He loved her most for her mind, for the marvelous, funny, clever things she said.

Such as . . .

That was odd. When he imagined her speaking in her high-pitched English, he couldn't remember any of the witty things she'd said. *Ah, but that's because she's a spy in the daytime,* he remembered with a grin. *All of the delicious things she says are at night, when we're alone. How funny to think that if I only knew her in the daylight, I wouldn't love her at all!*

Night grew deeper under the slim sliver of newborn moon, and still she did not come. It would be dawn in a few hours and he'd have to leave, again. He thought back wistfully to those endless holidays of his youth (as he thought of the time only a year or two past) when he would lounge at home for weeks, playing rugby and cricket with the village boys, swimming naked in the pond, with that last mad dash of cramming to do his Latin translations before the new term. If only he'd met Anna then, so he could woo her properly, instead of all these moments of interrupted bliss.

Maybe he should tell Burroughs he didn't want any part of this spying business. It had all been so exciting—it still was, for as things in Europe got worse, he knew how vital his sub-rosa role might be. But it pained him nonetheless to think of finding love only to leave it behind to play his very serious, very dangerous game.

I'll talk it over with her after I propose and see what she thinks. He honestly didn't know what her opinion might be. Oddly, when he thought of her answering in English, he thought she would insist that he stay safe in England. When he imagined her replying in German, he was sure that, whatever sorrow it might cause them both, she would urge him to continue his undercover mission.

He heard steps and his heart lightened. (And sank, too, in some way he didn't quite understand. Was he doing the right thing, proposing to a girl he hardly knew? It felt so right, so perfectly right . . . most of the time.)

But no, there were voices too, those rising and falling tones of the tipsy trying to be quiet, and laughter. It was a couple, he was sure. Who? Two of the servants? Some lingering guests? They were going to the glass hothouse. Ah, yes — Anna had mentioned that Hardy had a paramour. He heard a little shriek, a moment of silence, and then more laughter. Whatever was going on didn't concern him. Where was Anna? Why didn't she come?

He gave it one more hour, and then took a small notebook and pencil stub from his pocket.

I waited for you, he wrote. That sounded petulant, but he was on his last piece of paper and couldn't tear it up and start fresh.

Marry me, he added, to make up for it.

Then he felt along the inside of the yew bole until he found a loose piece of bark and fixed it in place.

As he walked back to Starkers he almost turned around to retrieve his scrap of a proposal. *She deserves better,* he thought, and then: *She doesn't deserve that much, because she didn't come.* He thought of the unkind thing she'd said about his beloved old governess, of the misguided (and sometimes frankly stupid) things she'd said about politics, the lower classes. It was an act, he knew, but if she could act that part so well . . .

Will she think less of me if she learns I can act like a perfect Nazi? Will I be a different person because I pretended to be a different person?

Tired of thinking, and simply tired, he made himself stop worrying. *You don't have to think about love,* he decided. *You love, or you do not.*

He remembered the night she called him an ass and told him *tschuss,* not *auf Wiedersehen,* then assured him that they were no longer formal. Her *tschuss* had been like a kiss. *I haven't even kissed her,* he realized. *Not really. Only her hand, that precious scar on her left thumb.* No, it was the right. Was it? If only she'd take off those damned gloves during the day so he could have a proper look.

Half an hour later his Bugatti was purring toward London and Burroughs.

Tschuss, he whispered to the wrong window, a kiss of promise blown through the cold, sharp air.

NEAR DAWN, WALTRAUD LET HERSELF into Hannah's room. She looked at the girl's tear-streaked face and almost decided not to wake her . . . but really, joy should always defeat sorrow, she thought, so she sat on the edge of the narrow bed and shook her friend gently awake.

"Thank you!" she whispered as Hannah opened her eyes. "Do you realize what you've done for me?"

Hannah sat up, frowning, still lost in a confused dream. "What have I done to you?" she asked.

"*For* me, silly. You introduced us, and whatever you told him about me beforehand, he was primed, my love, simply primed. He has a reputation for favoring entertainers, but so fast! Perhaps royals move in different time frames. They have the money to do as they like, and then people to take care of any messy termination. Perhaps one day a large man will haul me out of my flat and a lawyer will explain how I have no recourse, and then if I protest or go to the papers I'll end up floating in the Thames." She gave a melodramatic sigh. "From cabaret trollop to mistress of a royal, can you imagine? Quite worth the looming faux suicide, don't you think? So exciting to be with a man who doesn't have to worry about consequences, or his wife. If I ever become a wife, let me not be a silly, jealous one. *You* must be, though. You must positively kill Teddy if he so much as looks at another woman. Like that fright of an Anna he was dancing with all night after you left."

She noticed Hannah's pained expression, and wondered if that was the cause of the tears. She had meant to stick to Hannah's side and do everything in her considerable power to make Teddy realize he simply had to propose, but things had taken such an interesting turn with His Royal Highness.

"I didn't hear about the pearl incident until later, and everyone was strangely reticent with details. I would have been there staunchly defending you, except I was ensconced with HRH, as I've decided to call him, doing . . . well, doing such as can be done with a hundred people on the other side of a curtain. Still, that's quite a lot. And then afterward, to have some real privacy, we went to the hothouse, only we found that dishy gardener Hardy there, tending his tubers by moonlight, and HRH and he got to talking about plants and I was almost—*almost*—jealous, but then Anna came, and a few other couples drifted in, and it was practically a nightclub. HRH is so kind. It seems to be his hobby to whisk people off to brave new worlds. He said he can get Hardy an apprenticeship at the Windsor gardens, and after six months of that, practically anyone would take him on as head gardener. I'm glad he didn't think to do anything for that Anna. Oh, darling, we leave for London this morning! Farewell to servitude!"

"You have the flat in Mayfair and the coupe?"

"Or Rolls, though I think I'd prefer to drive myself rather than have a chauffeur snooping, making notes whenever I visit a gentleman who's not my uncle, and of course I haven't any uncles."

Amid her own troubles, Hannah marveled at her friend, already thinking of infidelity when her adulterous affair had scarcely started.

"But what a pain for you to have been persecuted by that vile old harridan. I know it was all cleared up, but still. Was Teddy quite heroic? I didn't hear a thing while it was going on, and when HRH and I emerged you were gone and the party was winding down. Teddy was dancing with Anna, no doubt to please his mother, and I couldn't exactly go up and ask when the happy day was to be. But I can picture him charging to your defense like an enraged bull." Waltraud's cheerful voice started to get a little forced, and she realized her extreme happiness wasn't as important as she'd thought.

"Isn't it all arranged?" she pressed. "With that dress, I was so sure . . ."

"You thought a *dress* would make him love me?" Hannah asked with contempt, not for her friend, really, but for the bitter world. "You thought it would disguise the fact that I am a nonentity — a Jew, a foreigner, a cabaret singer? You thought a dress would give me an English complexion and blond hair and the right background?"

"What happened?" Waltraud asked gently.

"Oh, Traudl, they took me away, and he did *nothing!* That is what happens to us, in Germany and here — they take us away, and people do nothing!"

She thought she had run out of tears, but she wept again as she told Waltraud how Teddy had hardly acknowledged her in her hour of need, how he had clung to the beautiful Anna.

"They should be together," Hannah sobbed in self-pity. "Two shallow English people, making shallow English babies. I know now why my mother ran away from this country."

"Hannah, love, if he doesn't care for you then he's a fool, and you could never love a fool. The moment he spurned you, your heart should have been warded against all breakage, forever."

"It doesn't work like that."

"It doesn't?" Waltraud asked, genuinely surprised. She rarely failed to get any man (or woman) she desired, but lost interest the moment her target showed no reciprocal interest in her.

"He loves me. I know he does. But he can't bring himself to acknowledge it."

"Then you shouldn't waste your affections on him," said pragmatic Waltraud. "And what perfect timing, for my Mayfair apartment is to have two bedrooms. For when we have rows, you see. We shall be such an impassioned couple that we will throw things at each other and have tearing big fights, and each go to our own bedroom to sulk, and then creep into one another's bed at midnight to make up. Only, we won't for a while, because you will be in the extra bedroom. He won't mind at all. You can even . . ." But she wisely nipped that suggestion in the bud.

"No, I can never be the cuckoo in your love nest. But I'm still leaving. It was wrong of me to stay past the first day, when I saw how they would treat me. Or how *she* would treat me, and they all follow her. I will go to the refugee center and look for work like any other Jewish girl. That is, any uncertain child of agnostic parents of Jewish heritage. I wouldn't mind being a kitchen maid anywhere else. Only at Starkers does it gall."

"Stay with me just for a little while, then. HRH can find you work—good work, singing, acting. Or teaching children to sing. We'll get you in the Sadler's Wells Theatre eventually, or the D'Oyly Carte if you want something lighter. There's no need to slave, not with your talent."

Waltraud wore her down, though Hannah swore she wouldn't impose for more than two weeks, and during that time she'd be out night and day looking for work, and her own place.

Waltraud had some more packing to do, so Hannah said she'd meet her in half an hour outside the gates. She didn't want to say goodbye to anyone. She just wanted to disappear.

She paid one last visit to the twin yews. She knew he wouldn't be there. Even if he'd looked for her earlier, he wouldn't have waited all night. Still, there was a little part of her that knew she would forgive him if he was there, doing penance all that cold night.

No, he wasn't there. Of course he wasn't there.

She went inside the hollow bole and breathed in the memory of him, of those nights, so few, so precious, so misleading. It was only a dream, though, she told herself. A midwinter night's dream.

She was about to leave the place of her disillusion forever

when she caught a glimmer of white in the faint crescent moonlight. Her heart beating wildly, she held it an inch from her eyes and strained to read the words.

I waited for you.
Marry me.

If it had been a question, not a command, she might have torn up the paper and left with Waltraud and HRH. But that stark statement, with a period at the end, made it seem so very inescapable, practically preordained, that she never thought to question it. She didn't *want* to question it.

Yes, she whispered to the stars.

Then she ran back to tell Waltraud she'd be staying after all.

Waltraud argued, but in the end she shrugged and said, "Just as well. Because I only now remembered where Lady Liripip's pearls are, and someone has to tell her. You see, she wanted them cleaned, and scrubbing with soap didn't seem to help. I'm not very domestic, as you know, but I do recall an old, er, acquaintance of mine, whose name I can't recall though I still have the Mainbocher gown he gave me . . . anyway, he soaked his false teeth in vinegar to make them clean and white. So I tried it on Lady Liripip's pearls."

"You didn't!"

"How was I to know that pearls dissolve in vinegar?"

The Letters of the New Year

I DO NOT WANT TO BE *this kind of girl,* Hannah thought. *The kind who forgives weakness, the kind who waits, interminably, for a prince to deign to take her.*

I do not want to be the girl who loves without reason or sense, enduring.

When Teddy talked to her in the black of midnight, he seemed as brave as an entire Roman legion, ready to stand against any barbarian, to hold fast and true. Was he not going to Germany to do the work of the angels and white hats? Sometimes he made it sound like a schoolboy lark, but they both knew how dangerous it would be, particularly if it came to war, as everyone thought it must. He was not doing that from patriotism, or a sense of adventure, but from a passionate sense of right and wrong: where there was wrong, to put it right. How could the man who would defy a country and save the world, if he was able, not defy his own mother? How could he swear one thing in the darkness and act quite another way in broad daylight?

But I love him, damn it, she thought. *Why are the poets right— why does that conquer all? Why does it make his weakness less contemptible?* She loved him and despised him at the same time . . . but the love would not go away.

So she stayed, scrubbing and chopping, tending to Anna, and occasionally, in between, being waylaid by Lord Liripip to hear more of his memoirs. Some shred of pride still prevented her from revealing who she was, as well, she had to admit, as some scrap of mischief. Let Lady Liripip gloat in her subjugation. The look on her face would be that much more enjoyable when she found out Hannah and Teddy were to be married, and when she faced her husband's wrath at the deception, all at once. A creature of the stage, Hannah appreciated a proper buildup and stunning climax. Sometimes it was better to skip over the obvious and the immediate in favor of a delayed punch line. And what a punch line it would be!

But it was a long time until May, when Teddy would return. Scrubbing dishes helped keep her philosophical . . . and if her occasional tears fell into the dishwater, no one noticed them for the bubbles.

ANNA HAD VERY LITTLE to amuse her that winter. Teddy was gone, and there was no one else personable on the estate to even daydream about. Even the handsome and completely impractical under-gardener she liked to watch had left immediately after the Servants' Ball. She did not know where, and did not let herself ask. It was bad enough that he slipped into her thoughts uninvited, that every time she tried to imagine her future with Teddy, Hardy's low-class but undeniably dashing face and form intruded. His absence was a relief, she told herself. She wouldn't rub salt in a wound that shouldn't be there in the first place by asking about him.

In January, she received a note from her father, though the envelope had the return address of the British Ladies' Poetry Society. Even that received a suspicious look from Lady Liripip when she spied it. "I hope their poetry rhymes, at least," she sniffed. "I have no stomach for modern tripe." Not that she was an avid reader of poetry. She hadn't read a verse since escaping the schoolroom.

Anna opened the letter at the tea table and skimmed it, keeping her face serene. "They only want a donation to help them teach guttersnipes to recite," she said, and tucked the letter into her pocket. Which, fortunately, started Lady Liripip on another critical rant — she believed pockets were common — and let the letter evaporate from her notice.

Had she somehow managed to extract the letter or divine its

contents, Lady Liripip would have expired on the spot. For it said, tersely:

> *Write to confirm successful position re Starkers.*
> *Not necessary after all to eliminate Lord Liripip, as his*
> *heir is not congenial to the cause.*
> *Stand by for further instructions.*
> *Destroy after reading.*

It was unsigned, but Anna recognized her father's handwriting.

Anna's oolong rippled in its Limoges, but she managed to endure the rest of tea, and even choked down the obligatory biscuit before withdrawing to her room. Once there, she stood in the center like one of those empty-eyed Roman statues, staring at nothing until her eyes burned. She scarcely breathed. She felt like a fawn who believes with all her trembling heart that if she does not move, the wolf panting upon her throat cannot see her.

Finally, with the greatest effort, she staggered to the window. Her breath fogged the glass, and frost covered the garden, but she could just see the faint warm orange of the firepots burning inside the glass hothouse. She felt an indescribable craving to be there, surrounded by blossoms that should have perished a season ago, breathing the living air. She longed for a simple world of flowers.

They wanted me to kill, she thought numbly. Not flirt with a visiting diplomat, not whisper code or pass documents or ferret out secrets, but kill. No wonder the NAFF had told her nothing of their true plans. If they had, she'd never have agreed, no matter how many eligible young lords she might have met. And Lord Liripip, of all people? She could not think of anyone less political than Lord Liripip, bellowing for his dessert and scribbling his memoirs. But he was in the House of Lords, technically, though he hadn't attended a session in ages. Was the NAFF really going to kill anti-fascist lords in hopes that their heirs might be pro-German?

She stripped off her gloves, using her teeth when they stuck clammily to her fingers. They were big, strong hands, she thought. Hands that by rights should be digging potatoes or working in a factory. A lady's hands could never kill . . . but these could. They were the one thing about herself that effort and will could not change.

Hastily, she tugged her gloves back on, shuddering. How could he think it of her? How could he expect his own daughter to do such a horrible thing?

Never, she swore. *He can't make me.* Not for the cause, which she hardly understood. Not to be a heroine. She didn't want to be a heroine anymore, not at all. All she wanted was a good marriage. *Teddy,* she amended. *I want Teddy.*

Though for some reason she couldn't quite remember what he looked like.

Frightened, disgusted, hurt by what her father had almost asked of her, she would have left Starkers if not for Teddy. But surely now that the NAFF had abandoned its ludicrous plan to have her kill Lord Liripip, her job was all over. Maybe somewhere else in England, some poor girl was being asked to kill a liberal old man so a fascist son could take over. But as long as it wasn't her, she didn't particularly care. She would stay, and tell no one.

She wrote a hasty note back to her father, via the address of the poetry society.

> *I regret I cannot contribute to your scheme. However,*
> *should you ever require anything of a less extreme nature, I*
> *am here, at your disposal.*

She didn't dare state outright that she was through with the NAFF plans. Her father was a violent man, and though she'd impressed upon him before that her face was her fortune and must never be damaged, she now knew that his cause meant far more to him than his daughter. If she refused to help, if he thought there was any danger of her alerting the authorities, there was no telling what he might do . . . or whom he might send. The NAFF had some unsavory members.

Anna rested easy until March, when she received another missive from the poetry society.

Have been told His Majesty often visits Starkers.
Advise when.

IN APRIL, WHICH HANNAH NOW heartily agreed was the cruelest month, mixing memory and desire, she walked past the burgeoning lilies that lined the lane. She was heading to the village to fetch a bottle of vanilla for Sally, and she was deep in thought.

Hannah was getting to be well known in the little village that abutted the grounds of Starkers and was, in that old feudal way, owned, more or less, by Lord Liripip. The baker shouted a greeting, and several scrubbed, apple-cheeked heads peeked out of the schoolhouse to grin at her as she walked by. Her hopeful longing, her fitful depression, began to subside in the wake of all the peasant cheerfulness, and she had a nice chat with the grocer as he fetched her bottle of vanilla.

"Someone was asking about you the other day," he said, after telling her a scintillating tale about his wife's bunion surgery.

"Me?" she asked, flush with the hope that hung around every corner, emerging again and again like a perpetually eager puppy, though it knew it would probably be kicked. Her parents? Someone from Germany who knew her parents? Teddy?

"I suppose he meant you. He was asking about the newest kitchen maid at Starkers, anyway. Said he thought he might know her, and could I deliver a letter to her. What's her name, I asked, but he wouldn't say. Just the newest kitchen maid."

"Who was he?" she asked.

The grocer shrugged. "Strange fellow. Shifty-eyed. I suppose he was an admirer and wanted to make your acquaintance. He couldn't just walk up to Starkers, though, could he? So he wrote a note. I didn't care for his looks, Miss Hannah. He had that stoatish look, if you know what I mean."

She didn't, because though her English was near perfect, she still didn't know if a stoat was a rabbit or a ferret or a badger. Though any one of those, she supposed, would make for an unpleasant admirer.

The grocer gave her the note, which she took with some reluctance. "Thank you." She waited until she was on the jonquil-lined path back to Starkers before she tore it open. It certainly wasn't in Teddy's hand.

> *The time is near.*
> *Be prepared.*
> *Meet me at the gate.*
> *Sunday midnight.*

She chuckled. Perhaps her admirer was Lord Baden-Powell, founder of the Scouting movement.

Or—Hannah's spirit danced, her heart grew lightsome in the giddy spring—could it be Teddy? Was it like in the novels? Was he planning an elopement? The stoatish man might just be his messenger.

She couldn't let her hopes rise too far. Maybe the note wasn't even for her, but for Glenda or Judy. Maybe Waltraud wanted to whisk her away to London . . . though that wasn't her pretty, careless script, and she probably would have written in German, which was by far her stronger language.

Tomorrow was Sunday. Hannah would simply go to the gate and see for herself. She didn't have to actually meet whoever it was; she could hide in the shrubberies or behind the wall. The gate was locked at night, with a bell to summon some hapless servant in case of nocturnal emergencies, so whoever it was couldn't get at her.

But a sense of caution made her want to tell someone, just in case. Sally or Coombe would prohibit her from going — servants have a strict curfew, and though in those modern days they weren't exactly forbidden to have admirers, it was certainly discouraged. Judy or Glenda, troublemakers both, would snitch. With Waltraud gone to her glamorous London life (she was dancing burlesque in a fashionable nightclub, she wrote, when she wasn't — ahem — serving the Crown) and Hardy away at Windsor perfecting his vegetative knowledge, Hannah didn't know whom to turn to, except . . .

Hannah's Salad of Bitter Herbs

ANNA HAD SETTLED INTO THE LIFE of an aristocratic hanger-on with comfortable ease. For most of the day she trailed Lady Liripip, running little errands for her, blandly submitting to her stinging criticisms. These were easier to bear because they were mostly about her parents—her supposed parents, that is. Her father was a Jewish swindler, while the woman Lady Liripip thought was Anna's mother was a disreputable minx who led men on. Anna asked in all innocence whether it was considered more acceptable to fulfill a man's expectations than to lead him to believe he had any and then thwart him, to which Lady Liripip gave a shocked glare.

"I only want to learn what's proper, my lady," Anna said with sweet innocence, and Lady Liripip congratulated herself that she'd picked a companion too stupid to cause any trouble. *It's the clever ones who muck things up,* she thought, remembering Caroline Curzon.

Anna never took offense, because she wasn't who she pretended to be, and it is easy to ignore things that are done to others, no matter how terrible. She kept such a good disposition under the barbs and stings that the fun quite went out of them, and as spring progressed Lady Liripip hardly bothered to insult her or her parents anymore.

But though her life was easy, and for the most part pleasant, many troubles dogged her. Least of them was the fact of her impersonation. She'd only been scared for the first few days. After that, it seemed that discovery was unlikely. Hannah, who should have been in her own position, seemed to completely accept her role as kitchen maid. And if she did, then who was Anna to take her out of it? Her father said that people must rise or fall to their proper social place, regardless of their birth . . . though some people, like her, must pull themselves up, while others have to be shoved down. It was not that Hannah deserved to be lowly, exactly — only that the alternative was for Anna to be the kitchen maid, and that certainly couldn't be allowed. She did not have the slightest idea who Machiavelli was, but she firmly believed that the ends justified the means, and her only end was to marry rich — to marry Teddy.

Which brought her to her other worry. On their last night together, things had not gone nearly as well as she'd hoped. Yes, they'd danced nearly every dance together, even after that embarrassing interruption from Hannah, who looked like some kind of tart but who did have some rather nice pearls, after all. Then, before parting for the night, he'd whispered to her to meet him in their usual place.

Well, if one could say "usual" when they'd only met there once. But, oh, that once! Her body still tingled with the passion of it. She'd never thought it would be so wonderful, so natural. In fact, thoughts of "it" had hardly entered her considerations. She hadn't improved herself, raised herself so high, for "it." Any poor handsome boy could give that to her — the florist she'd been so in love with, for example, the one she'd spurned because of course Anna Morgan could never be a florist's wife. Or that manly gardener with his broad shoulders and dirt beneath his nails . . .

All she cared about now, she'd lectured herself, was to marry a wealthy lord and be set and safe for life.

But that night in the greenhouse had set her afire.

She'd never dreamed that cheerful, charming Teddy could be so romantically aggressive. He seemed to hold her in chaste respect during the day, but when they were alone in the hothouse, in the pitch blackness where they could know each other only by touch, he'd possessed her with a passion that amazed her, and she responded in kind. Almost wordlessly, they had made love, and when near morning they'd gone their separate ways there was only a murmured "I love you."

After the Servants' Ball, she'd gone back for more. But Teddy never showed up. Instead she found the under-gardener, Hardy—who would have been even better-looking than Teddy if only he hadn't been so poor—and the Duke of Kent with a slim, willowy housemaid who Anna instantly decided was trashy-looking. Answering the lure of a warm, secret place, some of the younger guests had joined them. They'd chatted, and shared swigs from a bottle of champagne the royal supplied, but all the while Anna looked out for Teddy, ignoring the gardener's impertinent winks and ham-handed attempts to get her alone. She and Teddy might not have the time or privacy for a reprise of the previous night, but surely as soon as he got her alone, he'd propose.

But he never came, and in the morning he was gone before she woke.

He'd written to her since, but she had an odd feeling there was something missing from his letters, something he was not saying, or perhaps waiting for her to say. They were a little dry, telling her about his classes, his professors, his friends. There was nothing really intimate.

He'll be back in May when he graduates. Surely things will be finalized then.

Those two things troubled her. The one thing she scarcely worried about was the NAFF. The preposterous idea of murder was now vague and distant. Naturally her father had thought better of that. She'd written that the king would be visiting Starkers soon. Probably the NAFF would give her a secret treaty to present to him.

"I would like my hair down today, Hannah," she said when she sat in front of her vanity. "Gathered over my right shoulder. No, my left." She frowned, then smoothed her brow when she noticed the little wrinkles in the mirror. "Which side do you think, Hannah?"

"Does it matter?" asked Hannah, who had never learned the handmaiden's proper demure behavior.

"Of course it matters. Well, not so much now, as there's no one to see it. But in general, yes, a great deal. Is one side of the face better than the other? Hair on the right shoulder exposes the left profile, you see. I have a beauty spot on the left side that I like to play up. But then, my left breast is also slightly better than my right, and the line of hair draws attention down to the bosom, so perhaps the curls should be gathered to the left side." She looked at Hannah in the mirror behind her. "Now do you see how important it is?"

"Oh, yes," Hannah said with only the slightest smirk. "In the grand scheme of things it is very important indeed." But she did not mock Anna outright. For all her ignorance and her many foibles, there was something refreshing in her unthinking self-centeredness. You knew where you stood with Anna. There was no guile. She was not good, but to be bad required the ability to notice things besides oneself.

Besides, she knew that Anna was in the same position she was. Her beloved was gone. She noticed that Anna began moping as soon as Hardy left for his training at Windsor. She never thought Anna would succumb to Hardy's charms, but evidently she had, and missed them. Hannah certainly sympathized. Until that day, she wondered if she'd made the right decision, putting her faith in Teddy's love instead of going to London with Waltraud and looking after herself. Since the mysterious note, though, she had fresh hope.

"Speak to me in German," Anna said. "I need to practice." She had kept up with her studies in a desultory way, even though Teddy had never seemed to want to practice with her. To her surprise she was getting quite good. She did not have a brain for reasoning, but she could memorize and parrot any information that would help her fit in with the world she coveted.

Hannah was still dwelling on the mysterious letter the grocer had given her. She didn't want to take anyone into her confidence, exactly, for she'd read too many stories about elopements being thwarted at the last moment. But if perchance it wasn't Teddy, she did think it might be a good idea to let someone know she was meeting a mysterious stranger far from help at midnight.

"Here," she said, "I have a note. I will give you the German, and you will translate to English if you please. And we will dress your hair on the right. Your bosoms do not need any more attention, neither the right one nor the left."

She read the first line.

"The hour is . . . on top of me?" Anna ventured.

And the second.

"To be in readiness?"

Close enough. And then:

"Meet me on the . . . Tor? Does that mean the Glastonbury Tor? My father was in Somerset giving a talk and I *so* wanted to go to the top of the Tor, to see if I could feel the ghost of King Arthur, but my father said it was a waste of time."

This was the first Hannah had heard of Anna's family. She had rather thought Anna must be an orphan, to live in close proximity to Lady Liripip voluntarily. "What does your father do?" she asked.

"Oh, he lectures, mostly," Anna said with a wave of her hand, letting Hannah think he might be a kindly professor, not a vitriol-spitting hatemonger. "Did I do well with the translation?"

"Very, only it means meet me at the gate. Now one more. *Sonntag um Mitternicht.*"

For an answer, Anna gave a long and lusty sigh. How she wanted one more meeting at midnight!

"Wait," she said, catching sight of the paper in Hannah's hand. "Is that a real note, to you? Who are you meeting?" She snatched the note away. "Come on, tell me. Is Hardy back? I hadn't heard. Not that I . . . I mean . . ." She flushed. Why was she thinking about Hardy when it was Teddy she wanted?

"Anna, you don't have to pretend that you . . ." But she broke off. We all have our secrets, and if Anna felt it was safer to hide her relationship with Hardy by implying that he belonged to Hannah, why, let her. Hannah was sick to death of secrets, but this one wasn't hers to reveal. "No, it's not Hardy, I'm sure of that."

"Who, then?"

"I don't know."

"You're going, right?"

"I—"

"You have to!" Anna shrilled, clapping her hands. "You simply must! How romantic. Who could it be? The chauffeur, do you think, or the boot-boy?"

"I don't think—"

"I'll come with you. Oh, how exciting!" She was bored, restless, and the small adventure of a midnight walk, a tiny breath of scandal, would at least provide some diversion.

WITH NO TEDDY TO DISTRACT HER, Hannah had been getting months of uninterrupted sleep, so she was fresh and lively when they crept out of Starkers at a quarter till midnight and made their way beneath a moon-filled night sky toward the gate.

Anna felt like a schoolgirl—which she never really had been. She'd been to school, of course, early on, but for the most part she was self-taught, and that was more in comportment than actual knowledge. She'd never had close friends at school. Even as a little girl she had resented and disliked other girls. They were competition. She would bristle if the teacher praised them or someone admired their dimples. Then, sneakily, she would put tacks on their chairs.

But Hannah was different. Anna felt unaccountably easy with her. Hannah had a knack for friendliness, and then she was so different physically that Anna never worried that someone would look at the little dark sparrow rather than the grand white swan. Hannah never said sharp things to her. True, she had an idea Hannah gently mocked her from time to time, but it was so gentle, after all, and Anna didn't understand what Hannah was talking about half the time, with her obscure references to poets and artists and writers and politicians. (Anna was never sure which one Goethe was, since Hannah seemed to have a quote from him on practically every subject.)

When I am the lady of Starkers, I will be kind to her, Anna decided. How terrible to be so despised that you accept the idea of being put in a subservient position by your own relatives. She still didn't know why Hannah stood for it.

The walk was farther than Anna expected, and she had foolishly worn heels in case the secret admirer turned out to be worth her while.

"Here, take my arm," Hannah said, and helped her limp along.

When they got to the gate, there was not a soul to be seen. Disappointed, Anna sat down heavily inside the little decorative guardhouse just behind the iron bars and took off her shoe. She felt the fat, fluid-filled blister with her fingertip. If she'd been dancing—with anyone in particular, that is—she would have gone on no matter how much her shoes hurt, until her feet were bloody. She felt a sudden mad desire never to wear heels again. How lovely it would be to dress in trousers and clogs and nice thick socks and never have to totter again. She hated heels. She hated dieting. She hated having to always think about maintaining a posh accent. But there was no rest for her. Not until she said *I do.* No, better wait until *he'd* said it too, just to be safe.

"Who's there?" she heard Hannah ask from outside the guardhouse. She heard tires crunching through the gravel—a bicycle—and then heavy footfalls approaching the gate. "What do you want?"

"You're the newest kitchen maid?" a Manchester voice asked, incredulous. "You're supposed to be a drop-dead looker, innit? Well, to each his own. Listen: The king is coming soon. Give him a salad of bitter herbs, with yew. Got it? Say it back."

"Look, I don't know what this is about, but—"

"You're the kitchen maid what isn't one, really, eh?" he asked. Anna peeked through the clouded guardhouse window and saw the burly man look around nervously. "The one what been to Germany and that?"

"I am," Hannah said uncertainly.

"Then the message goes to you. Give the king a salad of bitter herbs," he repeated as if reciting from a script. "Sprinkled with yew. Just for the king, see. A special dish just for him. Now say it so I know you got it."

"A salad of bitter herbs," she repeated, "with yew, for the king. But what . . ."

He'd already hopped onto his bicycle. "Ta-ra," he said, and pedaled into the night.

"Oh god, oh god, oh god," Anna moaned, calling on a deity more primal and powerful than the benevolent uncle of the C. of E. For this, she needed one of those old gods who came to earth with their spites and jealousies and vengeance. She needed Zeus. She needed Loki. Nothing less than divine intervention would save her from this.

For now the third of her troubles, the thing she should have worried most about but had hardly considered all these months, had come to pass. She had been given her orders from the Von and Lord Darling and the NAFF, that great and terrible thing only she—a great devotee of the cause who happened to be placed in one of the greatest houses in the land, one that the king frequently visited—could accomplish. And only if she were ensconced in her menial position as a kitchen maid.

Anna's brain was rarely swift and clever, and then only when it immediately concerned herself. Now she knew exactly what they intended her to do—kill the king.

Were they mad?

She'd rarely listened to her father's rants. They all sounded the same to her, and she had other, much more important things to think about. But she did recall one common thread that popped up again and again—Edward, who had briefly held the throne before abdicating for that crass American Simpson woman (whom Anna pretended to despise but envied with every fiber of her being), would make a much better king than his brother, the second son, King George. (Who wasn't Georgie, the fourth son, whom she'd met before, but Bertie . . . so perplexing, these royal names.)

Edward was known for his Nazi sympathies. He had shaken hands with Hitler, and was openly in favor of appeasement. The papers said that was only because he'd seen the horrors of the last war and for the sake of humanity couldn't bear to have them repeated. But her father assured his followers that Edward and Hitler were like *that* — here he crossed his fingers in intimate digital embrace — and in a perfect world they would work jointly for the betterment of the people who mattered. There were a great many people who wanted Edward to rule Britannia again.

King George had an heir, of course — young Elizabeth. But if there was a strong enough movement behind Edward, it was just possible that he could retake the throne. There was no precedent for it, but it could happen. His marriage to Wallis Simpson could be annulled, and he could be king again. At the very least it would create such controversy and uproar that the nation would be in turmoil. Competing factions, a pubescent queen in the hands of her ministers. At the worst . . . civil war.

And they would have me *be the murderer who brings it all about.*

Anna didn't feel a surge of heroism, not a trace of solidarity with her father's cause. She didn't want to kill anyone. She *liked* the new king. He looked like a gentleman, and she had cut out pictures of his daughters. Edward, on the other hand, was a funny-looking milksop of a man with bad taste in women. And he liked Hitler. Anna used to not know who Hitler was, vaguely assuming him to be a friend of her father's, perhaps a like-minded grocer from back home. Now she knew better—from Teddy, from Hannah, and from the papers she occasionally read so she'd have some slight idea what each of them was talking about.

She had come to the conclusion that Hitler was no gentleman. Not very attractive, either, and that was important too.

I don't want to kill the nobility, she thought wildly. *I want to be the nobility!*

If they caught her—succeed or fail—she'd be shot. Or hung. Either of which would leave her a disgustingly mutilated corpse. Death is only attractive in a fashionable dress, with lilies and an open coffin.

But she remembered the peculiar, feral intensity of the Von's eyes . . . the way her father had struck her so savagely at the first sign of dissent . . . the alarming bulk of that night's messenger. *What will they do to me if I do not make the attempt?*

"What on earth was that all about, I wonder?" Hannah asked when the man was gone.

Again, Anna's brain worked with unaccustomed speed. *Maybe I don't have to do anything myself at all,* she thought. Anything— *anything*—rather than that!

"You are not familiar with English traditions," Anna said carefully. "When the king visits he is given special ceremonial food. Things just for him that other people aren't allowed to eat."

"Ah, like the nectar and ambrosia of the gods," Hannah said. "And that Norse goat who gave mead from her udder. But why tell me about it? And why at midnight, with such secrecy?"

"It is the English way," Anna said, praying she could pass it off as one of the national eccentricities, like Morris dancing. "Commoners aren't supposed to know, but as a kitchen maid of course you have to. You are the newest, so you had to be told in this private ceremony." She gave an unnatural laugh. "And here we thought you had a secret admirer! What a disappointment, only more work for you. But what an honor to serve the king."

"Bitter herbs," Hannah said musingly. She thought of the *maror* of the Seder plate, the herbs symbolizing the bitterness of enslavement endured in Egypt. Her family did not celebrate Passover, but they were part of the community and were often invited to other people's houses for the ceremonial Seder dinner. Hannah remembered her first stage fright as a little girl, asking, "Why is this night different from all other nights?" before hearing the story of the Exodus. She recalled the strange way the *afikomen*—just a piece of matzo—tasted unaccountably delicious just because it was treasured, and hidden, and called dessert.

"Why does the king eat bitter herbs?" she asked. "Is it in sympathy for the sufferings of the world? So that although he is king, he can try to understand the bitterness of the rest of us? Or is it to show us that although he is king, he has bitterness of his own?

Really, you English are surprising. I never dreamed you had such depths of tradition. Well, I will tell Sally, and together we will prepare the grandest bitter salad for His Majesty. With the yew. I must not forget the yew. I have such a soft spot for yew trees now." She indulged in a secret little smile. "But I did not know you could eat the leaves. Sally will have to tell me how to dress it."

"No!" Anna cried. "It . . . it's just meant for you. You were told in secret, so you must prepare it in secret. These are very old customs. They go back to . . . oh, I don't know, but a very long way. That man who came was probably an equerry. It is royal protocol. You don't question it, you just do it."

No one would buy that, Anna thought, on the verge of panic. Not if it was on sale.

But she had not counted on Hannah's lively imagination, her sense of the absurd, and her operatic acceptance of strange plot contrivances. She was also from a culture deeply steeped in ritual. To secretly serve a king bitter herbs with yew made as much sense as dipping parsley in salt-water. She never mocked other people's beliefs.

"Then I will make his salad alone, and sneak it on the board for Corcoran to serve. Sally need never know." Hannah looked pleased to be involved in the royal plot.

I could tell her, Anna thought. *I could confess all. I could tell her what every English child knows, that yews are deadly poisonous.* Children would dare one another to eat the sweet red berries, which alone among the tree's parts were innocuous, and in fact delicious. But the seed within was deadly—just one could kill. Schoolyard lore had it that the seeds would pass whole through the body, but if they didn't, one was fatal. All other parts were almost as toxic. Don't make your dog play fetch with a yew stick. Don't toss clippings in the sheep meadow.

Don't feed your sovereign yew leaves in his salad.

It won't be my fault, Anna told herself resolutely. *That man told Hannah—she's the one who will do it. No one will punish me, not the NAFF, not the hangman. I will marry Teddy and be able to forget the whole thing. It won't matter to me who rules, who goes to war, who is jailed or enslaved or oppressed. The world will muddle on one way or another. As long as I marry Teddy, I won't have to be a part of it.*

But she looked at Hannah's face, so lively, so amused at the idea of the innocent conspiracy, and felt as if someone had just spit on her—debased. *Anything to achieve my proper place in life* had always been her motto.

Anything . . . but that?

THE KING CAME WITH A small party two weeks later, at the end of April, to stay one night. In the afternoon, Hannah wandered through the lettuce beds, plucking and tasting. Umbel, the head gardener, who guarded his produce like his children, stopped her with a gruff command, then softened when he saw who it was. He'd had many a pleasant chat with the little German maid about *Wurzelpetersilie,* the root parsley popular in Germany, and the beauties of mashed celeriac.

"I am making a bitter salad," she said, omitting whom it was for. "Romaine, frisee, sorrel . . . what else?"

"Escarole, maybe," he said, pulling on his beard. "Herbs would round out the flavor. A bit of rue, a bit of yarrow. Not too much, mind, just a pinch. They can do a mischief if you have too much. Hmm . . . you need color. Marigolds, mayhap?"

"You can eat them?"

"Aye. Take a few of those at the edge of yon bed. Lemony, a little sour to counter the bitter. What will you use for the dressing? Vinegar, oil, and a bit of sweet? I have some clover honey I save special for my cough. It would do nice."

"Thank you," she said, following him to his cottage, her basket swinging over her arm. "And I need yew leaves, too. I'm told they will go nicely."

"Yew? Who's been feeding you that daft story? Yew's a death-herb. Why do you think they grow it in all the churchyards? Rue and yarrow are poison if you have too much, but tonic if you have a little. They freshen up the blood. But yew? You'll kill some-one if you feed him yew."

Hannah frowned and gulped. She was so sure the man had said yew. He'd made her repeat it to be certain.

"Though I have heard," Umbel went on, "of using yew as a decoration. Some ladies find them real stylish. Why, the Bowles had a yew centerpiece in the table setting they featured in *Country Life*. Yes, miss, real fashionable. I'll make you up a cluster if you like, tied with a red bow."

That must have been it, Hannah thought. What a disaster it would have been if she'd killed the king! She laughed at the absurdity of it, and at the funny way life has of skirting disaster. *How often have we come near to death or tragedy without knowing it?* she wondered. The world seemed to run on accidents.

"I can do it," Hannah insisted. "I don't want to put you to any trouble."

"Nay, miss, I'd rather do it myself. A few stray leaves in the feed and we have a lake full of dead ducks. Best not to risk a mistake. I'll bring them up to the kitchen in a bit. Keep them well away from the food, now."

THE KING TASTED HIS SALAD, with its contrasting flavors and jaunty marigold petals like droplets of sunshine, and pronounced it delicious. He went so far as to call out Sally to offer her his compliments . . . and was impressed at her humble, diffident manner, pretending she had nothing whatsoever to do with creating that interesting salad. It was not good form to steal another man's cook—wars had been fought over less, before the Magna Carta—but he might put out the word that there was a place for her elsewhere, if Starkers ever began to pall.

Anna and Hannah Get Engaged

〜

Dear Anna,

I will pay a flying visit to Starkers on the seventeenth of May, arriving early in the morning and departing again, alas, the next morning. And they say that the British aristocracy idles its life away in unrelenting leisure! For reasons of which you are perhaps aware, I would love to spend months and months lolling at home, amusing myself and those around me. But for other reasons, of which you are equally aware, I cannot. I must trade my innocent schoolboy life for . . . But I preempt the censors.

Yours,

Teddy

P.S. You remember Hardy, the gardener the Duke of Kent took a fancy to? I'll be picking him up when I stop at Wind-

sor. I'm sure there are many among the below stairs female
population who will be delighted to have him back, if only
for one night. He will visit his old friends before resuming
his training. He has some very interesting ideas about eat-
ing weeds.

One day! Only one day! Anna clasped the letter to her breast and determined to make the most of it.

For the week between the receipt of the letter and the seventeenth of May, Anna engaged in a flurry of beautification, slapping cream on her face and lanolin on her elbows, looking into the mirror at every conceivable angle to pluck unsightly hairs. She pumiced her feet and anointed her hair with beer to make it shine. (That last she'd learned about serendipitously when her father, who became emotional in drink, once flung a full pitcher of ale at her head.)

The night of the sixteenth, she called Hannah into her room.

"Hannah, I need to look absolutely splendid tomorrow. I need to look better than I ever have before. I need to dazzle!"

"Whatever for?" Hannah asked.

Anna could control herself no longer. It had to happen tomorrow night, and then he would tell his parents and they'd print the notice in the papers and the whole world would know! Right now, she had to share it with someone.

"Look," she said, thrusting the letter into Hannah's hands.

"Do you see? He's coming tomorrow. Oh, I'm so happy — so very happy! He's everything I've ever dreamed of." She watched Hannah's expression eagerly as she read the missive. It wasn't much of a love note, Anna had to admit — he'd written infrequently and his letters got progressively more formal, addressed to *dear Anna*, not *my dearest Anna*, and signed *yours*, not *your very own*, which made considerable difference. But still, enough for her to gloat over.

"We are so madly in love," she went on as Hannah read. "He's as good as proposed."

"And you've accepted?" Hannah asked carefully. It was hard enough to believe that posh Anna stooped to consort with the under-gardener, but to marry him?

"Well, I'll just say that we understand each other, and leave it at that. He's said such things already that it only has to be formalized this time when he comes. I just wish he didn't have to leave so soon."

Hannah, reading through the letter a second time, saw nothing more than a perfunctory letter one writes to family or some obligatory social contact. There was nothing romantic in it to clue Hannah in. She assumed Anna was excited about Teddy's postscript.

Feeling a rush of sisterly camaraderie, Hannah said softly, "I think I might be in the same boat as you."

"Really?" Anna asked, her joy in Teddy's letter deflating a

little as she felt again that surprisingly sharp stab of jealousy at the thought of Hardy admiring anyone but her. Poverty usually made people so ugly in her eyes. Why hadn't it done so with Hardy? "I'm so . . . happy for you."

"You won't tell, though, will you? I'd rather keep it a secret until it is official, and I think he would too."

Anna understood completely.

TWO GIRLS, ONE THOUGHT: Wait for night.

They were used to nothing happening during the daytime. Full light was for formality. Hannah's work kept her out of the upper crust for most of the day, and though she hoped to run into Teddy while she tended Anna, she never did. She was tempted—oh, how she was tempted—to seek him out, to creep into his room or beard him publicly, his note with its imperious command in her hand, and say loud and clear, *Yes, I will marry you.* But her pride, which had kept her in her place of degradation, rebelled. *He will come to me,* she insisted. *If he loves me he will come to me.* She would go so far as to wait in the yew, nothing more.

Neither did Anna get any satisfaction by daylight. She too was sorely tempted to sneak into Teddy's room in a robe and nothing underneath for a reprise of that glorious night. But ladies did not behave that way, however much they yearned to, and she had to remember that she was a lady. Well, a lady by proxy, by will and ambition.

It is for him to come to me, she thought. *If he loves me, he will. And if he cannot manage to get me alone today, I will find him by night in the greenhouse.*

Their paths crossed, of course. He arrived at breakfast and sat down to nibble toast and tell about his graduation. Then, after he freshened up, he and Anna and his stepsisters played billiards, then lunched together. Her hopes rose when he suggested a walk, but he spoke too loudly and all of the little nieces and nephews heard and clamored to tag along. Proposals among the nursery set simply aren't possible.

Night could not come quickly enough.

ANOTHER BLOODY NEW MOON, Anna thought as she sneaked out of Starkers. Though there *was* something romantic about it, touch and sound alone.

But we are both so beautiful, she thought. *We should be able to look at each other.*

Now, where was that greenhouse? It should be easy to find — an entire building — but there was no glint of moonlight on the glass, and none of the low-burning fires that had kept the interior warm on winter nights. She could scarcely see her hand in front of her face . . .

Then, without warning, there *was* a hand in front of her face. It clapped hard over her mouth as she tried to scream. Another hand circled her neck and tightened, and a voice said into her ear, casting spittle, "Come quiet-like or I'll slit that pretty throat."

She smelled tobacco—not the comfort of a pipe or the wealthy associations of a fine cigar, but that rank old tobacco smell of fingers stained by chain smoking. Muscular bulk pressed against her back, and stubble grated against her cheek. Her first thought was ravishment. Her second, that Teddy must never know. Her third, that if she resisted, her beauty might be spoiled, but if she acquiesced, she might escape with nothing but her dignity crushed and broken.

She allowed herself to be dragged deep into the semidomestic woods that lay beyond the Starkers gardens.

"I'm going to let you go now. Make a sound and I'll break your nose. That don't look so pretty on a gal. Savvy?"

Anna nodded, and the clutching hands released her. She turned to find the same burly man who had told Hannah to prepare the salad of bitter herbs.

He looked her up and down and let out a low whistle. "Now that's what I mean by a looker. I got a little suspicious when I talked to that other bird. They said the one I was to contact was a real stunner. So I went back and asked, and they gave me a better description. Big, blond, tits out to here. Weren't my fault. They're the ones just told me to ask for the new kitchen maid. Whoo, you sure don't look like a kitchen maid."

"As it happened I took another position," Anna said weakly. "With the family."

"You're supposed to be in the kitchen. How can you poison someone if you aren't handling his food?" He slapped his forehead. "And the NAFF says I have to work my way up—they're the ones who've bungled the business. Did that other skivvy do what I told her to? That would be a lark."

"She tried, but someone told her yew was poisonous and—"

"Someone being you?" he said, and in an instant had her by the throat again and up against a tree, breathing his tobacco breath into her face. "You were there? You heard?"

"I . . . I was hiding. I heard."

He knocked her head against the tree. It didn't hurt, much, but made her see how very easily it could.

"And you let it get mucked up? Thought you were supposed to be a clever girl. Your da says you are. What do you think I'll do to you if you don't cooperate, eh?" He pressed himself closer. "Whatever you're imagining, it's only the beginning. This is the real thing, doll. You do as you're told or you die, and it won't be quick, and it won't be fun. Not for you, anyway." He gave her a leer. "Maybe for me."

"B-but no one said I'd be asked to commit murder," she stammered.

"Not asked," he corrected. "Told."

"I can't kill anyone, especially the king! Are you all mad? It's treason. You'll be hanged."

"Desperate times, my dove. There's a war going on."

A war? She hadn't read the papers lately, but surely someone would have said something.

"A class war and a race war and a war to keep the bloody Jews and reds from taking over the world. Killing a king is nothing. A man stands in your way, you kill him, king or beggar."

"Then *you* kill him," Anna said miserably.

"Look at me. You think the likes of me can get anywhere near a king? He goes from fortress to fortress, with guards all around him. You have to plant someone in the fortress. That's you."

"Get someone else. I can't do it!"

"There is no one else. The NAFF is counting on you."

"But the king came and left. I won't have another chance."

He gave her alabaster throat a squeeze. She could feel her pulse on either side beating madly against his hand. *He'll kill me,* she thought. *He really will, if I don't do what he says.*

"You get the king back to Starkers, and you kill him. Plain and simple. If you don't, I'll cut off that pretty face bit by bit, and then afterward I'll . . ." He whispered something in her ear, something so inhumanly filthy that if she'd had the means she would have killed herself right then, just to escape the merest possibility of that ever coming to pass.

When he finished whispering he let her go, and she sank to her knees in the grass and nettles.

"Well?" he asked.

All she could do was nod, once, in utter submission.

"I'll be watching," he said, and stalked off into the night.

For a moment she froze, trembling, unable to move, although

she was afraid he'd come back with more threats, or worse. Finally her body seemed to unlock, and with a low shuddering wail she staggered back toward Starkers.

Safety . . . where can I find safety? She could not do any of the things she knew — scream for the police, ask some man to defend her. The obvious thing to do was to run to the first person she could find, babble out her terror, admit to the plan, and beg for mercy and protection. That would save the king, but would it save her? She believed that man's threats. Was the law a match for him? He would come after her, she was sure. And if not him, then someone else in the NAFF. The organization that had once been her salvation, raising her father and thus raising her, was now her enemy. They would hunt her down if she betrayed them. Her father himself would kill her with his own hands if she betrayed them.

And what of Teddy? After they were securely wed she might be able to confess her real name and position, but would he forgive her before? Afterward — well, she might be in love, but she was pragmatic, too, and there is no such thing as an aristocratic union dissolved without a big payoff. She desperately wanted Teddy and the title, but a great deal of alimony would suffice. He could cast her off, but only after they were married.

She could tell no one. She was in this all too deeply — in her deception with the Liripips, and her mission for the NAFF. She would have to at least bring the king to Starkers. She would have to . . .

"But I can't!" she wept. "I just can't." She ran and fell and ran again, bruising her knees and cutting her hands. She felt the gravel path beneath her, and at least knew where she was. She'd been running blind, but now she realized the greenhouse must be just ahead.

There was only one way to be safe. Ladies—real, titled ladies—are not murdered by tobacco-scented thugs. The chatelaine of Starkers does not have her face cut off.

"Where are you?" she cried into the night. "My love . . ."

She ran headlong into strong, comforting arms and was pulled against a broad chest. For a moment she fought, but there was no tobacco smell, and a voice said, "Is it you, sweetheart?"

She was weeping so loudly, she could hardly hear him. She knew those arms. She couldn't wait for him to ask her.

"Marry me," she begged, falling to her battered knees and clutching at his legs desperately. "Please, oh please marry me. I'll die if you don't."

She heard him chuckle, low and loving.

"Since you put it that way," he said, and drew her into the pitch-black greenhouse, where he lay her down among the nasturtiums and made her almost forget her fear.

She ran away from him before they could talk about their future together. She did not want to give herself the chance to confess—or him the chance for regret. They had agreed to be married. If she had her way, no words would follow until they both said *I do.* She curled into a tiny ball in her bed and did not let herself think of anything at all, only chanted the name Lady Anna, over and over.

"Yes," Hannah said in her tender German when Teddy called her name softly, dropping the *H* in the way she found so very appealing.

"Yes, my morning star?" he answered in the same language. He reached into the dark yew bole for her hand.

"Of course yes, you fool, despite what you have put me through. Do you know, if you weren't going to be a spy I would think you quite a coward, refusing to admit our love to your mother. My position has not been an easy one, you know."

"I imagine not. Will you say it one more time?"

"Yes," she breathed, as he stroked the scar on her thumb, his favorite spot. "Oh, yes!"

He gave her a tug. "I want more than your hand now."

But she would not be drawn out of her hollow. "No. That is very hard to say after my emphatic yes, my a-thousand-times-yes, but you must be punished." She said it flippantly, but she was serious. She had been deeply disappointed, and he had to prove himself before she said yes to anything else. "Not until you announce our engagement to your mother." She remembered a prim phrase from one of those English books she'd laughed at as a child. "First you must make an honest woman of me." She chuckled. "Then I can be as dishonest as you like. Though it doesn't sound as good in the reversal. I mean to be honest with you, ever after. After you tell your mother."

"I have to leave in the morning."

"More cloak and dagger?"

"Yes. I'll be going to . . . well, I oughtn't to tell you exactly. You shouldn't even know I'm doing spy work, but I trust you not to blab. I won't be able to write often, if at all. I'll have to put it out that I'm on a walking tour of the Lake District, complete with pastoral picturesque ecstasy, so don't mind if my letters don't sound like me. All part of the cover. I'll be learning radio operations and code and how to use a gun. I've missed every pheasant I've ever aimed at, so that might be hopeless, but we shall see. They promised me at least a few days at home before I'll have to go to Germany. In September, I think. May I tell her then? I'll arrange a party, ostensibly a welcome-back party, and invite simply everyone. I'll try to snag some royals, too. They always make good witnesses. Mum can't kick up much of a fuss with a Highness in attendance."

"She will so hate that I am marrying you," Hannah said, unable to hide a note of gloat in her voice.

"And I will so love it, my morning star," he said, kissing her hand. "Really? Engaged, and this wee hand is all I get?" He sighed, but kissed it again. "Then I'll just have to make the most of it."

Hannah's Glass of Champagne Changes History

～≈～

On September 1, 1939, Germany invaded Poland, Starkers prepared to celebrate Teddy's homecoming with a banquet and dance on the lawn, and Anna utterly failed to close the zipper on her dress.

Only the last caused Anna any concern.

She'd always relied on her own discipline to keep her body in its proper shape, but lately she'd had to resort to a snug girdle to fit into her clothes. Today, even the girdle didn't do the trick.

"Hannah, do you think they'd have a corset in the village?" she asked on the day of Teddy's homecoming. "A real honest-to-goodness corset with laces that I could make as tight as I like? I have to fit into my dress tomorrow!"

Hannah gave her a sympathetic smile. Teddy had not written — that was no surprise — but she'd heard from kitchen scuttlebutt that he would be stopping at Windsor first and bringing up a party to stay the week—several young royals, including Waltraud's HRH. (Though he would certainly come with his wife, not his mistress.) Hardy would be coming too, Sally had told her. He'd been recruited to join the Ministry of Agriculture to advise them on alternative crops in case of war. And now that Germany had invaded Poland in defiance of England and France, war was all but inevitable.

"Do you think it is such a good idea to compress yourself like that?" Hannah asked. "In your condition? You might do harm."

"In my condition?" Anna repeated sharply. "What are you saying?"

"Well, you had been meeting . . . someone. And you last saw him nearly four months ago, so it is only natural that you are starting to show."

Anna buried her face in her hands and sat down heavily on the bed. Pregnant! She hadn't let herself think about the possibility, telling herself that it was only nerves that upset her cycle, made her eat too much. She was mortified, and yet . . . it seemed just one more protective layer of security. No matter what Teddy found out about her, he'd never cast off the woman who was carrying his heir.

Hannah sat beside her and put an arm around her shoulder. "It's not as bad as all that."

"No," she sniffed. "We're getting married, you know. He will be announcing our engagement today."

"What a coincidence!" Hannah cried. "So will—" She was

interrupted by a rap at the door. A housemaid came in with a letter on a silver salver.

Anna looked at the envelope with a tense expression, then relaxed. It was only a note from Lady Liripip, who would rather send a servant on an errand than walk to the next wing to tell someone something.

Thank goodness, Anna thought. Too many letters had been from the NAFF brute, who had established himself in a cottage in the village. One was simply threatening. The next insisted on a meeting, and when she ignored it another threat came. Finally she slipped to the village to meet him and did her best to play on his more tender emotions, crying and pleading. Apparently he had no tender emotions, so she tried another tack, swearing she wanted to serve the cause, but was afraid she'd make a mess of it again. There was some sense in that, and she eventually managed to convince him that the NAFF would be better served if he did the killing. But the man insisted she must get the king alone. When was he coming? When she confessed she hadn't managed to arrange it yet, he grabbed her arm and dug his fingers into the soft flesh of her inner wrist. "Then arrange it," he'd said coldly. "Soon."

She did her best, writing to Teddy repeatedly, telling him what an honor it would be to have the king in attendance for her engagement announcement, but he couldn't guarantee anything, and Anna was feeling desperate.

Now, though, the gods seemed to be conspiring in her favor. She tore open Lady Liripip's letter and read the lines.

> *His Majesty and family are attending. Due to the trouble on the Continent they are sending their children to Windsor and visiting here en route.*
>
> *Wear wool, not silk, so you don't overshadow the queen.*

Hannah read it over her shoulder. "I would wear silk anyway," she said, rummaging through Anna's closet. "This one, with the drape. It is more forgiving of your delicate condition."

When Hannah had gone, Anna penned a quick note to the NAFF brute and had a boy deliver it to the village. It said, in their agreed code: *The stoat has flushed the leveret.*

The party would provide the perfect opportunity. She had hoped the king would come that day, and they had planned for the possibility. The NAFF man had marked his place of conceal-ment. All of the gamekeepers and groundskeepers would be at the party, for Teddy had written to his mother that he had good news to relate and insisted that it must be shared with everyone at Starkers. The estate would be unguarded, and if she could only lure the king a few yards away from the others, it could be done. She hardly cared anymore. So long as it was not by her own hand, so long as she got Teddy.

"You've been salting that soup for five minutes!" Sally snipped, and gave Hannah a gentle buffet with the back of a ladle. Hannah was drifting through the day in a happy daze. Already she'd confused baking powder and baking soda, and scalded the milk, and absently chopped the walnuts into a fine powder. "Go and change into your clean dress," Sally said, wiping her hands on her apron. "They'll be calling us out to the garden soon, and you're no earthly use here. I can get by without you."

Hannah changed into her slightly less hideous print kitchen dress and scurried out to the garden, where she could observe the Liripips and their guests finishing their informal dinner on the lawn. In a moment dessert and coffee would be served, and after that there would be dancing, but in between Teddy planned to make his declaration. He hadn't told her, of course, not exactly, but all the staff knew there was going to be a big announcement. Teddy had arrived early that morning and as before, she hadn't seen him. But that was all right. After tonight everything would be fine. More than fine. She hugged herself, took a deep breath.

There he was, wiping his smiling mouth with his linen napkin, sitting between Anna and a pretty woman with a wry, lopsided smile who she thought might be the Duchess of Kent, Georgie's patient wife. Just another moment and they would be united forever. This meant more to her than any marriage ceremony. That was for other people. This public acknowledgment was for her.

Oh, how they would joke of it in their later years. She would mock-scold him before their children, their grandchildren. *One moment I was the kitchen maid; the next, your mother.* Of course, people always fudge the biology when they speak to children . . .

The tables were efficiently cleared, and then the tables themselves were whisked away. Dancing would soon begin.

She saw Anna—in a flowing eau de nil dress that didn't reveal a single scandal—sidle up to the king, who listened with well-bred patience to whatever she was saying. *Poor king,* Hannah thought. That very morning Anna had said she didn't see why everyone was upset with Germany invading Poland, when they were practically the same country anyway. Hannah guessed from His Majesty's slightly pained expression that Anna might be saying something similar now. She seemed to be directing the king to another corner of the garden. What was she up to? Hannah wondered. Seduction? She could never be so brazen. Maybe just angling for a royal engagement present. Oh, and there was Hardy, standing with the other servants, though he technically wasn't one anymore. He was splendidly dressed with a cream-colored rose boutonniere, and he rocked from toe to heel, grinning like an idiot, trying to catch Anna's eye. Why didn't she look at him? Even a king shouldn't distract her from her true love. Anna had her hand on the king's arm, pulling, and his patience looked to be wearing thin. An equerry was approaching, uncertain whether to be amused or alarmed.

The other servants and staff were gathering, lining up in order of importance, waiting for the announcement. By the time Hannah noticed, it was too late to join them without causing a disruption, so she stayed where she was, half hidden in the shrubbery.

Lord Liripip pinged his fingernail against a wineglass, and all was silent except for the trill of songbirds.

"Most honored guests," Lord Liripip began, rising unsteadily to his feet. "My son will have news of his own, I am told." He cast a deliberate wink at Teddy, who blushed. The guests laughed politely. "But age before beauty, pearls before swine and all that rot, what? Please join me in celebrating the fruit of my labors — and right fruity they are, too, as you will discover for the mere sum of seven pounds sterling, paid to the publisher or your favorite bookseller. In short . . ." He summoned Coombe, who staggered forth under the weight of a massive tome, practically dictionary-size. "I present *The Scandalous Memoirs of a Life Well Lived,* by yours truly. Printed, I might add, in large type for all of my contemporaries who might otherwise miss out on some of the dirtiest parts."

Here the king had to physically shake off Anna, who looked on the verge of tears and kept glancing into the shrubbery in Hannah's direction.

"If you will indulge me," Lord Liripip went on, "I will regale you with one of the choicest bits of my history. Nothing lewd," he added, nodding to the queen and her charming daughters, Lilibet and little Margaret.

"Just about the time I had begun to grow weary from a lifetime of amorous vigor—no, no, I shan't go beyond euphemisms," he said to the tight-lipped queen. "I met a girl. Ah, what a beginning for a tale: I met a girl."

And he told them about the sprightly younger daughter of one of the county families. Her irrepressible joy had won him, as had her singing. "She was a handful, leading the lads on a merry chase, she and that sister of hers. Elspeth was the real hellion, but Caroline was the one for me. I pursued her, like a winsome little fox, that girl half my age, and thought I won her. I loved her. Loved her more than any being on earth, until my son was born."

My mother, Hannah realized.

"I loved Caroline Curzon, and she left me. Ought to hate her, what? But no, nothing's changed. Can't have her, can't forget her." He whipped out a large handkerchief and dabbed at his eyes.

Lady Liripip empurpled like a beetroot.

"She asked a favor, though. Went down on her knees. Marry my sister, she said. Elspeth was the wild one, and she'd been a mite careless." He described a big belly with his hands. "Save the family honor, she says. What can I do? I'd do anything for Caroline. I marry the girl, and she dies, and the other man's child dies, and here I am, a washed-up seducer stuck with this old piece of gloom." He nodded to Lady Liripip. "I mended my ways, and live through my memory. Hundreds of girls, all in here." He tapped the tome. "But none to match my Caroline. Now, unless I miss my guess, where the father failed, the son will succeed. Teddy, my boy, tell us!" Lord Liripip's fallen old face was alight with happiness and hope.

Teddy beamed at his father, not at all distressed at his mother's putting-down. "Gladly," he said, "but first, champagne all around."

Soon guests and staff alike had glasses. Hardy noticed Hannah half concealed in the bushes and snagged one for her.

"Is it what I think it is?" he asked.

She nodded.

"To you, then!" he said, raising his glass to drink.

"No!" she whispered with a little laugh, catching his arm too late. "Not yet. It's bad luck to drink before the official toast."

"Sorry," he said. "Though I doubt anything could spoil your happiness. Or mine."

"Double congratulations are in order for you," Hannah said slyly.

"What do you mean?"

But just then Teddy smiled at the assembly and said, "I am young, and have not yet had experience to fill more than a pamphlet." He looked at his father's memoirs. "But I was lucky enough to find love early. You will say she is beautiful, and that is of course true, but I did not fall in love with her beauty. That will change and fade. I love her for her lovely thoughts, for her ravishing understanding, for her pulchritudinous compassion. She sees the world clearly, how it is and how it should be. I want to join my mind to hers, my soul to hers, to make this world a better place."

Hannah, her face warm and her eyes stinging, felt like the light princess from the fairy tale, untethered to the base earth. She gazed at him, waiting for him to seek her out. Could he see her? She stepped out of the shrubbery.

Teddy reached for the woman beside him, and took her gloved hand. "My friends, meet the woman I will marry."

"What's going on?" Hardy asked, his fists clenching.

Hannah didn't hear him. Gravity returned, leadening her heart so she felt she must sink into the earth. *He lied to me. It was all a lie.* The trill of birdsong, the drone of crickets, became oppressive, deafening, filling her ears. She could hear nothing but the sound of her heart breaking.

"I lied," Teddy said just then, seeming to echo her thoughts. "I said I didn't fall in love with her beauty, but there is one part of her that is absolutely irresistible." He grinned at the sniggers from the younger guests, and, shockingly, even the king, who caught himself and changed it to a cough.

He pulled off one of Anna's gloves. "Do you see this here, this little thumb? This is the sweetest spot in the world. There is a little scar, just here."

He caressed Anna's thumb, then stopped short, bemused. He dropped that hand and caught the other, laughing at himself as he tugged at that glove. "I mean this hand, of course. I fell in love with her thumb, so I had to have the rest of her."

He bent to kiss her scar, but when he raised his head he looked at Anna as if she were a stranger.

"Where is the scar?" he asked in hushed perplexity. "Where is the woman I love?"

All of the hints, all of the inconsistencies, which had been like so many scattered pebbles underfoot, now coalesced into a mountain. Yet even from that high vantage he could not quite see the truth.

He looked at the woman he thought he loved, the woman he had just asked so publicly to be his. Each of her features seemed separate now, not a lovely whole. Yes, that was a fine nose. Yes, large blue eyes certainly had their appeal. But they didn't combine to make a woman anymore. They were like things at a jumble sale, valueless and piecemeal.

"You can't marry Anna!" Hardy suddenly shouted, and shoved his way through the crowd. "She's already promised to marry me."

Anna's jaw gaped and closed and gaped again. "Go away!" she snapped, her eyes opened very wide.

"I . . . I'm not sure what's going on here," Teddy began.

"You know exactly what's going on!" came a clear, even voice from the shrubbery. "You will make a perfect spy when you go to

Germany," Hannah added, taut and trembling with the effort not to break down. She had been humiliated long enough. Now she must be strong. "You managed to fool *this* German completely." Then she whirled and ran into the bushes, flinging her champagne glass blindly ahead of her. She heard a small exclamation, more surprise than pain, and caught sight of a figure blurred by the foliage. She saw a large man stagger back, almost catch himself, hit a root with his foot, and lurch forward, falling heavily on the ground.

Thus is history made, Hannah would think in the years to come. *A king has a love affair, and a nation shows its teeth instead of its belly. A disappointed girl pettishly throws her drink, and an assassination is thwarted.*

Just then, though, all she thought was *Even my sadness must not make me stop feeling compassion for others.* She pushed her way through the branches and knelt to touch the man's burly shoulder. "Are you all right?" With some effort she rolled his bulk over. His face, turned toward her, glistened with dripping champagne, and the tiny sliver of glass embedded below his fixed, staring eye caught the light of the setting sun. When he stumbled, he had fallen on a long knife, piercing his belly just above his navel.

"Oh, I'm so sorry," she began, before she recognized the face.

"Hannah?" came Teddy's tentative voice behind her.

Hannah uncoiled from her crouch. "I've killed a man. The king's equerry." Her voice was shaking, and not just from the sight of the blood that oozed in viscous finality across the grass.

King George, flanked by his real equerries, approached. "He is not one of mine. I don't know him."

"But he once came here and said I was to . . . Oh!"

A man with a knife hiding in the bushes near the king. *How stupid I was,* she thought, *to believe a king would send a servant by cloak of darkness to tell me a recipe. Bitter herbs with yew—how very bitter it would have been had I succeeded. This man tried to get me to poison the king! How stupid I was to . . .*

Her eyes sought out the tall golden girl, alone and forlorn on the green.

How stupid I was to believe Anna.

Anna must have ordered the note to be delivered to her, the newest kitchen maid, ignorant of both cooking and English custom. It was Anna who told her that ridiculous story, so blithely, without a blush or stammer. She and that man had planned to poison the king and pin the blame on Hannah.

And now—she'd heard from the below-stairs talk that it was Anna who had persistently begged that the king be invited to Starkers again; Anna who wheedled Lady Liripip into making this not an indoor dinner and ball, but a garden party where an interloper could easily creep across the densely wooded grounds to within sight of the monarch. And Anna had been urging the king to go with her, and looking anxiously toward the very shrubbery in which Hannah—and the assassin—had been concealed.

Hannah brushed past Teddy, wove among the equerries, and passed the king without so much as a nod.

"Assassin!" she hissed, so low that only Anna could hear it. But before she could denounce her to the assembly, she saw Anna's naked terror. Chalk white and trembling, Anna reached out an uncertain hand to touch Hannah's.

"Please help me," she mouthed without a sound.

That beseeching touch, that plea, stopped Hannah cold.

Anna was a vain, selfish egoist, but Hannah could not believe she was an assassin. At least, not voluntarily. That very vanity, coupled with her foolish ignorance, must have trapped her somehow. She thought of Buchenwald, of all the innocent people who had been cast in there. She thought of the night of broken glass when her world had been torn apart. This was not the same, not nearly, but there is a parallel in all pain, and all the cruelties of the world rhyme with one another, have the same flavor. Hannah knew that though Anna wasn't quite innocent, she wasn't guilty either.

Just as silently, Hannah asked, "Did you want that to happen?" She gestured over her shoulder to the corpse, the king, and beyond them all the looming specter of the brooding yews.

"No!" Anna swore. "I never wanted any of it to happen." Tears like crystal drops rolled heavily down her cheeks. "All I wanted was to get married, to be taken care of."

Hannah could have been cruel. With her own hurt smarting so freshly, she could have condemned Anna simply out of spite.

But then she would not have been Hannah.

"We must talk of this, and soon," Hannah said. "Finish celebrating with your betrothed." She swallowed hard, and thought she could not go on. But she did. "Meet me in the kitchen later," she managed at last. "That's where I belong." Then with Herculean effort she choked out, "I hope you will both be very happy."

Anna held fast to Hannah's hand when she tried to go. *This is my chance,* Anna thought. *I can be good. I can make everything right.*

But Teddy was coming, beautiful Teddy, her lifelong insurance against want and humiliation.

He will forgive me everything, she thought. *After the wedding.*

She composed her face into a smile—a smile that almost made Hannah regret her generosity—and said, "Thank you, Hannah," before letting her go and opening her arms to embrace Teddy . . . who sailed right by her.

"Hannah? Are you—"

"Leave me in peace, Teddy," she said in German, and tried to flee.

She was as fast as a deer for the first three steps, but when Teddy cried, "Stop her!" the king's equerries, army and navy men all, instantly surrounded her and seized her. They weren't sure what was happening, but there was a dead man near the king, and a girl who had confessed to killing him.

"Let me go!" she cried, struggling against their strong grips on her arms and wrists. She cursed at them, creatively and fluidly, in German.

At that, Teddy was almost sure. There was only one thing left to discover.

"Whatever you do, don't let her go," Teddy said softly, never taking his eyes from Hannah's exquisite little face.

He extricated her hand from their grip, and looked at the delicate waist of her thumb.

His face fell. There was nothing there.

"It is the other one, *Dummkopf*," Hannah said.

"So it is," he said, taking it into both his hands and holding it like a jewel beyond value. Then he looked up at the girl whose price was above rubies. "You were the one in the yew?"

She nodded.

"Then you are the one that I love."

He pushed back her dark hair, took her sweet face in his hands, bent, and kissed her. "Will you marry me, my morning star?" he asked.

"I already said yes," Hannah answered. "Perhaps you should not ask me any more times in case I change my mind."

Hannah Is Forgiving

⌇⌇⌇

HANNAH'S BLISS WAS INTERRUPTED by a high, uncanny scream.

"No!" Anna shrieked, her white face streaked with red, the veins in her neck raised and throbbing. "You marry *me!* You asked me before all of these people. You have to!"

"Anna, I don't know exactly what happened, but it is the woman I met by night that I love. I don't know how I was so blind. You're an excellent girl, Anna, but I don't love you. I love Hannah."

"The kitchen maid?" Anna snorted with disgust, almost forgetting the truth. "You could love a lowly kitchen maid?"

"I hope I could," Teddy said. "But Hannah is much more. I have heard her talk. I've heard her sing. She . . . Wait, Hannah, you are the contralto singer, from the cabaret? But I thought . . . my cousin . . ." He looked from one girl to the other, and then at the perplexed but deeply fascinated guests who were drinking in every word of this exciting scandal. "Let us go inside where we can speak in private."

But Anna thought publicity was her best weapon. He had made a public proposal to her, and she meant to force him to carry it through. And when she dropped the bombshell, in front of all these earls and dukes and royals, he would have no choice but to marry her.

Very loudly, very clearly, Anna announced, "You must marry me, Teddy. I'm carrying your child!"

At that, even the birds stopped chirping.

Then, very kindly, Teddy said, "I'm sorry, but that's not possible."

"Oh no?" Anna said, reverting entirely to her fishwife voice. "I might not be as clever as that kitchen maid, but I know how babies are made, and we made one in the hothouse!"

"I've never even—" Teddy began, but Hardy interrupted him.

"That was me," he said, looking very proud and manly, and to Anna, utterly irresistible. Except, he was not a lord.

"Teddy," she said imploringly, "I gave myself to you, because you said you loved me. You said you would marry me. This is your child, and you can't forsake us, Teddy. Please. You wanted me. You sent me the flowers and asked me to meet you."

"It's Hardy who loves you," Hannah said. "I delivered the flowers to you, from him. Didn't you know?"

"You mean," Anna said, dismayed, disgusted, "I gave myself to the under-gardener?"

Hardy took her hand. "I love you, dearest. You aren't what you pretend to be. You act like a lady but you're not, and there's no shame in that. Not these days. A man is what he makes himself, and a woman too. I've got a good job now. Come to London with me, Anna."

"No, I'm meant to be with Teddy," she moaned. "I'm meant to be the Lady of Starkers."

"Over my dead body!" came an aristocratic voice that still managed to be every bit as fishwife-ish as Anna's. "I take you in from Germany, from your nasty little Jew father and your trull of a mother, and this is how you think to repay my kindness? Caroline was a blight on the Curzon family, and you're no better. How *dare* you think to insinuate yourself into this noble family!"

Hannah drew a breath to reply, then realized with shock that Lady Liripip was talking to Anna.

"No, no," said Lord Liripip, hobbling over. "She's not at all like Caroline, but she is welcome in this family. Unhand her, Hardy. She will marry my son. I loved her mother, you know. Now Teddy will have the daughter. It is right and fitting."

"Sir," Teddy said, "that is not the girl I'm marrying."

"Eh?"

Teddy presented Hannah.

"But the gel's a floozy!" Lord Liripip cried. "No offense, Hannah, and I'm sure you're a splendid one, but my son can't marry a floozy. He marries Caroline Curzon's daughter."

"But I *am* Caroline Curzon's daughter," Hannah said, those simple words that could have prevented such a world of trouble had not pride forbade her to say them.

Then Anna did something unfashionable, something that ought to come back into fashion, because it is really one of the very best ways for a woman to delay having to answer for the consequences of her actions: she fainted.

Into Hardy's arms.

IT IS EASY TO BE FORGIVING when one has one's heart's desire.

"Now, are you sure you want to stick to that ridiculous story you concocted?" Lord Liripip asked as he drank in the delightful sight of his son and Caroline Curzon's daughter cuddled on a bench overlooking the Liripip Yew. "I've no objection to seeing the scheming hussy tossed in the Tower. You should hate her for what she did."

I should, Hannah thought, but she'd spent several hours alone with Anna after the garden party engagement debacle, and instead she felt profound sympathy for her. Anna had been shanghaied into her mission, threatened with her life. Of course the wise thing would have been to run to the authorities, but it was no more Anna's fault that she was stupid than it was Hannah's that she was Jewish, and she was sick and tired of people being condemned for accidents of birth. Teddy told her it was nothing like the same, but Hannah stood firm.

"Being born foolish is like being born blind," she said. "We must protect the less fortunate, and make sure they are taught, so they can live full lives."

"You think Anna is teachable?"

"Well . . . she still thinks the Sudetenland is in Africa, near Swaziland, but there is hope for her."

The story Hannah told, with an absolutely straight face, was this:

When they first met at Starkers, Anna came to Hannah to confess her secret mission. Hannah, seeing hers as the superior intellect and loving the country of her mother's birth, volunteered to play the part of the kitchen maid until the details of the treasonous scheme were revealed. She thwarted the poisoning attempt easily, but was unable to identify the perpetrator, so she waited until the second attempt.

Asked why she didn't alert the authorities, she pleaded British pluck. "Would Boadicea have run to the other kings and chieftains before fighting? Would Grace Darling have stopped to call the coast guard?"

Luckily the dead man had a letter in his pocket, proclaiming his beliefs and calling for all his brothers to join the NAFF and fight for a fascist England and a restored King Edward.

"It bothers me, though, that they think I killed that man on purpose. I couldn't have. The only heroic thing I could have done was shriek for help, which might have been enough with all those guards around, but still. They think I'm a heroine."

"You are," Lord Liripip said. "But in any event, the whole thing is being hushed up. The monarchy can't afford to look vulnerable just now. It's happening, you know. Tomorrow or the next day His Majesty will make the announcement. We will be at war." He tottered off to examine some withering ferns.

"If she hadn't lied, we might not have fallen in love," Hannah said when she and Teddy were more or less alone.

"I would have loved you no matter what," Teddy said, nuzzling her cheek. "Even if my mother approved of you, I would have loved you, though it would have been very hard."

"I hope your mother is feeling better soon," Hannah said, doing her best to sound sincere. Lady Liripip had followed Anna's example, but regrettably everyone's attention was on the young people and no one happened to notice and catch her. The doctor said she'd broken her collarbone and would have to keep to bed for weeks. (Actually, he'd first said she's bruised her collarbone and ought to be careful for a day or two, but after a charitable donation from Lord Liripip he amended his diagnosis and prescription drastically.)

"What Anna did was not so bad," Hannah mused, snuggling comfortably under Teddy's arm. There was just enough light to see each other's faces.

"She stole your life and tried to kill her king!"

"In one way," Hannah said slowly, putting her thoughts together. "But she didn't lie, exactly, did she? Not at first, any more than I did. I showed up and they thought I was one person and

I accepted it. She showed up and they thought she was quite another person and she accepted it. Then we both filled in the details to stay in our places. We each were where we thought we deserved to be. You must admit, she makes a much more convincing daughter of an English aristocrat than I do."

"Stuff and nonsense," said Lord Liripip, limping out of the gloom. "I know quality when I see it, and you, my girl, are it."

"With respect, sir, you thought I was a floozy."

"But a *quality* floozy, my dear," he said with a rakish wink that he'd been saving for twenty years.

A Sudden Need for Flowers

WAR CAME ON SEPTEMBER THIRD, and with it the impossibility of receiving any letters from Germany. It was very hard for Hannah to be happy, but despite the uncertainty of her parents' safety, she was—blissfully happy, and terribly guilty.

"But I won't marry you until I know they're safe," she insisted to Teddy.

She might have been persuaded if Teddy had to go to Germany, either as soldier or spy, but after the engagement debacle, when Hannah in her deeply injured wrath had spoken openly of Teddy's spy work, all that was nixed. A furious telegram had come from Burroughs after a paragraph appeared in the next morning's gossip column. All that work wasted on a spy who was outed before his mission began! When Teddy wanted to enlist, Burroughs told him not to be a fool. He was far more valuable at home managing other spies in the ranks of the Special Operations Executive than volunteering to be cannon fodder.

So Teddy, seeing all of his friends join up, and half of them killed in the first year while he stayed safe at home, had a burden of guilt all his own.

THE FIRST LETTER CAME IN the summer of 1940, via the Red Cross.

> *Darling Hannah,*
>
> *I'm having the most jolly time as a prisoner of war. No, the guard looking over my shoulder to censor any dangerous bits points out that soldiers are prisoners of war, while mere civilians such as I are internees. In any event, I find myself in a most wretched place called Tost, in Upper Silesia. (My censor says I may say the name of the town. I suppose you might tell any RAF boys you happen to meet not to bomb it.) To my delight, the population is predominantly male. Apparently I was sent here because of a clerical error, and it would be too much trouble to remove me at this point, so here I stay.*
>
> *You'll never, ever guess who is here with me, at this very moment, sitting at the next camp table and looking hungrily at my fresh paper supply. Old Plum himself! Mr. Pelham*

Grenville Wodehouse! Apparently he and wee wifie were in France when it was invaded and they refused to leave their little dog, so they were snatched up. Wifie is in Paris, Plum is here, and the poor dog is probably eaten by now, for I've heard there are grim food shortages in France, and everywhere else too.

(Here my censor insists that everyone under the Reich eats like a king. Perhaps the Reich has not yet found Tost, for we live mostly on potatoes and rumors.)

Poor Plum! He is such a charming innocent, and I fear he will catch it after the war. He's so chummy with everyone, friend and foe alike. I personally keep a certain frosty distance between my captors and myself, as I am still technically English. Only occasionally do I accept chocolate or lipstick from an officer. Then I barter them for paper for Plum. I dare not eat chocolate. The perpetual potatoes have gone straight to my hips. Your papa will not know me when he sees me again.

I am well, though unutterably bored in this dreary place. What a dump! I had never even heard of Upper Silesia before, and now I know why. I told Plum, if this is Upper Silesia, I'd hate to see Lower Silesia. He said he will steal that for his next book. So you see, there are bright spots. My quips will be immortalized. I must be like Plum, and not see problems and enemies, but people and opportunities. He's *like a puppy, endlessly optimistic. You must be like a puppy*

too, love. Be happy, for all is well.

Write to me, beloved girl.

Cora

"He's alive!" Hannah said, beaming through tears as she handed the letter to Teddy. "My father is alive!"

Teddy held her hand as he read through the note, absently stroking the little scar. "She doesn't say so," he began uncertainly.

"Oh, no one says anything outright in wartime. But look here—he won't know her when he sees her again. That means she's sure he *will* see her again! And here—all is well. She's afraid to give any details for some reason, but she believes he's perfectly safe. And if she believes it, I believe it." Hannah flung her arms around Teddy.

THE SECOND LETTER CAME AT the end of that year, when Starkers had just thrown open its doors to a herd of Cockney urchins sent to escape the Blitz. It had a California postmark and positively reeked of sunshine.

Liebchen,

Siberia is not all it's cracked up to be, so I'm giving

California a try.

There's a fellow here, Preston Sturges, who makes the

funniest films that just can't seem to get past the Hollywood

morality police. I talked Pres into letting me tackle a

rewrite of a flick called The Lady Eve, *and now I have a*

real studio job — I write sex scenes so no one can be sure

whether the lovers have actually had sex. Still the same

tricky old Teufel, *you see, in the same funny old world.*

Write so I know you're still safe at Starkers. Maybe the
Yanks will step in and hurry this damned war along. Out
here, though, most of them don't seem to notice.

All of my love, dear heart,

Aaron

Much later Hannah learned of her father's harrowing journey
to Russia, of the golden promises and black betrayals that country offered . . . of the midnight escape, crossing the Pacific curled
up in a bulkhead . . . of destitution in the golden land of oranges
and sunshine . . . of his work as a shoe shiner . . . how an offhand
quip about polishing shoes shiny enough to see up a lady's skirt
led to a stellar Hollywood career as script doctor, then writer,
then director, with a gracefully aging Cora Pearl as his star . . .

But now, her happiness complete, Hannah consented to be
married in a fortnight.

"Over my dead body!" said Lady Liripip, who had spent the
last year campaigning against her son's intended. Good to her
word, she died the morning of their wedding. No one noticed

for hours; her stiff posture and rigid smile were nothing unusual. In fact, everyone was impressed by her remarkably pleasant behavior.

When she was discovered, the family shed a few obligatory tears, and Hannah placed another order with the florist who had served them so ably at their wedding.

"Hannah, is that you?" squealed the voice over the phone line. "Lilies? She did? Cor! How very thoughtful of her. No, no calla lilies in stock, can't abide them, but I have heaps of lovely white stargazers. I'll make up a few wreaths, and maybe some big pots of mums. Ha! I don't imagine she invited you to call *her* mum, did she? Of course not. Condolences and whatnot, but it is for the best, I believe. Oh, I'll send you a spray of lemon blossoms too, just for you, luv. Is there any welcome news yet? Silly me! That's only a great idiot like myself who walks down the aisle with a big belly. You'll wait your proper nine months, I'm sure. Eight? You devil! Can you hear mine over the wire? He's got a handful of peonies, the terror, tearing them to shreds like they don't cost half a guinea apiece this time of year. Yes, Hardy is splendid. Always away growing his war weeds for the Ministry of Agriculture, but I have the flower shop to keep me occupied. Give my love to Teddy, will you? Not too much, though! Oh, I forgot to tell you last time we talked: Hardy said that his new strain of pigweed is such a success, they're thinking of knighting him. Fancy that! I'll be Lady Anna after all. Ta!"